ANGEL FALLING

EMBERS DUOLOGY

BOOK TWO

by Victoria Larque

BUTTERDRAGONS
PUBLISHING

Title: Angel Falling (Embers Duology Book Two)
Series: Embers Duology
Author: Victoria Larque
Copyright © 2021 Butterdragons® Publishing
All Rights Reserved

This is a work of fiction. Names, characters, businesses, places, events, locales, and incidents are either the products of the author's imagination or used in a fictitious manner. Any resemblance to actual persons, living or dead, or actual events is purely coincidental.

No part of this book may be reproduced or used in any manner without the express written permission of the publisher except for the use of brief quotations in a book review. This includes, stored in any retrieval system, or transmitted in any form by any means – electronic, mechanical, photocopy, recording, or otherwise.

Published by Butterdragons® Publishing

https://butterdragons.com

ISBN: 9789493229334 (ebook)
ISBN: 9789493229341 (paperback)
ISBN: 9789493229358 (audio book)

Cover Design by: Dazed Designs

Audio book narrated by MJ Webb and Joshua Schubart

For those who helped me write this book.
It carries pieces of my heart.

I feel the ground beneath my feet
I feel the wind beneath my wings
I feel the Demoness by my side

We are an unlikely pair
Fighting Heaven and Hell
Striving to save the world
But falling in love at the same time

****

I see the fight ahead
I see the Angel beside me
I see the world we could have

Our skills mix in a bloody symphony
Battling darkness and light
For our chances to live as we wish
And love with all the might

by Helle Gade

Chapter One

Mihr

The Surface, in the Namib Desert,
close to the sea, Namibia

The full moon sat fat and round in the sky, drenching the normally reddish dunes in silver and black. Their sharp-edged backs wound along like the bodies of gigantic snakes, on and on, past the horizon. From above it was a surreal sight. An ocean of sand, next to an ocean of water. Wastelands teeming with both life and a sense of utter emptiness.

I beat my wings once, then glided by using the strong coastal wind. It was chilly and misty, covering my skin with a film of moisture that grew to droplets, feeling like icy fingers running over my face and arms. I tasted the sea in the air, remembering the last time I had flown down this coast at night. Back when I had been part of a different world, believing different things…

With a loud *whoosh*, Kasha – my Hellcat – beat her huge wings to keep up with me. Her large black body and even larger wings looked out of place and right at home at the same time. She was like an ancient beast of legend, belonging to this beautiful wasteland. Mysterious and breathtaking. Strange to think that she was only a few weeks old. Evident in the way she kept on 'running' while flying. Her effort to copy my wingbeats coupled with her lanky paw movements – which were still a bit big – brought a smile to my face.

Kasha was almost the size of a grown horse, and one of two beings I had fled Hell with, not long ago. She had picked me as her warrior upon meeting me, and we hadn't really parted since. The resulting bond we had formed with each other manifested as a warm tug, right beneath my rib cage. A tug pulling in her direction.

Tonight was the first time I took her out in the open, the thick mist covering the city we hid in a perfect cover. She needed to learn how to truly fly. The reason why I wanted to teach her sooner rather than later was an uneasy feeling, knotting my stomach ever since getting here. We were not safe. I knew it. And contrary to Fane, I was not about to sit back and relax.

Fane... The other being I had escaped Hell with. The reason I had been able to in the first place. She had freed me, in exchange for my angelic blessing. A Demon, an Angel and a Hellcat. Our kind wasn't supposed to be in this plane. Earth. We had no business being here, but we had nowhere to go either. I just knew our current cozy life – together with two Humans – was not going to last. Our worlds would come for us. Which was the exact reason I was out here, to train my Hellcat some maneuvers. This place was far away from any living Humans, so it was perfect. And Kasha needed an opportunity to stretch her wings. She had been cooped up most of the last two weeks.

I blew out a stream of air and beat my wings hard once, shooting up, then I pulled them flush against my sides and dove down. With exaggerated movements, Kasha copied me.

The second we sank lower behind one of the dunes, the sound and wind from the sea cut off abruptly. I had anticipated it and watched as Kasha floundered for a few seconds before catching herself.

"That's my girl," I told her, opening my wings to stop short before my feet hit the impossibly soft sand.

A mewl answered me and she landed gracefully. Her face was almost at the height of my own and when she came prancing my way, her black horns blinked in the moonlight like blades of obsidian. Her mane of black hair, fanning around her perfect feline face, gave her the same sense of royalty lions had. Red eyes blinked at me before her heavy head bumped into my shoulder, nearly knocking me off balance. A loud purr vibrated from her chest, sounding like the engine of an old beetle.

I laughed and grabbed two hands full of her mane on either side of her face. Digging my fingers into her silky fur, I scratched and petted her, then pressed my forehead to hers.

Another mewl came from my large, beautiful beast. I quickly kissed her between her red eyes then let go and pointed to the sky. "Up!" I shouted.

Without hesitation, Kasha sprang into the air, leaving a bout of wind and fine-grained sand to billow around me. She hovered above me, her paws treading air softly, a curious expression on her face.

I spluttered, shook off the sand and wiped my face. "Yeah, didn't think that one through," I murmured, running my fingers through my hair to shake out some of the sand. "Time to play and learn."

With a lunge, I launched straight at her, prompting her to roll out of the way in mid-air. Over the course of the next few hours, I taught her how to dodge, chase, and race. Normally, she would be trained alongside her kind, trained to carry her Demon warrior into battle against Angels. Hellcats were considered dangerous beasts amongst my kind, but their training was lacking one specific thing – flying and fighting without a warrior as well as with them. Their normal warriors – Incubi and Succubi – didn't normally have wings.

Contrary to them, Kasha and I would become a symbiotic entity of the sky. Having wings allowed me to show her how to use them, as well as train her to react to a flying opponent. It was all fun and games for her, and she had fought at my side before, both Angels and Demons. But now, since she was almost grown, she would be a force of her own.

When the horizon began paling, I flew above her, easing down onto her broad back for the first time. She rolled over, giving me her belly and pawed at my face playfully. Like a backstroke swimmer, she glided through the morning on her back, swatting at me.

I turned my index finger, indicating for her to turn around again.

It took me almost a full hour before she didn't try to bite or paw at me when I hovered on her back. The first time she landed with me seated on her back felt bumpy and had me grabbing hold of chunks of mane, but I couldn't wipe a stupid grin from my lips as we galloped through the dunes together.

The sun poked through the blanket of mist and I decided it was time to head home.

"Up!" I commanded and Kasha took us both to the sky. She leaned to the side and craned her neck to look at me, nearly making me teeter off to one side. Quickly, I opened my wings and slid from her back. She twirled around, and I winked at her, before barreling past, having her chase me.

When we reached the city, we wove through the mist, shrouding us in secrecy. I could will myself invisible, but Kasha was a different story. As a kitten she'd been visible to Humans as such, but now? It wasn't like we could show her to someone and ask what they saw, and Cam and Dax knew what she was, so they saw her in all her hellish beauty. And no matter as what she appeared, how did one explain a flying cat to anyone?

As I watched her overenthusiastic air-paddling, her pink tongue lolling out to flap in the misty wind, I felt my heart swell with love for her. It still baffled me how I was able to love one of her kind – Hellspawn. The old me certainly wouldn't have thought it possible. But she was just Kasha. The Hellcat who had chosen me as her warrior, who had fought by my side, was loyal to a fault, and who had saved my life. Loving her was as easy and natural as breathing.

Kasha's ears strained, her mouth closed and she looked down, her nostrils flaring. She smelled home.

I lifted a finger and she flapped her mighty wings to stay in place as I sank down through the blanket of mist, to see if the coast was clear.

A figure in a hoody, wearing mittens and a dashing, multicolored, knitted beanie, slunk along the outer wall of our house. White breath billowed out from underneath the cap and the figure shook itself, rubbing their fists to warm them. I waited until they turned the corner, then whistled softly. Momentarily, Kasha dropped from the coat of mist above and we landed on the terrace of our house together.

I opened the sliding glass-door and before I could utter a word, Kasha pushed her huge body inside, hitting her right horn on the aluminum frame audibly. She hissed, ducked her head to the left and vanished into my room.

I sighed and followed, coming to face Kasha sniffing at the bundle of blankets and red limbs in bed, before she pressed her head to it and purred. A red hand rose and patted around until finding Kasha's head and scratching her behind one ear.

"Soft kitty," a raspy voice murmured. The slight gravelly quality, mixing with the sensual velvet sound, made a warm shiver fork over my back. I loved her voice in the mornings.

Quickly, I pulled off my damp shirt and shrugged from my pants, before tugging on the covers and sliding into the bed.

Kasha pulled her head free and blinked her red eyes at me once, before she grunted and walked to the door. She always fled the room when Fane and I were in the same bed. Smart cat. She flicked the doorhandle with a huge paw and pushed the door open with her shoulder, then exited silently.

I waited until she bumped the door closed behind her – something she had started doing not long ago – before I dug beneath the blankets for Fane. My Demon. My Ember.

My fingers met hot skin.

"Sulfur and ash! Are you trying to kill me?" she cried.

I chuckled and pulled the blanket down, revealing auburn hair, a set of amber eyes and a very pretty snarl. Ignoring her lamenting and cursing – both very colorful – I snuggled closer, pressing my whole body to hers. She was naked as sin and hot as a bed of coals. I was naked too, but my skin was chilly from the hours outside.

"Mihr, you son of a dungheap! Get your freezing self off me, right now!"

"You are in my bed, that means you have to warm me."

"Says who?"

"It's a very common rule."

She wriggled in my grip but I pulled her closer until her back was flush against my front. I gasped when her butt smoothed into my crotch.

"Liar," she said breathily, no doubt feeling what her hot wriggling was awakening.

"I'd never."

She groaned, arching her back, adding pressure to exactly the right spot. "Curse the saints, Angel. Isn't cold supposed to make things shrink?"

"Ah, but I am not cold." I slung both arms around her and slowly ground myself against her. "Not anymore, at least."

She sniggered. "I can feel that." Fane turned to me a fraction and threw her upper leg over mine. I peppered her shoulder with kisses and inched my hand down her body, letting my fingers dig into her soft flesh here and there, making her breath hitch each time. Her heartbeat picked up as my palm skimmed over her stomach and dove lower.

Pure heat zinged through me when I felt how ready she was for me already.

"Quit the foreplay, my angelically endowed nightly visitor, and get to it," she uttered in a breathy voice.

"Why so eager? Want to get it over with?" I teased.

She moaned in answer and trembled at my touch. I always marveled at how sensitive and receptive she was, and how completely she could give herself over to the experience. There was no wall with her when it came to physical intimacy. Never had been. I still worked on lowering mine in this particular regard, and it was frustrating.

"Less talk more – oh!" She hissed and rolled her hips. "That's the spot." My Demon slid a hand behind her and down my body, her fingers skimmed over my skin, making her touch feel like sparks of electricity. I gasped when her hand closed around me and she guided me exactly where I wanted to go.

She was slick heat. Fire, that fanned the flames of my own passion to unknown heights. Familiar by now and yet mind-blowing each time. How could one person feel so good? So right? We fit like pieces of a puzzle. Worryingly perfect.

A sigh left me when I was seated deeply within her. She pulled her hand back and moaned in answer. For a second, we both held very still, relishing the feeling we inspired in one another, then she bumped into me and wriggled a bit. The movement alone had me nearly seeing stars and I started moving. Slow. Languid. Enjoying every second, every slide of heated skin, and every minute shiver running through her. Her soft skin erupted with goosebumps and her veins subtly started glowing, starting from her hands and running up her arms, back, and to her neck.

I continued my lazy pace and traced her glowing veins with my fingers, lips, and tongue. She tasted the same as always – like sin and secrets. I bit into the side of her neck softly, eliciting a purr-like growl and a serious tremor.

Fane bent forward and thrust back hard. "More," her gravelly demand and movement caught me off guard and I had to concentrate and reel myself back in before I lost control. My fingers bit into the soft flesh of her hip and ass to slow her down. It was no use.

Fane snatched my hand and drew it over her stomach, up her chest and to her lips, she sucked my fingers into her mouth, letting her tongued dance around them, all while moving against me with increasing speed and urgency.

My control snapped and I turned us both over a bit, so she was on her stomach and I above her.

"Oh, yes, just like that!" Fane cried when I pummeled into her. Her body stiffened, her hands gripping the sheets, her hair bouncing with each move, fanning over her face and hands. Coiled like a spring, she received me, low moans tumbling from her. Then I felt her release. All of her relaxed, then convulsed beneath and around me. The feeling of her, the sight, and the sounds nailed me in the back of my spine. Within a few more thrusts, I exploded. For a moment my world splintered apart until it was only me and her, riding the high of our passion together. How was it possible that my need for her didn't seem to dim? Each time was like the first. Like entering a part of life I had never experienced before.

Sweaty and out of breath, I rolled from her and onto my side, taking her with me. I slung one arm under her neck and my other over her, hugging her to me. Close to her, our legs entwined, our bodies pressed to one another, I felt safe. Where I belonged. A feeling that had eluded me for centuries.

True, I had known where I belonged, and I'd had a purpose, but everything had been grim, the future dark and uncertain. The only constant had been battle and death. I had been whittled down to near nothingness, until my will to live was only fueled by rage and hatred.

Then a Demon – of all beings – had rescued me from Hell. A Demon who made me question everything I knew, who made me feel joy, safety, and fear. Because for the first time in almost forever, I had something to lose. Something precious and coveted. My heart fluttered painfully. I had been right that night in the forest hut – I couldn't sustain a casual, physical, relationship. The Demon in my arms already commanded much of my stupid heart. But she'd laugh at me if she knew. So, I was not about to tell her.

A small chuckle shook her frame and she laced both her hands with mine, pulling my arms tighter around her. "Can we make this a thing? You waking me like this?"

"As you wish," I murmured.

Fane turned in my arms and blew a lock from her face to look at me. Her amber eyes found mine and latched on, searching for something. "You okay?"

"Yeah," I said, wary of her searching gaze. "Why?"

A crease appeared between her slender brows. "You look... broody. Did something happen during your training sesh?"

I stroked her hands with my thumbs. "No, Kasha is learning very fast, and I think she had loads of fun."

"Then what's eating at you?"

For a second, I debated if I should throw caution to the wind and tell her how I truly felt. The moment seemed appropriate. But I knew I couldn't take her face changing from curious and worried to closed off. There was no doubt in my mind that my feelings for her would scare her away. She had been very clear on what she wanted from me, and what not. I opted for the second thing troubling me.

"We'll have to plan our next moves soon," I said. "I think our time here is running out."

The groove between her brows deepened. "Already? I don't think so. We are protected. Dax shields this house, no one can find us. Besides, it's been maybe two weeks."

"Exactly. We fled Hell, I killed an Archangel, and we not only revealed ourselves to Humans, we are living with two. Your and my people will be on the hunt for us. Constantly. Our only chance is to strike before they do."

Fane wriggled back a bit and turned, so she could look at me fully. Her expression was not happy. "I asked for a reprieve. And all you want to do is risk our lives? Again? We could just hide forever."

"You know we can't."

Her lips thinned. "We can damned well try. Why stir up shit if we don't have to?"

A smidge of annoyance laced through me. "You know why, Fane."

She rolled her eyes at me. "Because Michael was – maybe – stealing souls?"

"Yes, and not maybe, he was definitely building an army God has no knowledge of. Plus, your kind is out looking for Angels to bless them so they can take a stroll outside. Imagine what happens if they capture enough.

Imagine how many Humans will be killed by plundering Demon hoards."

"Uh hu, right. And why exactly is that our problem? We–"

"Seriously, Fane?" I pulled my hands from hers and propped myself up on an elbow. "You are asking me to justify why we have a responsibility?"

She said nothing, her amber gaze defiant.

I heaved out a sigh. "Fine. We have to do something, because if we hadn't escaped, your kind wouldn't be able to massacre Humans in this realm."

"But your buddy would still have stolen souls to build his unsanctioned army, so that is not our fault."

I gaped at her, momentarily at a loss for words. "This is not about fault, Fane. It is about doing the right thing. We know what the repercussions could be, and we should do something about it. You came to help me fight the Demons back in that village, remember? To save the Humans and do the right thing?"

An indecipherable expression flashed across her features, then she glowered at me. "I was coming for *you*. Not those people. Those I care about come first. Why is that so hard to understand? Right now, we are safe. If we go out looking for trouble, we are not. It's simple."

"You think I want to put you in harm's way?"

An icy feeling stole itself into my chest when she shrugged. "I know you don't, but it sure fucking feels like you don't care for our lives very much." She slipped from the bed and pulled on pants and a shirt.

"Fane. Come on, you know I didn't mean it like that."

"Don't care, Angel. Thanks for the fuck." She stomped through the room and was gone within seconds. The sheer anger and frustration I felt at watching the door close kept me from going after her. All the safety and calm she had brought was ripped away, as I turned on my side and stared through the glass doors at the misty sky.

Chapter Two

Fane

The Surface,

a coastal Namibian City

In the back of my head, I knew Mihr was right. I didn't much care for him bringing up the topic though. Especially after a bout of great sex. *No manners, that guy.*

We were safe, we deserved a bit of freedom and downtime. I certainly did, especially after spending my life in servitude. It was incredible for me to be able to do what I wanted. The only thing bothering me was that I had decided not to use my powers for the time being, so we couldn't be found by any Ember feeling the earth for me. Which meant not feeling my surroundings outside of the house. Which meant – shoes.

I grimaced, hating the numbness each step carried, and my thoughts snapped back to Mihr and our fight. Why was he so eager to jump right back into his old life? Wasn't what we had now enough? Wasn't I?

I trudged on listlessly, following Cam and Dax through the blinding midday sun, my back slumped like a question mark. He had not meant it the way I decided to take it. Mihr was worried about my people – Demons – coming for us, because clearly Lucifer was taking the loss of a born Angel and a traitorous Ember hard. And my Angel was devastated about uncovering his former – now dead – best friend, Michael, being a soul-stealing pissant, who had built an army of his own Angels. Although, I was certain there was a lot of sadness and disappointment swinging along in that particular package, which Mihr had not yet looked at too closely. I knew all about unpacking shitty truths, but my Angel wasn't ready for them. Maybe it was part of the problem, or part of why he was so adamant on us doing something.

Still, as I hiked my slipping bag back up on my shoulder and peered past Cam's bouncy curls, glimpsing the market we headed toward, I felt a sense of inadequacy. It had taken him mere days to suggest risking our lives and our new-found freedom. Even after what we've been through. And while the nightly sex was ah-fucking-mazing, we had not talked about us. Which was a package *I* wasn't too thrilled to look at.

No matter how much our fight pulled at me, rolling around the pit of my stomach like a stone, I woke from my musings and dark thoughts bit by bit as smells, sounds and vibrant colors attacked my senses.

It was curious how, after three hundred-something years in Hell – not to mention bound in slavery – it was impossible for me to stay glum while in the earthly realm.

The scent of roasted meat mixed in with the one of heat-baked tar, twisting into an intoxicating combination, the sound of vendors conversing loudly in unknown languages, the colorful clothes and trinkets blinking from both people and stands… It made me perk up and excitement flit into my chest, where it fluttered around like a small butterfly. Gentle, but there.

"It's a shame Mihr didn't want to come," Dax said, grinning at me.

"He was up all night training Kasha," I said, winking with a confidence I didn't feel in the slightest.

Cam raised a brow at me, giving me a disbelieving smirk. I could practically see the dirty thoughts she was thinking and stuck my tongue out at her.

When we walked into the market, diving headfirst into a cacophony of voices and impressions, I pushed my fight with Mihr firmly from my mind. I knew we would have to talk it out, and I knew I had to make concessions and apologize for some of the things I said, but right now, I didn't feel like thinking about it. Not. At. All.

"What are those?" I exclaimed, heading for a stand where a woman was busy cleaning mushrooms the size of soup plates. Next to the board she was cleaning and cutting on, was a gas-stove with a pan. Behind her, on the far side of the stall, countless plastic-woven bags containing more of the mushrooms, blankets, and other unidentifiable things, were propped up and stacked over one another.

She smiled at my enthusiasm kindly, showing off a row of perfectly straight, white teeth. A million-dollar smile, for sure. "Omajovas," she said, her kind brown eyes twinkling with mirth. "They grow on or next to termite hills. Want to try?" She cut off a piece and held it out to me.

I took it with a smile and bit into it. My teeth squeaked on the raw mushroom, and a "mhh" escaped me when the unusual taste hit my tongue. "This is amazing," I said and waved Cam and Dax over. "Guys you gotta try this."

The woman behind the stall winked and held up a finger. "Wait a second, then you can all buy a schnitzel."

She quartered one of the mushrooms, dunked them in flour, egg yolk and breadcrumbs, before letting them slide into the pan along with a healthy helping of butter. The scent erupting from her efforts was amazing.

"A schnitzel?" Dax peered at the sizzling mushrooms. "Isn't that supposed to be meat?"

The woman laughed, a warm and agreeable sound. From behind her, one of the blanket heaps parted with another – wheezing – laugh. An old woman emerged, thin as a stick, with countless lines on her expressive face. She wore a long dress and a type of headscarf many older women here seemed to wear. It was a bright-red color and suited her well. "Ijo, axarob, but anything can be a schnitzel if you cover it in breadcrumbs and fry it."

"Etse." The younger woman clicked her tongue. "Dahi oussie. Sit back down, you always scare the customers away."

"Not us, promise. What language was that?" Cam asked.

The old woman side-eyed the young one and crinkled her nose. "Damara." She looked at Cam and thumped her scrawny chest with a frail fist once. "The language of my people."

Her dark eyes floated over us and stuck to me. They narrowed. "You." She pointed a gnarly finger at me. Next to her the younger woman sighed and rolled her eyes while turning the mushrooms over, but the older one seemed to either not care or notice as she rounded her to stand opposite me.

Her wrinkled lips pursed and relaxed repeatedly as she sized me up. "You have the energy. Special. Like a magic man I know."

"Dahi, oussie!" the young woman hissed, this time clearly agitated. "Jy weet mos…"

"Ja, ja, nie die blankes bang maak nie," the older one answered, in another language altogether.

I was extremely talented with languages, one of the perks of being a Demon, and I was sure I had heard the cadence and flow of that last sentence before. "Afrikaans?" I asked.

The older woman gave me a near toothless smile. "Special energy." She wagged a finger at me. "You know. They always know. Hulle weet."

"Moenie!" the young woman said, banging the pan on the stove loudly, her voice hard and exasperated. "Nou gaan uit!"

The granny smirked, but hobbled from the stall and vanished in the crowd as if by magic.

"Here are your Omajovas, fifteen dollars." Cam was handed three makeshift plates fashioned from aluminum foil, in which our mushroom-schnitzels steamed. The young woman smiled ruefully as if to excuse her older companion when she accepted the money I dug from my bag.

A little unsettled, we left the stand to stroll over the market. Not even the phenomenal taste of the mushrooms – they positively melted in my mouth –

could help me forget the knowing smirk of the old woman. Her words about the 'special energy' echoed in my mind.

"That was weird," Cam said after a while of me being quiet. "You think she knew what you are?"

I shrugged and stuffed the last of my meal into my mouth. *Delish*. "No idea, but I wondered that myself. How would she know though? And what is a magic man? Did she mean Warlock, or magic user?"

"She didn't seem scared of you," Dax said. "So, I'd say she doesn't know what you are." He licked his fingers clean and grinned at me. "She did say 'blankes', so it appears the riddle is solved."

"What are you talking about?"

"Well, blankes means whites in Afrikaans, and since mom and I aren't white, she meant you. You're white, Fay."

I blinked at him, then at my red skin. "I am?"

Cam giggled heartily. "God, Fane, you haven't noticed people staring at you?"

Looking around, I squared my shoulders, meeting many eyes from every angle. "Of course, I have."

"You thought it was cause you're hot, didn't you?" Cam asked, wiggling her brows.

"I *am* hot," I mumbled.

"Yeah. Apparently, you're also white."

I bumped my hip into hers, sending her stumbling to the side, cackling like a swamp-hag.

"Asshat," I grumbled.

The revelation about how Humans – other than Cam and Dax – saw me, made me forget the unsettling encounter with the older woman. And we spent a good portion of the morning trying, tasting, and buying our way through the market. There was roasted meat, spices, fabric, beans, corn and corn flour, something called milliepap, made from corn flour, and worms that had been cooked in saltwater and dried, sold in plastic bags as snacks. Dax took one look at them and shook his head, lips thin, but Cam and I tried one. They weren't bad. Crunchy and salty. Very dry. A full-bosomed, infectiously happy woman told us that they made great snacks while sitting on the couch watching TV.

Dax grimaced and decided that no movie night in the immediate future would host any worms.

On our way home, our mood was light and our hands filled with countless bags we acquired. I was especially psyched about a huge piece of fabric I bought that I would turn into shorts at the nearest opportunity. I had even conceded toward Mihr so far, that I'd bought him a bag of biltong. Dried, seasoned meat. He loved the chili bites especially.

Talking and laughing, we entered the house with our treasures and headed for the kitchen to unpack.

I loved everything about the house, from the way it smelled when we entered, to the tiled floors, to the white walls littered with pictures of landscapes and animals. The gray tiles spanned the entrance and led to a huge open room containing the living room – which was set in a square space two steps down from the rest – and an open kitchen behind it. Off to the left, a long table stood beneath a beautiful hanging lamp, and was decorated with an assortment of driftwood and seashells we had collected from the beach. The furniture – couch and kitchen – were held in tones of gray and white, which the dark wood of the table and chairs complemented.

It wasn't so much about what it looked like, but more about the memories and feel. We ate and played games at the table, we snuggled on the couch and had movie nights – with a lit fire in the hearth – and we cooked in unison. Mihr and I were learning from Dax. It was a space filled with laughter, warmth and family. A space and life I would never willingly give up.

We found Mihr sitting on one of the high stools next to the counter, Kasha next to him. Even sitting down, the Hellcat towered over him. It was a good thing that the ceilings were unusually high.

"Kasha!" Dax exclaimed and dashed at her. He dove into her belly-fur, hug-snuggling her. The huge cat purred immediately and licked him across the head, making his curls stick up at one side.

"Nice hairdo, kiddo," Mihr said and smiled at the boy.

Dax laughed, stroked over his head and went to hug the Angel. "How was your training?" he asked.

Mihr, who had reciprocated the hug, let go of Dax. "It was good. She is very playful still, but learns quickly."

I placed down my bags and crossed my arms. "Well, technically, she's still a kitten, you should cut her some slack."

His gaze found me and hardened. "She does have to be ready if we need to fight. Because there will be battles coming. I will not let her be helpless when they do."

Knowing that he wasn't only talking about Kasha, but me, I glared back. "You'll be putting her and yourself in danger, though. You know that, right? Danger no one has to be in."

"She is a warrior, it's who she is at heart."

Cam looked from me to Mihr and blew a strand of curls from her face. "Oh-kay. Clearly you two have something to work out. Dax, leave your stuff here, I'll pack it away later, let's go play a round on the console."

I nodded at my friend thankfully. "I'll do the packing away, thanks Cam."

Dax pulled his fingers through Kasha's fur, standing next to her. "Are you guys about to fight?" he asked, his eyes big.

"That depends," I said.

"On?"

"Daxter," Cam said. "Let's go."

Dax sighed deeply. "Come along Kasha." He trudged off after his mother, the Hellcat strolling along at his side. "I'd rather do some reading, if that is okay," Dax said to his mother.

Cam reached out and drew her arm around him as they walked to the stairs. "Sure thing, bud. I think Imma watch a movie for now."

Once they were upstairs, Mihr raised a brow at me. "I'm curious too, Fane. What does it depend on whether we fight or not?"

"On how fast we find common ground."

He huffed out a joyless laugh. "That seems unlikely."

I pulled one of the bags over the counter, started unpacking the goods and sorted them into two categories – fridge, and not fridge. "Listen, I know you didn't mean it like I decided to take it. I know you don't want to put us in danger, but when I told you I needed a break, I didn't mean two weeks. And it felt like you were discarding it as unimportant." I placed the stuff from heap number one in the fridge, snapped it shut, and rolled the empty plastic bags into little sausages and stuck them into the bags bag for reuse. The part where I felt like he was disregarding *me* specifically, I left out. There was always a distance between us, one he erected. And that, more than anything, made me feel like I was not enough. That this slice of paradise we had found was not enough.

"I feel like you are discarding what we have found here – the peace, the way of living – because of a cause I have never believed in."

Mihr hopped from his stool and opened one of the other bags. He pulled stuff from it and lined it up, sorting it as well. "You should know by now that I'd never do anything to jeopardize anyone in this household. But we do have a responsibility."

"I know," I mumbled.

"Think of what could happen if things escalate."

"I know."

"We are the only ones who actually have the knowledge and means to do something about it."

"I. Know." With a grunt, I gathered his sorted things and made another trip to the fridge. "But what do you suggest we do? We can't run around warning

Angels of Demons out to capture them for a blessing. And we can't–"

"We'll have to go to Cyrisas. Or rather, I have to go. Someone has to tell Him about the stolen souls. The secret army."

A pack of spices slipped from my fingers as I went rigid with terror. Shock iced up my limbs with lightning speed and I had to take a few deep breaths before my throat loosened enough to utter a word. "Are you fucking insane? No. Absolutely not, Mihr."

"I don't think I have a choice, someone has to–"

I wagged a finger at him, a shrill laugh rolling through my chest. "You are not going back there. You are a fallen Angel. They would kill you on sight."

"I have to try, Fane."

Wrath mixed with the stiffening shock and my veins started lighting up as a result. "I am so done with you placing so fucking little value on your life. What are we going to do without you? What am I–" I stopped myself. Nope. Not going there.

My Angel opened and closed his mouth, his face a mix of warring emotions, surprise prominent, then a sly expression took over, morphing into a cocky smirk. "Don't tell me you have come to actually care for me."

"Don't be ridiculous." I snorted. "But I like Kasha, and she would follow you right into Heaven. What do you think they would do to her? Huh? I won't be able to keep her here. Not now, when she has grown into stallion-size."

For a moment he was quiet, then he opened his mouth. I would never know what he'd wanted to say, because a blood curdling scream ripped through the house, bouncing off the walls and refreezing my limbs.

A heartbeat of silence followed. Mihr and I stared at each other. "Dax!" we said at the same time and started running.

My heart beat behind my ears and what felt like an iron band closed around my ribcage as we sped up the stairs and barged into Dax's room. What we saw took my breath away and made me want to sink to my knees.

Cam was cradling a writhing Dax, whose arms flailed as his body was shaken by tremors of what looked like unbelievable amounts of pain. His sharp yells sliced straight into my chest.

"What is it, darling?" Cam asked, her terrified eyes meeting us, asking silently for an answer.

Mihr crossed the room and sank down beside the bed, gently nudging Kasha out of the way, as she loomed over the bed, her whole body tense. The Angel grabbed hold of Dax's arms, which elicited another sharp scream.

"Fane, look," Mihr said, urgency coloring his voice.

I dashed over and gasped when I saw Dax's arms. Mihr had peeled back part of the long sleeves and gashes, welting at the sides, looking sickly red, with black, gooey centers, covered every inch of Dax's open skin.

"Saints and Cherubs," I gasped.

"What is it, Fane?" Cam asked, tears rolling down her face. "I-I heard a strange noise, then a voice I didn't recognize. I went looking a-and found him like this. What is happening to my little boy?"

"I... I have no idea," I said.

"I might," Mihr said, his face pale and grim. "These smell like demonic magic." He indicated at the gashes. "They look like tithes. Magical payment for demonic spells."

Chapter Three

Mihr

The Surface,
a coastal Namibian City

Frantically, I searched Dax's room for the grimoire he always used. Maybe I could somehow break the spell shielding us. It had to be the thing affecting him. I hoped.

The boy's cries had turned to heart-wrenching sobs and while Cam rocked her son back and forth in her arms, cooing and whispering to him with a teary voice, Fane had gone to get the first-aid kit. It would do no good. Those wounds were clearly magical and no amount of iodine or any other Human medicine would help. Kasha had taken up vigil next to the bed, towering over Cam and Dax, her body rigid, safe for her tail flitting around nervously. The boy didn't react to his mother's questions and words, his eyes were firmly closed, his skin pale and sweaty. From time to time a yelp would break through his constant sobs.

Fane sped back into the room and threw a kit on the bed. She sank down on her knees and opened it, speaking with Cam in hushed tones as she pulled cotton, plasters, bandages, and tinctures from the pack. She gingerly pulled Dax's sleeves up, her face grim as she began to clean the gashes.

I refocused on my search and rummaged through Dax's school bag and the stuff on his desk.

"There you are," I mumbled, finally pulling the tome from a drawer in the desk. I placed it on the table and flipped through the pages, looking for something resembling the spell shielding us. My breath hitched. Dax had given the tome a serious workover. Countless pages had side notes, scribbles, and sticky notes all over.

I cursed, searching for the spell I guessed was draining him. But the more I saw and read, the clearer it got that Dax had not only searched for something himself, he had used spells to get there. Lots of them.

"Heaven preserve us," I whispered.

"What?" Fane got up from her kneeling position, a ball of cotton drenched with iodine in her hand.

I carried the tome over and placed it on the bed, so we could all look at it. "Dax has been using spells. Quite a few," I explained, pointing at his scribbles. 'No results' or 'try again later' was scrawled next to listings and spells such as 'magical ailments,' 'search and reveal,' and 'universal translations.'

"What were you trying to do, sweetie?" Cam asked, wiping Dax's sweaty brown. She got no answer.

Fane flipped through the book and tapped a finger to a spell. "Here is the one I think he used to shield the house."

"Let me see," I said and pulled the tome closer to take a look. "Hmm, it states to use carvings to map out the circumference. I'll go look for them and erase them, see if that does something. If this is a result of the magic draining him, maybe one less will be enough to help him."

Cam cradled her son closer and nodded at me.

"I'll help," Fane said and together we headed from the room.

I grabbed her hand when she wanted to go downstairs. "Look for carvings in doors and windows. They could be very small."

She gave me an affirmative nod and squeezed my palm quickly, she looked as worried and helpless as I felt. "I really hope this helps," she said.

"Me too."

Fane blew out a shaky breath, then let go of me and vanished down the stairs.

I turned and searched through Cam's room, the bathroom, and the upper study. In each window, I found a small carving beneath a windowsill and scratched it away. Done with the rooms upstairs I sped down to help Fane.

Together we made quick work of the tiny etchings Dax had done, before we went back to his room. His window was the last and once the carving was erased, we all watched him closely, hoping for… something.

Nothing happened at first. Daxter still writhed in his mother's hold, sobbing and whining, his complexion gray and sickly looking. I was so focused on him, I didn't notice the strange atmosphere stealing itself into the room. The hair on my nape rose and an icy shiver tumbled down my back. It felt like the warmth was sucked from the room. As if the walls around us didn't exist.

"Something feels off," Fane said, obviously feeling it too.

"Maybe it's the protection vanishing," I suggested, though it felt more sinister than that.

"Could be." Fane shrugged.

A huge gasp came from Dax. The boy sucked in air until his back arched from the bed, then he exhaled and sank down, silent. His sobbing stopped, as did his tremors and wines. The gray complexion and beads of sweat stayed, though. Underneath his lids, his eyes jerked from left to right in rapid succession.

"Dax? Honey, are you okay?" Cam asked, shaking him softly. No answer, no reaction. She looked at me. "Did it help?"

"I seriously have no idea," I told her truthfully. "All we can do now is wait."

"And maybe look through his book again to see if there are other spells we can break," Fane suggested. She rubbed her upper arms with both palms. "Is anyone else cold?"

Cam nodded. "Let's go to the living-room and light the fireplace."

Dax stayed in his new quiet, unresponsive state. Even when I picked him up and carried him downstairs to lay him on the couch. Not even a twitch. His skin was chilly and looked waxen. The only thing moving was his chest rising and falling with deep breaths, and his eyes darting back and forth behind closed lids.

Cam tucked him into a blanket and pulled his head on her lap. She stroked his messy hair and dabbed the sweat from his face. Fane had brought her arsenal of bandage material and continued to clean Dax's gashes.

I got a fire going and sat down on the couch at Dax's feet. Kasha was sitting behind us, watching Dax closely without a sound. She loved the boy dearly and our connection was heavy with worry, stemming from both sides.

I opened Dax's grimoire that Fane had brough along and started reading.

"I should never have let him keep that thing after we got here," Cam said. "But he was so passionate about magic." A single tear ran down her stricken face, which looked almost as pale as her son's. "He wanted to learn all he could. I was okay with him learning…" her lower lip trembled and she trailed off.

"You couldn't have known, love," Fane said. "He was so proud to be able to shield us, and you did forbid any other spells."

"Should have taken it away," Cam said, eyeing the tome reproachfully.

I agreed, but it wouldn't do any good telling her that.

While Fane swiped the black goo from Dax's cuts, then dabbed iodine on them and bandaged everything, I dove into the book.

My eyes narrowed when I came to a portion that I couldn't read. Most of the spells were in Latin, but this… This language was nothing I recognized. I remembered Dax asking me about one of these pages, whether or not Fane or I could read it. Neither of us could. What kind of language was it? Maybe I could find something to help if I was able to decipher this part. I frowned. If only I had access to the library in Cyrisas.

"What is that look about?" Fane asked watching me, her gaze suspicious.

"I wanted to go anyway," I said in answer. The graveness with which I said it, tipped Fane off as to what I was referring to.

Her eyes rounded. "No, Mihr."

"What? Go where?" Cam asked.

"Heaven," Fane said. "You would be killed instantly, and even if you weren't and you'd reach your head honcho, who is to say he would listen, or care?"

"He is God, Fane. He always cares."

This time Cam snorted. "If God cared about the fate of Humans, He is either pretty powerless, or a sadist."

Her expression dared me to counter her words. It was the age-old discussion and I was tired of having it. Tired of protecting and justifying His actions, or lack thereof. Truth be told, He had stopped truly caring ages ago. For individual Humans, that was. He did send us out to dim the bigger problems. Sometimes. Sometimes some of us went to help of our own volition. But there was only so much we could do, only so many of us free that weren't busy fighting against Hell.

"I will make him care," I said.

"The fuck you will," Fane growled. "You will not go near that place. Promise me."

My gaze met her amber one. "You know I can't."

"Then we find another way," Fane said. She placed Dax's bandaged arm down and strode to me. Plopping down at my side, she snagged the book from my lap. "Lemme take a look."

"Knock yourself out," I said. "But if you come up empty, I will go."

For a while there were no sounds other than the periodical hiss and pop from the fire, pages turning and the occasional sniffle from Cam. I felt utterly helpless as I placed Dax's feet in my lap. They were growing long, preceding the rest of his growth. Right now, his feet looked disproportionally long. Soon the rest of his body would catch up. Still, he was little more than a child, his demeanor so young, almost naïve. It was one of the things I loved about him. He saw no evil in anyone or anything, which could be the reason he had thrown caution to the wind and tried so many spells. What had he been doing, though? And had the cuts been there already, or had they materialized today? I bit my teeth together. I really needed to do something. If Fane didn't have such a good point – namely that I'd probably die before ever reaching God – I would have been on my way by now. Maybe I could sneak into Cyrisas if I was careful. I nearly snorted at the thought. No one snuck into the holy city, and Fane had brought up something else earlier. Maybe I'd be able to command her staying behind for a while, but eventually Kasha would follow, no matter how clear I made it that she shouldn't.

"Huh," Fane made next to me. "I think this... there is a listing here. A summary of magic users in this realm."

"Humans?" I asked.

"Probably. It doesn't say, but what else would they be?"

"Nephilim? Half-breeds?" I suggested.

Fane raised a brow at me. "Really? You think there are many in this realm? I don't even know of any that exist."

"Well... I know that Nephilim definitely exist. From time to time, Angels have been known to... fornicate with Humans and produce offspring. Of course, those Angels and their children are killed, but I think some must have slipped past during the years."

Fane blinked at me.

"What? It has been known to happen." I scooted from side to side in my seat uncomfortably.

"I knew your kind was naughty," Fane said. She looked back at the book and frowned. "But I'm unsure whether or not there are any demonic Half-breeds. I mean... The Demons would have to be visible to Humans and able to interact in order to *fornicate and produce offspring.*"

I rolled my eyes. "I have known half-Demons to exist, so there is a way. Through summoning, I guess."

Fane suddenly scrutinized the page closely. "I know this word... Damara... land?" She leaned forward so she could look past me at Cam. "Didn't the old lady at the mushroom-schnitzel stand say she was 'Damara'?"

"Mushroom-schnitzel?" I asked, but was ignored.

"I think so," Cam said. "But do you know if that tribe is indigenous to this country or not?"

"Hmm." Fane worried her lower lip. "I'll just go and ask. If so, there is a magic user hiding in that place."

"And you're going to go there? Not knowing what or who you are walking into? Aren't you?" I asked when she snapped the book shut and got up.

"Still a better idea than banking on entering Heaven as a fallen Angel," Fane said.

"Then I'm coming with you," I said.

"You should stay here with Cam and Dax. The shield is down, this house could be vulnerable."

I crossed my arms, feeling a sour heaviness enter my chest. "Seems sensible. But so are you when you go out."

My Demon walked to her friend and placed a palm on her shoulder, squeezing it repeatedly. Cam reached for Fane's hand and took it, her gaze hopeful.

"I will find a way to help him, Camille. I promise," Fane said. She looked up to me again. "Vulnerable or not, no one will notice. I'll just not use my powers, I'm guessing my people have sicked another Ember on my tail again. Dunno if they even have a way of finding me without looking for anomalies concerning my powers."

"I don't like it," I said. "But we have to try everything to help Dax.

"Exactly." Fane passed Kasha, stroked her shoulder and stepped behind me. She bent over me and hugged me from above. "You take care of my peeps, ya hear? And yourself." She kissed my forehead and I skimmed both her arms with my hands. "Be careful," I told her.

My Demon winked, lacking her usual cheek. "Always am."

"Liar." I wanted to hold her to me, to not let her go, but she was right. We had to do something, and it didn't feel right leaving Cam and Dax alone without the shield. There was no way of knowing if we could be found and by whom. I told myself that Fane was clever and resilient, and she was only out for a bit, traversing the same streets and places she had this morning.

Still, the sour heaviness didn't leave my chest.

Chapter Four

Fane

The Surface,

the streets of a coastal Namibian city

The moment I left the house, I drew my jacket tighter. The chilly atmosphere I felt since the shield was down was amplified by the cold wind coming from the sea. It was always a bit cold in the wind here, but now… I felt the chill whistle through me and sink into my very being.

Contrary to what I had shown Mihr and Cam, I wasn't confident at all as I walked from the yard and closed the high, wooden gate behind me. I glanced up and down the street before taking a left. A bout of paranoia engulfed me, making my steps unsure and my shoulders clench. I felt watched, even though the possibility was unlikely. At least Cam and Dax were relatively safe with Kasha and Mihr in the house. Certain

Demons could use magic, and I loathed to think what would happen if they found us here, or the house, or me alone on these streets. *How would they know?* I held on to that question as hard as I could.

I passed many small shops and nearly jumped when a metallic squeak to my side sounded off with all the subtlety of a thunderclap. It was only a rotating stand made of painted wire, hosting postcards of Namibia and – I smiled – maps of the country itself. Quickly, I snagged one and entered the shop. It was empty so buying the map was the work of a moment. Content with my acquired loot, I continued on my way. The respite from my paranoia was short lived and soon my steps quickened, as did my heartbeat. Whether I was being watched or not, Dax needed help as soon as possible.

Once I reached the market, my breath came easier and I quickly found the stand from before. This time there was a line in front of it and the old flour bags containing the Omajovas had shrunken in numbers quite a bit. Glancing past the customers, I couldn't help my heart skip a relieved beat when I spied the older woman, perched in a corner, grumpily glowering at the people in the row.

I thought back to this morning and rounded the stand to come up on the side of the old lady. "Oussie?" I asked. "Do you remember me?"

Her brown eyes flashed to me and a toothless grin lit up her wrinkly face. "You. The one with the energy." She scrambled to her feet and hobbled over, bumping the younger woman to the side a bit.

"Etse!" the younger one lamented before she saw me and just shook her head.

"What do you want?" the older woman asked me.

I leaned on the stand to close the distance between us, feeling the eyes of the other customers on me. This time it wasn't paranoia, everyone was looking. "I wanted to ask you a few questions if I may? About the..." I crinkled my nose in concentration. "...the Energy? And the magic man?"

"Ih, the energy," the old woman said and nodded once.

She scrutinized me for a few heartbeats, her ancient gaze seeming to look past and into me. I felt curiously bare to her perusal.

"Come," she finally said and exited the stall. She led me to the back, where a few empty bottle crates were stacked. She pulled two from a stack, sat down on one and gestured to the other, offering me a seat.

"Thank you," I said, sitting down opposite her.

"What do you want to know?"

I chewed the inside of my cheek for a moment, not knowing where or how to start. "You said you are Damara?"

She nodded once. "Yes, my people."

"So, where is the place called Damaraland?"

"Northwest. It is the homeland of some of my people. I come from the village Khorixas myself. If you have a good car, it is about four hours away."

So far so good, sounded like it was in this country. I wrung my hands, anxious about my next question. "Is that where you met the… one with the energy?"

Her grin was back. "The magic man? No, he is further north. I once visited my tannie. She lives close to the Torra conservancy." She placed her bony hands on her knees and leaned forward. "I wanted to see the fairy circles, they say God walked the Earth there and those are his footsteps. But I know different." She held up an index finger. "The energy is strong, there is magic. I got lost and when I climbed a hill to see my way, I stumbled into a pack of lions." It was hard not to be spellbound by her expressive face as she ripped open her eyes and clamped a palm over her mouth. "Atatata, I tell you, they wanted to eat me. I couldn't run. You don't run from a lion. So, I found a stick and," she clapped her hands, "I bliksamed it on the ground and yelled at them." As she got even more animated and lost in her memory, her accent thickened and a few words of Afrikaans slipped through here and there. "They skriked a bit, but soon hitting the ground with my stick didn't work anymore." She shook her head. "I thought it was my time and I prayed to ti !khutse!" She looked up and pointed her finger at the heavens. "He didn't care, but the magic man did. The lions came closer, I could feel the breath on my neck." She slapped the side of her neck with a palm. "Hot and stinky. Like aas. Like death. And then," she clapped her hands together, making me jump, "they ran away."

Her eyes wide open, she stared into the distance, her memory coming to life in her mind. "There stood the man… the magic man. Eish, he was young, but old. Mooi, but scary. He looked at me and said, 'Axsa, go home. Your way is clear now.' He showed me," she indicated ahead with a hand, "and I saw. I ran home to my tannie as fast as I could. She told me he was a magic man, and I was lucky he hadn't eaten me, or put a curse on me. He can do that, you know. The energy, it is groot!"

"How long ago was this?" I asked, spellbound by her animated storytelling.

"Ach," she waved me off, "fifty years, for sure. But my tannie told me the man was already there when she was a girl."

"Huh," was all I could say. That was fascinating. There were two options. Either the woman before me had seriously lost her marbles, or I had just found the location of another magic user. Human or not, it didn't matter. Neither Mihr nor I knew enough about magic to really help Dax. And he needed help now. So, I was going to chance it.

"Can you show me on a map?" I asked, leaning to the side to pull free the one I had bought and stuffed into my back pocket.

She looked from the map to the pen in my other hand, to me. "Why?" Her gaze narrowed.

I sighed, deciding that time was of the essence and I didn't have enough of it to convince her. *Surely this miniscule use of power won't register*, I thought picking up a stone to my feet. I let my power leak into my fist, warming it. I placed the map on my lap and formed, molded and shaped the stone with my fingers. Finally, I held out my palm to her and she gasped when a small statue rested upon it. A statute resembling her.

The woman took the miniature of herself, turned it over in her fingers, ogling it. Then – without taking her eyes from the thing – she reached out a hand for the map.

Once done marking the map and writing down a few instructions, she tucked the miniature away and stood. She reached out a hand and pulled me up with what little strength she had. Her gnarly fingers clasped mine even as I stood, at least a head taller than her. "You honor me. I will keep your present close. If you come back from your search for the magic man, you may find me and we'll talk about your adventure. If you're not getting gryped by a bunch of lions." She winked. "Come find me when you get back. Ask for Anna and Lizette, that is me and my granddaughter who runs the stand."

"Thank you, Anna," I said and shook her hand.

I received one last toothless smile before she waddled off, back to the stand.

No matter if I ever saw Anna again, she had gotten me a lead, and for a moment, hope surged in my chest, tugging at my anxiety, but unable to vanquish it completely.

I hurried back as fast as I could. The feeling of eyes following me didn't leave and I was covered in goosebumps from head to toe by the time the wall enclosing our house came into view. Oncoming fog, blocking out the sun, coupled with the ever-present wind, whistling through the alleys, added to my discomfort, and for the first time I felt it as being truly cold and damp. Not livening, but foreboding. Nerves. Had to be.

I hopped from the salt road onto the pavement and nearly jogged the last few steps before opening the creaky, wooden door sitting inside the high wall. Feeling for the ridges of the map I had stuffed in my front pocket, I hurried to the door, my mind already far inland, searching for the unageing magic-man.

The situation in the living-room was much the same as I had left it around an hour ago. Cam was still cradling Dax on her lap, Kasha still loomed behind both like a living statue, and Mihr paced the length of the room to the kitchen counter and back. His movements were sharp and his wings softly flapped in his wake. For a moment, I stopped short at the sight of his angelic form. As always, he looked out of this world, too magnificent to be real.

Upon me entering, all heads turned and I walked over to Cam, pulled the map from my pocket and spread it out on the coffee table before sitting down on the couch.

"I got a lead," I announced.

Cam leaned closer and Mihr dashed toward us to bend over the table and take a look. I poked a finger at the cross Anna had made on my map. "X marks the spot," I said and tapped the paper.

"The spot? To what exactly?" Mihr asked.

"A magic man, or magic man, as my newest friend Anna has told me," I answered.

"Aha, and how does *Anna* know a magic man?" My Angel raised a brow, his expression doubtful.

"He saved her from a lion attack once, and apparently, he never ages."

Cam placed a palm on my arm. "You think he can help Dax?" Her voice was small and unsteady, brittle with fear and uncried tears.

Covering her hand with my own, I gave hers a squeeze. "I don't know, sweetie, but it's the best lead I've got. And I will go look for him immediately."

"So let me get this straight," Mihr said, crossing his arms, his wings rising so the tips nearly brushed the high ceiling. "You are getting ready to take a stroll through the middle of nowhere to search for some 'magic man,' not knowing what – or who – you might run into? But you have a problem with me going to Heaven for help?"

"Right on the money, Cynthia. I'd rather risk searching out *one* man, who might be able to help, than have you fly into certain death." I tried hard to keep my facial expression in check as he glared at me reproachfully. "And you better can the attitude, you can't expect me to jump for joy at your harebrained plan."

"You know why I have to go," he said.

"I know why you *think* you have to. That is not the same. And your kind will not listen to a thing you say. *He* will not listen."

"Well then, I'll go where I think I ought to, and you can do the same."

Anger shot through me like lightning, making my veins shine with what looked like lava. Damn, this Angel had a way of getting under my skin, it wasn't even funny. The anxiety in face of Dax's condition, coupled with my jog through paranoia-land had been bad enough, but this gave me the shove over the edge. "Satan's ass, Mihr, you are a pain in the neck. Fine. You can flap off to wherever you want to, I don't fucking care anymore. If you'd rather die than help Dax, you are welcome to go ahead. But do me a favor and leave Kasha here, she doesn't deserve to share your fate."

"Fane..." Cam said at my side.

I twisted my head to the side and looked at her. "No. I have had enough of his stupid heroics." My eyes snapped to Mihr. "You care so damned much for the poor fucking souls your former bestie stole, you'd leave all of us behind and risk your life. I'm done standing in the way of your suicidal tendencies." I felt my skin heat to unnatural proportions. Cam hissed and pulled her hand back, but I was too angry to really notice. "You have wanted to get back up there to die since I got us out of Hell, and I am done trying to stop you."

His irises darkened until they mirrored the gray of his wings, while the white of his eyes turned brighter, making them almost shine. "You think I'm suicidal? You think that is why I want to go back? I want to help Dax, I want to make things right. How dare you accuse me of not caring?"

Had I been in my right mind, I would have cowered beneath his glower and imposing appearance, alas, I was pissed beyond reason. Springing to my feet, I got all up in his face. "You asked me to leave you behind to die, you ran head-first into danger – against fifteen Demons – and you have been wanting to tell on Michael since we got here. Don't pretend different. I notice the way you try to hide your nervousness. If you want to leave me so badly, go ahead. Go to your all-caring God and see how well that turns out for you."

"You know what? I will."

"Fine!"

"Fine." Mihr stomped through the room, heading for the exit. With his hand on the handle, he turned to glare at me. "I know what this is really about, Fane. But unlike you, I will refrain from throwing baseless, hurtful accusations at you." He pointed a finger at Kasha, who had gotten up to follow him. "You. Stay."

A questioning mewl floated from the Hellcat, but she stopped in her tracks and watched her Angel slam the door behind him.

"Ugh! That complete asshat," I fumed. "Can you believe him?" It was my turn to pace the length of the room.

"No. In fact I can believe neither of you," Cam said, her voice oddly calm. And cold.

I spun to face her, and recoiled at the look in her eyes. Pure anger shone from them. "My boy is… obviously dealing with something and I have no idea what that is. It scares the pants off me. And you two have nothing better to do than bicker and accuse each other of stupid things? I get that you are scared for him, but maybe you should tell him why. And not be a downright asshole." Cam huffed out a sharp breath, then her shoulders sagged. "Why the fuck am I even humoring this? If Mihr can find help for Dax in Heaven, isn't it worth the risk?"

The anger rushing through my veins only moments before drained from my system as though someone had pulled the plug on it. All that was left was shame, and near-crippling fear. "Of course, Cam. Everything is worth the risk for Dax. I didn't mean–"

"I know." Tears glittered on her face as she looked at me, her wrath replaced with stark fear. It slammed into me and left me breathless with its magnitude. It was a kind of fear I had never known myself. Bottomless and terrible. "What if... what if he never wakes up, Fane?"

I stumbled over and sank to my knees in front of her. "He will. If it is the last thing I do, I promise you, I'll fix this." Reaching out a palm, I cupped her cheek. "I swear to you, Cam."

"He's my boy, Fane. My boy." Cam's lower lip quivered and I hugged her to me. She shook with sobs, slowly wetting my sweater with her tears.

Unable to hold my own tears, we sat together, Dax's between us as we cried. I would not fail either of them. Ever.

Chapter Five

Fane

The Surface,
Somewhere in the air above the Skeleton Coast,
Namibia

It had taken me hours, but finally Kasha allowed me on her back while in flight. Taking off had been interesting, all five times. But now we flew steady. She, frolicking with the wind, doing a weird paddling-air movement with her paws and biting into clouds as though they were solid. And me, packed into jackets, my two whips strapped to either side of me, the hoods – yes, multiple – pulled around my face so only my eyes and nose poked out. I ducked into Kasha's mane-fur, my fingers – gloved – wrapped into it, frozen stiff. My teeth chattered as I adjusted our course a bit, orienting myself along the roads beneath us.

We were lucky. It was one night after a full moon so we could see our path clearly, cut into the desolate sandy ground like sliced-open earth. From time to time, I fiddled out the map and made sure we were on the right road.

Beyond that, I could only hold on, try not to freeze and fall off, while avoiding thoughts of Mihr. He must have reached Heaven by now. But had he already crossed into the holy city? Was he still undetected, or had they found him? Was he – I forced my thoughts away. He had chosen – admittedly with a bit of my help – to take off on his own. Once in the air, there was no way for me to follow without risking not only my, but his and Kasha's life too. He had gone where neither of us could follow.

It had been hard to relay that fact to the Hellcat, though. She had been adamant to find her Angel. I think what had swayed her was how I had told her we needed to help Dax first. Eventually, she seemed to understand where we both went was important, even if that path didn't lead to Mihr.

Now as my ire had cooled some, I felt awful. "Shouldn't have said those things to him," I mumbled into the cutting wind. "Shouldn't have lost it like that. Cam was right, I'm a major asshole."

A soft, inquiring mewl came from Kasha, sounding curiously like a dove's coo.

"What was I thinking? Yelling at him like that when we needed to work together, to help Dax? Stupid, stupid, stupid."

What if the last things I said to him were words of anger? Just because I felt like he was pulling away? Like I wasn't enough for him? Because I had fallen for my Angel.

I pressed my face into Kasha's fur. As frustrating as it was that he put the lives of unknown people first, his genuine compassion was one of the things I loved about him. It was a foreign concept to me, but I did like it. Yet, I had to wonder if I was right. Did Mihr have a death wish because he felt like he needed to be punished for what happened? For Michael? For being with me? No, certainly not that last part. We weren't together like that, the only thing he might feel guilty about was the sex.

Groaning, I unearthed the map and looked it over, then steered Kasha a bit to the left. I had bigger things to worry about right now, like Dax holding on until I had dragged back the magic man, and Mihr surviving the holy city and his God. Fear riddled me mercilessly and my throat, tight as it already was, squeezed all the way shut. It took me three tries to swallow.

"I hope we find him, Kasha," I said.

The Hellcat dropped in answer, then beat her mighty wings to surge up once more. In my current state of mind, it made my stomach sink with nausea. I felt like tilting to the side and let gravity take me. Shame and fear danced cha-cha upon my conscience. For now, all I could content myself with was freezing and waiting until we reached our destination. Pity, I had wanted to see more of this spectacular country, but not like this.

****

We arrived shortly before dawn and when Kasha landed, I nearly toppled off, stiff as a board. Carefully, I slid my aching body from her back. My face tingled and burned from the sudden lack of the constant wind and my joints cracked when I took my first uncertain steps, hanging onto Kasha for support.

From down here, the surroundings looked unreal. The soft rosy glow on the horizon revealed red stones upon red sand. Grass – yellow, with silvery tips – covered everything. The blades stubbornly growing around the stones let a sea of semi-see-through silver dance in a slight breeze. Here and there hills rose, and in the distance, a huge mountain reached into the pristinely clear sky. I was sure I had never seen a clearer sky since being on the Surface. It was magnificent. But looking at it had my thoughts firmly steering into Angel territory and I yanked my mind back.

With a deep breath, I pulled my hoods off, combed my fingers through my hair and walked in the direction of a settlement I had seen from above, hoping the people living there could help me find my magic man.

"Kasha, you should better hide while I talk to them, I have no idea how they see you, and I can't help to think that no matter what form it is, it wouldn't help our cause much."

The Hellcat threw me an offended look, but seemed to have gathered my intent when I told her to stay out of sight behind one of the hills.

I rounded the hill and came upon a slowly waking village. It was more a gathering of tiny houses really. Some of the houses were made of bricks, some of sheet metal, and others – as I could see from a half finished one – had a skeleton of long sticks stuck into the ground that where closed by a mix of grass, dried mud and cow-dung. Those also had reed or grass roofs. Small as the houses were, I saw satellite dishes sit atop many a roof. The scent of smoke and fire wafted through the air, originating from the countless fireplaces all around.

A brown dog, snoozing next to a bone, lifted his head abruptly when hearing my steps. He blinked at me, then sprang up and barreled toward me, yapping and barking, with rising hackles. I stopped and waited. Within seconds, more dogs emerged from everywhere, and I was surrounded by a crowd of barking and snarling pups.

Alerted by the ruckus, people stuck their heads from the houses and came outside to see what was going on. As soon as they beheld me in my furry circle, they began waving their arms, shouting and chasing the dogs away. Soon, I stood in another circle, this one made of curious Humans. Most smiled at me shyly, except for the kids, who grinned and surrounded me immediately, chattering and laughing. One of them even boldly poked my hand with a tiny finger and giggled. I smiled, my spirits lifting at their beaming faces.

"Are you lost, Miss?" a young man asked, making the children quiet down. He had a pleasant face and genuine worry shone from his brown eyes.

"Not lost, no," I answered. "I am looking for someone."

"Who might that be, Miss?" the same man asked.

"A woman named Anna told me there might be a magic man living around these parts." I felt weird saying it and my discomfort grew when the shy smiles morphed into worried expressions. Some of the women tugged their children from my immediate vicinity, anxiety sharpening their movements and faces. Others simply turned away and walked off. Talk about an atmosphere change…

A small, old woman fired a sentence at me in what I guessed was Damara going by the clicking sounds accompanying the words. Like Anna, she wore a long, flowery dress and a dark-blue headscarf.

The young man from before nodded and translated, "She says there is no one like that around here."

I gave the ancient woman my best smile. "I know there is. And I really need to speak to him. It is urgent."

She waved me off, firing another short-clipped tirade at me.

Again, the young man helped me understand. "She says no one goes looking for a magic man. Especially not this–" he stopped short, receiving a smack on the back of the head from the old woman.

"Especially not this one?" I suggested.

The woman glowered at me, then at the young guy. She motioned at me to follow and stomped off, surprisingly fast. My translator joined me, a sheepish grin on his face. Behind us, the other people dispersed slowly, but I felt their lingering looks glued to my back.

The tiny woman scuttled past the houses, her walking stick thumping the ground with each step, until we reached one that was painted red and a bit larger than the others. A little garden with succulents and strangely shaped stones – an assortment of quartzes and granite – lay to the right and the other side had a washing line filled with dresses and fabrics of exceptionally bright colors. A few stools, very close to the ground, sat in a circle in front of the entrance.

She sat and motioned for me to take a seat, as well. The young man stood behind the woman and waited for her to speak. Her eyes wandered over me, suspicious and a bit curious.

"Her name is Magdalena," the man said after she spoke. "I am Abraham, she wants to know who you are."

"It's good to meet both of you, I am Fane."

A long speech followed, during which Magdalena gripped her walking stick with both hands and waved it around. I liked the cadence of the language a lot, if I ever got the chance, I would like to learn it. Abraham slightly bobbed from one foot to the other, looking highly uncomfortable as he listened while trying to keep his smile in place for me.

When Magdalena was done, he opened his mouth and closed it again, then he took a deep breath. "Magdalena says you should go back where you came from. Talking about a magic user unsettles the people, especially since the recent happenings."

I doubted it was all she said, but Abraham's voice carried fear when he spoke. I couldn't be sure, but believed it was the same fear I had seen when mentioning the magic man.

"What recent happenings?" I asked.

Magdalena hissed and said something short.

"I'm sorry, but she says that is none of your business, you should leave." He nodded at me, a rueful expression on his face. "I can show you how to get to the nearest town and you can get a lift to wherever from there."

"Thank you, Abraham, but I really need to see the magic man." I stared straight at Magdalena. "I am not leaving until I have spoken to him."

My words were met with an angry rant and a waving, pointing stick. For a second, I was afraid I'd have to doge it, but the old woman flipped it over and drilled it into the ground repeatedly.

Abraham interrupted her with a calm voice, which resulted in Magdalena turning on her stool, poking her stick to his nose and yelling. An argument ensued at the end of which she threw her hands in the air repeatedly before turning to me again. This time, my nose made acquaintance with the end of her stick, but I stayed put. Magdalena huffed a few times, then prodded a stone with a foot. She let her stick sink and grumbled something that sounded defeated.

Abraham shook his head. "You should not search for him, those who have, haven't come back often. And since a while–" He said something when the old woman sucked in air to speak and she clapped her mouth shut. "Since a while, young people from our village have gone missing at night. Either he is the cause, or he is doing nothing about it. Either way, it is dangerous right now."

"I'll be fine," I assured him.

He smiled and nodded, but in a way that had me knowing he didn't believe me.

"Just… just point me in the right direction, I'll find him," I said. "Please."

Abraham and Magdalena shared a look.

"You need magic?" Magdalena asked, her accent thick.

"I do. Desperately."

"No good." She wagged her finger. "Danger."

"Don't I know it."

She crinkled her nose and frowned. "The circles. He is close."

"Circles?" I looked up to Abraham.

"The fairy circles," he explained. "They are one or two kilometers that way." He pointed north-west. "The magic man lives close to the circles. If he wants to meet you, he will find you."

I inclined my head once and got up. "Thank both of you so much. You have helped me a great deal."

"Careful. Magic not good," Magdalena said.

"You're a wise woman, Magdalena," I said. "Thank you." With one last smile, I walked away, heading in the direction Abraham had shown me.

Once I had left the village behind me, I whistled. I didn't have to wait for long and Kasha appeared from Saints knew where. Luckily, not the direction of the village.

When she reached me, she knocked the air from my chest by stomping her face against it with a purr. I almost toppled over from the impact, and threw my arms around her to steady myself. She pressed her head closer and mewled.

"You worried?" I asked, scratching behind her ears and around her horns.

Another meow.

I hugged her to me and kissed her between the eyes. "I'd never leave you behind. You know that, right?"

This time, I got a long mewl followed by serious purring action. "Let's go," I whispered into her fur before I let go.

Quickly, I pulled off my shoes and continued walking barefoot to feel the earth around us. We didn't need any surprises. And this way I could at least feel. I relished the stone and sand meeting my soles, and the knowledge that I could protect myself if need be. Using my power would have to be a last resort though.

As we braved the stony, desert-like valley, we saw antelopes in the distance and felt the heat of the sun as soon as she had risen fully. It was unbelievable what power she held here. I felt the shine burn on my skin, calling forth my inner fire in answer. Repeatedly, I had to dim it as not to burn off my clothes. I loved the feel though. This was where I was supposed to be. A habitat that complemented me. Made of stone, sand, and sun.

Anxious as I was, a sense of utter calm threatened to brim my mind at this place. It was unreal, beautiful, and harsh. Incredible. It felt right.

I frowned when my feet told me something was off. Not really off, but different. Like circles enclosed in nothingness. As soon as I saw them, I understood. There were circles of sand in the grass. Perfectly round patches where nothing grew. The roots of the grass cut off accurately, they were what felt like the nothing encompassing the sand.

Sinking down into a crouch, I dug the tips of my fingers into the sand and closed my eyes. Too perfect. This couldn't be natural. I frowned, feeling down. There was a foreign feeling looming deep underground. Something I couldn't really grasp or understand. Like an involuntary shiver, it danced over my skin, making it crawl. There was malice in the deep. And a certain feel reminding me of Hell. But what exactly, I couldn't say. All I knew was that none of these countless circles were natural.

"Are you the one who brought trouble, or are you then one seeking it?" a voice said behind us said, making Kasha and me spin around.

A man, tall and muscular, wearing a loincloth made of leather, stood before us. He looked perpetually ageless, and I couldn't decide whether he looked twenty or fifty. His face had no lines at all, his hair was twisted into dreads in some places and neatly braided in others. A cape of leopard fur hung around his shoulders and countless necklaces rested on his chest. For a second his body seemed to flicker before me, like a mirage, but when I blinked, the moment was gone.

All in all, I was sure I had found my magic man.

Chapter Six
Mihr

Heaven, The Burned Valleys

The Burned Valleys were an endless wasteland of softly wavering gray-white sand. Ruins of fallen temples and houses crumpled into themselves, their walls and roofs prey of destruction, time, and decay. Once, long ago, the place had been a bustling city. Lucifer's fall and the resulting war had reduced it to dust and rubble. Except for one of the old temples.

I stood, hidden in a partly destroyed house, spying through a gap in a wall. The live sand nipped at my heels gently, as if it recognized me and said 'hello.' Maybe it did, Fane did say it was alive and conscious, but I didn't pay it much mind as I had bigger problems.

It was true. Even after everything Michael had said, a part of me still wanted to have a reasonable explanation. Something that would brand him a liar, but not a stealer of souls. Yet, there it was, clear as day. The hidden compound. The evidence of his unholy betrayal.

Anger at Fane and fear for Dax's life had driven me to come, the last sliver of reason had brought me here, to confirm my suspicions. Faced with the truth, both momentarily took a backseat as utter wrath and the feel of betrayal washed over me, erasing the last smidge of guilt I felt for killing Michael.

I had known my former friend had built an army, but seeing irrefutable proof, was like finding out for the first time. Staggeringly devastating.

No matter what I had told Fane, I couldn't just creep into Cyrisas without knowing, without proof. And now I was looking at it. The old temple had been patched up and reworked enough to house people. Angels sporadically arrived and left. They did try to be inconspicuous about it, but it had been laughably easy to find the place. All I had to do was lie in wait close to the only intact portal to Earth, and soon enough, a group of young Angels had shown up and led me straight into this lost city.

This part of Heaven was forbidden, the exits to the realm of Earth had been closed off, leaving only one for emergencies. It was guarded by seasoned Angels, who had let the young Angels through. Things started to make horrible sense, the more I saw. Not only were young Angels trained here – probably stolen souls – but others of my kind knew about it. The guards for example. Meaning Michael had not acted alone.

Who else was part of it? How far up the line did this secret project go? A tiny part in me dared to ask the unthinkable – Did He know? The second that question wormed its way into my mind, I chased it out. But the damage was done. Doubt had entered me and wouldn't leave. I couldn't risk finding the Lord alone and confide in Him, as I had planned on doing. If I was to tell Him, many would have to be present. Because if He knew… He would have no qualms silencing me before more people found out. God was many things, forgiving wasn't one of them.

I ducked when the *whoosh* of wings sounded above me. A second later, an Angel swooped over the house I hid inside and landed not far away. She looked around with panicked eyes, her heeled feet clomping on the cobbled stone ground as she paced through the rubble. Flexing and balling her hands repeatedly, she seemed to wait for someone tensely.

I narrowed my gaze, that face... it looked familiar. Then I recognized her. She was the Angel who had turned on Michael, defying his orders to kill Fane and Cam, deciding to save her companion instead. What was she doing here? And who was she waiting for?

Since I couldn't leave without her spotting me, it seemed like I was going to find out.

As I was forced to watch her pace, chew her nails, try to sit on parts of crumbled wall, just to spring up once more, my anger settled enough to be bombarded by thoughts of Fane.

I clenched my teeth and concentrated on the she-Angel outside. Repeatedly, she gazed up then shook her head as if she was shaking away a thought or notion, making her dark-brown hair sway. Her dark-gray wings opened and closed with sharp movements, something I doubted she was aware of. But no matter how much I focused on the she-Angel's nervous demeanor, Fane was at the back of my mind. Nudging with the subtlety of a sledgehammer.

Had she found her magic man yet? What if she got into trouble? Knowing my Demon, I was sure of it. Fear scraped up my back like a set of rusty nails. I had to get going. But the more I thought about sneaking into Cyrisas and into the Lord's palace, the heavier the doubt from before grew, until it settled in the pit of my stomach like a pile of rocks.

I had been sure he didn't know. But now… just that little part of me wondering had been enough. If He knew, I would be no good to Dax or the souls being stolen – I'd be dead.

We should never have split up, we should have tried both our options together, the way we had gotten through everything. Her words though… Why? Did Fane really believe me to be suicidal? I didn't understand her reluctance to do something, she had agreed to two weeks ago. And I didn't buy her outrage at putting our lives at risk. Something else was up and I had my suspicions on that matter.

The she-Angel outside straightened and a smile stretched on her lips. It was too wide and morphed her beautiful features into a grimace. Her dark wings began seriously shaking, sealing the deal on how young she must be, my kind learned how to control the emotions relayed through our wings first. She was freshly turned.

A man landed a few feet from her and she jogged to him as though to hug him, but he stiffened and she stopped short.

"Thomas, thank the Lord! You got my message," she said, her words echoing off the ruined walls around us.

"That was careless, Karina," Thomas said. "You could have gotten us both in trouble." He shook his head then crossed his arms. "Why did you ask me to come? You shouldn't even be outside the compound, Shamal—"

My eyes widened in shock. Shamal was part of this? Another Archangel? Just who else was involved?

"Shamal threatened to kill me." The white of her eyes started glowing subtly, her wings shivering something fierce now. "Because I chose to save you. I am so relieved you have recovered fully, I wasn't sure." Karina's shoulders sagged. "I am confined to my room since…"

"As well you should be. You defied an order, Karina. Had you obeyed, Michael would still be alive."

Shock flitted across her features. "You can't mean that. I made a decision. I chose you."

Thomas inclined his head once. "I am thankful you did, but you shouldn't have. Michael was more important than I'll ever be. He was the champion to our cause. I heard some of the others say that he founded our order. We lost our greatest fighter and for what?" his voice grew bitter. "For a one in a thousand soldier like me? He was our leader, Karina. What were you thinking?"

Karina rubbed both her upper arms as though freezing, her gaze flew from Thomas' face to the tips of her shoes and back again. "You know why," she said softly.

"The Devil be damned, you can't be serious!" The Angel stiffened even more. "You have to forget about us. This… unhealthy obsession has gone on long enough."

"Obsession? Are you kidding me? You didn't think it an obsession during the times we hooked up." Karina frowned. "What is wrong with you?"

"That was before you dishonored us both by choosing me over Michael. Now your name spells disappointment and lack of commitment." He let out an exasperated sigh. "I shouldn't have come, but I wanted to make clear where I stood on the matter. Please leave me alone from now on."

"Thomas…"

"I mean it. Just…" He threw his hands up and stepped back. "Whatever was between us, is over, Karina."

Karina's face drained of color as she stared at the guy she'd saved, her unbelieving mien heartbreaking.

"Also, you should get back as soon as you can. If Shamal finds out you disobeyed him, there will be consequences." With that, the feathered idiot snapped open his wings and sprang into the sky, flying off in the direction of the compound.

Karina was left blinking at his shrinking form. She sagged like a balloon without air, her wings – which had stopped shivering, hung from her tall frame like washing cloths.

I couldn't help but feel sorry for her. Her decision had saved all of our lives, and while Thomas, the doofus, wasn't grateful – even though he said he was – I certainly felt gratitude towards Karina. Had she followed Michael's order to kill Fane and Cam – no, I couldn't even think about it.

As I watched on, I saw change roll over the she-Angel. Her desolation slowly but surely morphed into anger as she muttered to herself, her face turning darker.

"Obsession? Son of a biscuit. Who was the one chasing after whom?" She started pacing again and I hoped she would take off so I could too. Sympathize as I might, Dax still needed help, and Fane was still chasing after dubious magic users.

Something nipped at my ankle and I jumped, then looked down. A swath of sand had twirled its way into the ruin and gently ran over my feet. The touch felt like course wind, like desert sand being blown against me. A not-really-there touch. I felt decidedly stupid as I nodded at the sand as if to acknowledge it. The sand rustled excitedly and wound up my pantleg, coiling around my leg like a snake.

I stumbled back in surprise as it slid into my pocket, my heel hit a loose piece of stone, which bounded off the next wall with a loud, dull sound. Forgetting all about the sand, I spun around and ducked, hoping that Karina had either gone, or hadn't noticed.

Pressing my eye to the crack and spying outside, I let out a relieved breath when she was nowhere to be seen.

"You," her voice said behind me and I jolted upright, cursing beneath my breath. How in the nine circles of Hell had I – an over seven-hundred-year-old warrior – given up my position like a bloody newbie. The answer was as simple as it was irrelevant, live-sand.

Karina quickly recovered from her shock and pulled out her blade. "You are coming with me," she said.

"Doubtful, young one," I told her, and let my wings materialize, with one lunge, I broke through the derelict ceiling and shot from the ruin. I beat my wings as fast as I could, cursing myself and the stupid sand in my pocket, while casting back glimpses over my shoulder.

The she-Angel hovered over the ruins, then turned and dashed off toward the compound.

I doubled my speed. She was getting backup. I needed to get away as fast as I could. Out of Heaven if possible, there would be no place safe for me in this realm now that they knew I was here.

I made for the forgotten portal I had come from and sailed through to Earth as fast as possible. I had to find Fane.

Pulling my wings against my body, I barreled down like a bullet, concentrating on my connection with Kasha, letting the subtle pull to her lead me. As I crossed over barren land and stony hills, I wondered where they were. And hoped to high Heaven that Karina had not gotten hold of an experienced Angel in time, who could make an educated guess as to where I had exited.

I told myself that I had used one of the forgotten portals, trying to dim the anxiety stemming from seeing the evidence of Michael and Shamal's betrayal first-hand.

Chapter Seven

Fane

The Surface, Damaraland

"Depends on who's asking," I said.

The man in his loincloth tilted his head, then his eyes widened. "You are not of this place."

"You have no idea, buddy."

"What is that?" He pointed at Kasha, but before I could say anything, he held up a hand. Then he took a bit of powder from the countless little bags lining his loincloth and threw it in the air. He mumbled a few words and suddenly I felt a wave of pressure roll over my skin. It rebounded in my ears without a sound and I gasped, feeling dizzy.

The man stared at us, then stumbled back. "You are from beneath!" he yelped. "You and the beast."

Kasha shook her mighty head and squinted. Looked like the bout of pressure was affecting her too. She pawed the earth and wobbled a bit, unsure.

"Have they finally sent someone to kill me?" the man asked, proceeding to plunge both his hands into different pouches.

Judging by what only a bit of his powder had done, I acted fast and sank into a crouch. My fingers broke through sand and earth, cementing my connection to the surrounding. A rush raced through me as I reveled in my power, having kept from using it for far too long. I closed my eyes and felt around, then pulled at the ground the man stood on. The hard floor cracked open like an egg and he sank into the crack up to his hips, the air leaving his lungs with a heavy *umph*.

"Hold your powders, cowboy," I told him. "We are no threat. In fact, I believe we need your help."

He wheezed, patting around his hips trying to pull himself free. "Lying Demon. Your kind never needed the help of one such as me. If you want to kill me, do it, I have lived well past my years as it is."

"Listen man, you threw powder at us and were about to do so again. I only defended us." I twisted my palm and filled the crack, starting at his feet. I was careful to infuse as little of my power as possible into the earth, not knowing how many Embers were on the lookout to pinpoint me. But even as I felt connected again, a sense of doubt and foreboding stole itself into my chest. They had to be really good though, to be able to feel that slight tremor of power. Other than myself, I wasn't even sure an Ember existed who could. Even telling myself that, the doubt didn't leave. *Paranoid much?*

The man gasped when his body rose, until he stood before me, his legs caked in red dust, looking a bit disheveled, but unharmed.

"We are looking for a magic man, judging by what you can do, we have found you."

"Huh." He dusted himself off and grimly felt his – now empty – pouches. He sank to his hunches and gathered up some of the things that had fallen from his pockets. What looked like coal, leaves, sticks, and small bones. "What would you need me for?"

"I have a friend who is a magic user himself and I fear he has exhausted himself on magic. He has cuts all over his arms and fell into a trance from which he might not wake."

"Curious. Normally your kind can do magic a lot better than that."

I bit my lower lip. "He is not of my kind. He is Human."

The man's brows shot up, crinkling his forehead into countless wrinkles. "Human. A friend?"

"Yes. And I will do whatever it takes to make him well again."

"Very curious." He sniffed and gazed past me into the distance, then he sniffed again and abruptly turned from us. "Follow, creature."

"Come along, Kasha," I said, and the Hellcat cautiously placed one step in front of the other to keep up. I reached out a hand to stroke her head and to steady her if she needed it, as she still seemed to feel the aftereffects of the man's powder.

The three of us walked through the fields of accurate circles. With each step, I felt the resonance of something ancient beneath my feet, but no matter how deep I felt or how hard I concentrated, I could not decipher what it was. Like an itch at the edge of my mind, it kept me unsettled.

Once we left the circles behind us, we crossed a dry riverbed, the coarse sand crunchy beneath my feet, making a peculiar sound I had never heard before. Even as some greenery sprouted around us, and with it the feeling of life, the unease didn't let up. This land had been touched by something. Whether it was the magic of the man we followed or something different, I didn't know.

We clambered up the other side of the riverbed and came to face a hill made of stone slates. My naked feet felt the stone and I scrutinized the wall rising before me. There should be an opening. I felt it.

The man stopped and turned over one of his pouches, letting small pieces of coal rain into his palm. He drew a sign onto the stone, and what my power had told me to be true revealed itself. The stone flickered like heated air, then vanished, making an opening appear.

"Welcome to my home, cursed one," the man said and gestured for me to enter.

Kasha eyed the tunnel with clear disdain and I told her to stay and be vigilant. She mewled once and pressed her head to mine, before bounding off to climb the hill for a better vantage point.

"The beast listens to you?" the man asked as he looked on. "What is she?"

"A Hellcat," I said. "What did you do when you met us? With the powder?"

He led the way inside and said over his shoulder, "It was a spell that reveals, and stuns. Although, I think it worked better on the beast than on you."

I let my palm graze along the stone tunnel as I went, feeling it. Granite, marble, and pockets of ore, then a cave. I was led into it, light flooding our way from a slit in the ceiling. Fine sand caressed my feet and I looked around at what looked like a cozy home.

The cave walls were straight and smooth, low chairs made of wood sat around a fireplace, and on a naturally even slate of stone, lay a mattress and a heap of blankets. Next to it stood an old dresser with a shelf stacked atop it. The shelf contained books and small figurines. The slit in the ceiling was black with soot from the fireplace and all around the walls were drawings. Animals, people, symbols, and strange marks filled every single open space. The cave smelled like smoke and spices, sharp yet agreeable.

The man trudged over to the dresser and got out jeans and a shirt. "You may make yourself at home," he said as he swapped out his clothing and met my bemused look with a raised brow. "What? I have to look the part I play, doesn't mean it's comfortable."

I turned my back to him and plopped down onto the sand, sticking my fingers into the softness. Just feeling my element to this degree was marvelous. I had stayed inside a house for far too long.

The man rounded me – now dressed normally, safe for the pouches lining his jeans – and sat down on one of the boulders littered throughout the cave.

His dark eyes searched me for a while, and while I felt urgency burning within me, his perusal was strangely charged, making me bear it. His ageless face was handsome and the intelligence in his eyes felt more like the wisdom of ages. How come he knew I was a Demon, but not that Kasha was a Hellcat?

"Now what makes a Demon–"

"Ember. And my name is Fane." I grinned at him.

"Gabriel Gawaseb."

I raised a brow at that but kept my thoughts to myself.

Gabriel scrutinized me with a curious face. "Fane, why does a Demon care whether or not a Human dies?"

"He is my friend."

"Demons and Humans are never friends. One uses the other, or one corrupts the other, there is nothing else."

I sifted sand through my fingers, calming myself with the smooth feel and sound. "Clearly, there is. But never mind that now. Will you help me or not?"

"I might. If you help me first."

"How long will that take?"

"Depends on how fast you solve my problem."

The thought of Dax's waxen face made me swallow and anxiety clawed its way up my throat. "I really don't have much time, buddy. You either help me, or I make you help me."

"Careful, Demon," Gabriel said, "I have means to protect myself."

"Maybe. But I can cocoon you into the stone you're sitting on in a heartbeat."

He chuckled. "You do that, there will be no one to help you. And magical exhaustion is no small matter." He tugged at one of his necklaces with a finger, playing with the pendant. Once more, he seemed to flicker like a trick of the light, but it was so fast that it could have been my imagination. "Your friend might die if the magic stays intact and saps his strength entirely."

The anxiety from before doubled and I fisted the sand in my fingers, trying hard not to alter its form to avoid using more of my power. "What would you have me do?"

Gabriel continued playing with the pendant in his fingers, but his expression changed ever so slightly. For a second, I saw stark fear flash over his face. "There is a village nearby. I have long lived in peace alongside them. I protect them. They come to me for advice and favors sometimes, but recently… Every night, one of them vanishes. They get up from their bed, walk into the desert, and never return. First, they blamed me and some of them even tried to find me." A sly smile tugged at his face, only to vanish as fast as it had come. "But when they found what was left of the missing people… they were afraid to even look." Gabriel sighed and let the pendant sink. "I set up protective spells, to keep them from wandering off, but one always slips through. I followed once, I know where they go, but the energy surrounding the place that calls to them is far too powerful for me to counter and not of this plane." His gaze caught mine. "It is of yours. Your kin roam the place nightly and take mine. I have felt demonic presence before, but they have never killed. Now they rip my people apart. I can't drive them out, but maybe you can."

I snorted. "Me? Okay, so you seem to not know too much about Hell and Demons. I am an Ember, I am one of the weakest Demons there are. Depending on what you are dealing with, my chances are slim."

"But you have weapons," he pointed at my whips, "powers to shift the earth, and the beast."

"True, but I can't use my powers. Not extensively, at least." I gave him a most winning smile. "How about you help me and I will do what I can once we get back?"

Gabriel crossed his arms. "No. There is no telling how many will die if I leave them unprotected."

"One a night?" I suggested, making him glower. My shoulders sank. Prepared as I might be to make him sink into the stone to force him to help, I shouldn't use my powers, and I heard Mihr's voice in my head, telling me to do what was right. Mihr... who I hoped was safe. Guilt bombarded me anew, making the anxiety spike to new heights.

"Fine," I grumbled. "I will check out this place and see if there is anything I can do."

The magic man nodded once, then he stiffened and sprang up. "Someone is here."

"What?" I stuck my hands into the ground.

"Close by," Gabriel said, and this time I was positive that his form flickered. Dark-black skin blinked through, to be replaced by his normal brown. I even glimpsed a hint of red eyes. But that couldn't be, could it?

Gabriel dashed through his cave, took a long stick, leaning against a wall and pressed it against the drawings on the wall in rapid succession, making the symbols gleam and sparkle. His voice turned low and dark as he chanted in a language I had never heard before.

A rumble of pressure prickled across my skin as I felt the sand for clues.

A set of feet hitting ground out of nowhere. Outside. Paws drumming over us, launching Kasha into the air. She landed close to the intruder and – they ran for each other.

"Stop!" I shouted and sprang to my feet.

Gabriel, stick in hand, threw me a surprised look.

"I know who's coming," I told him. My heart fluttered as I turned and sped from the cave and into the tunnel. Was it him? I ran headlong for the mirage of stone and crossed it. A chill hit me, like a curtain of water, as I passed the magic and came to face the glaring sun.

My eyes adjusted just in time to see Kasha and Mihr clash in a mix of limbs, wings and fur. Relief flooded me like a tidal wave and tears sprang to my eyes. A tremor took hold of my body and my knees knocked together with weakness. He was okay. He was back. My Angel was unharmed.

Chapter Eight
Mihr

The Surface, Damaraland

Kasha's chest rumbled with purrs and I hugged her huge head to me and scratched behind her ears and horns. "Found ya," I said to her. She leaned against me and I had to fan out my wings to stay upright as her weight caught me off guard.

With a relived chuckle I stepped back to look at the place I had landed in. The barren, beautiful land around me lost focus when my eyes landed on Fane. She stood in front of a stony hill, tears glimmering on her face. Her fists clenched at her side, she looked like she wanted to make a dash for me, but didn't. As angry as I had left, outraged by her accusations, I wanted nothing more than have her running to me, to hug her, feel her body in my arms. Safe and sound. I held back though, the bitterness her words had left me with still prominent.

"You're alive," she said, her voice breaking.

"I am."

"Did you..." She swallowed. "Did you see Him?"

"No, but I found the compound."

Her relieved expression changed to rage within seconds. "You went looking for it? Are you crazy?"

"I needed proof."

"Mihr, I swear to everything that is stone and metal, if I wasn't so happy to see you, I'd wring your neck right now."

"You wouldn't even be able to reach, Tiny."

She actually stomped her foot at that, and my anger at her paled even more as fondness and mirth flooded me.

Suddenly, a man appeared out of thin air, as if he had just walked from the stone behind Fane. I opened my mouth to warn Fane, but the man robotically walked up to stand next to her, his eyes glued to me with utter shock and surprise.

"An... Angel?" he said.

A sharp smell reached me and I recoiled. "You're a half-Demon."

The man reached for one of the countless pendants around his neck and rubbed it between his fingers, the look of shock morphing to one of fear. "How do you know?"

Fane glanced at him, her brows pulled up. "So that is what the flickering was about. I knew there was something off about you. A half-Demon, hey? I had no idea such a thing existed."

"I told you it occasionally it happens, just like half-Angels," I told her. "It was part of my job to find them and…"

"Kill us," the man finished on my behalf. "Is that why you have come?"

Fane waved him off. "Not everyone is out to get you, Gabriel."

'Gabriel?' I mouthed and Fane smiled. "I know, right? Quite the angelic name for a magic man, or half-Demon, as it were."

"You and your beast know this Angel?" Gabriel asked, pointing at me. "Aren't you supposed to be… mortal enemies?"

"Kasha is his beasty, to be precise, and his name is Mihr, fallen Angel and Hellspawn blesser. We are… companions of sorts," Fane said.

"Yeah, you could say that," I murmured. "I see you have found your magic man. Will he help?"

"Gabriel is being tetchy. He wants me to clear out a Demon presence of unknown origin and kind. All I know is that people from a nearby village vanish nightly and turn up in pieces." She turned to the man at her side. "Right so far?"

Gabriel had not ceased staring at me. He swallowed and nodded absentmindedly, letting the pendant sink to his chest. "I have to protect my people," he rasped.

"Huh. A half-Demon who protects," I mused. "Not a common thing."

"Oh, come on, Paige." Fane rolled her eyes. "When will you learn to not judge people just because they come from Hell? In one form or another?"

I narrowed my gaze at her. "The day you start showing compassion for those you don't know."

The veins of her hands snaked up visibly, glowing subtly with anger as she glared at me. "Satan's asshair, I knew you'd endorse this unnecessary detour, even though Dax needs help as soon as possible." She blew out a breath and her veins stopped glowing. "Fuck it, lead the way, Gabe. The sooner we get this over with, the better." Fane turned to the man at her side, making her skin light up fully. "Mark my words, halfling, we do this, you help. Or I will personally make you a part of the wall inside your own cave, *capisce*?"

Gabriel, who seemed to have come to terms with my nature, looked at Fane. "There is no need for threats. Once you have done your part, I will do mine."

My Demon grunted. "You are no fun. The one half-Human who sees me for what I am and I can't even scare you." Her gaze swiveled to me. "I blame you. After seeing you, I am just a little red woman who throws rocks."

Had the situation and the overall circumstance been less tense I would have laughed at her disappointed and disgruntled face, but as it was, unease pulled at me with untold heaviness. The relief at finding Fane and Kasha unharmed was overshadowed by what I had found in Heaven, and Dax's situation. I could only hope our mission would go undetected by my kind. Once more, I told myself I had been fast enough, there would have been no way they could tell where I had exited.

Kasha leaned her head against my shoulder with a purr, breaking my glum trail of thought.

"Follow me," Gabriel said and traipsed off in the direction of a distant mountain range.

Fane, Kasha, and me followed suit. The moment we walked next to one another, the wish to reach out and touch her, to pull her to my side, became nearly unbearable. I was still angry at her, and judging by the glances she threw up at me, she was too, which didn't dampen the need, but made me decide to not act on it. We would have to talk soon, about many things.

****

We followed Gabriel through a near vegetationless valley for about half an hour, then we came to a set of small gatherings of red rocks. They looked odd, as though giants had stacked them together willy nilly. The half-Demon lead us around one of them and halted. Before us, the ground fell off into a canyon riverbed and on the other side sat a house. Or what was left of it. A square foundation of cement was encased by walls on three sides. The roof was completely gone and most of the walls had crumbled into red dust. Bricks lay strewn where they had broken from the walls and the cutouts of two windows faced us like two misshapen eyes watching. Even in broad daylight, the ruin exuded a sense of inexplicable evil.

"The villagers have come here," Gabriel said. "I can go no further without being pulled myself."

"What do you mean, pulled?" Fane asked.

"I told you, I do what I can to lessen the unholy pull of this place, but I am not immune to it either. I hope you three are. If not, you will know soon enough. Here." He drew two of the countless necklaces over his head and handed one to each of us. "These might help. The spell woven into them is a powerful protection. It might lessen the pull, or deflect it. For you it might be enough." He sighed and let his shoulders sink, his ageless face suddenly looking a lot older than seconds ago. "I will wait for you at the circles. Find me when you're done."

The half-Demon pivoted around and sped away as fast as he could without running.

"Seems eager to be anywhere but here," Fane observed, weighing the necklace in one hand. She closed a fist around the small pendant made of bone and horn and closed her eyes. "I can feel the magic inside. He was right, it is pretty strong."

I scrutinized my own pendant with a raised brow, unsure whether I wanted to trust the magic of this half-Demon. But what other choice was there? None of us knew what we would be walking into. "Let's hope it works," I said and drew the thing over my head. "We should take a look. Need help crossing?"

My Demon furrowed her brows and scrutinized the canyon. "I might," she said after a moment. She reached out both arms and wound them around my neck. I bent my knees and picked her up. As if on reflex, Fane circled my hips with both legs, making my breath hitch. Her face was inches from mine and her eyes caught me. Her lips opened slightly in a small 'oh' and I fought the urge to close the distance. How could you want someone so badly and be mad at them at the same time? It made no sense.

Staving off the need, I averted my gaze, sprang up and opened my wings. We glided over the canyon effortlessly while Kasha paddled the air at our side, her pink tongue lolling out.

As soon as I landed, I let Fane slide down and stepped back. Her lips had turned into a tense line, and it looked like she was biting them to keep from saying something. I still felt her skin on mine, her breath fanning my face and her lips so damned close, but I wouldn't be the first to talk. Not this time.

I shook out my fingers and trudged toward the house. Whatever pull Gabriel had spoken of, I felt nothing but the ever-growing sense of evil, paired with Fane's presence. The atmosphere of the house was chilly, my Demon's presence like a fire in comparison. I cursed myself for letting her distract me. But the strain of unsaid things between us was like sand beneath my skin. Irritating.

Fane's bare feet slapped stone audibly as she jumped from rock to rock like a cricket until she hopped onto the foundation. She glanced up as she slowly snuck past a crumbling wall and into the ruin. Kasha trotted along at her side, but when they entered the ruin, Kasha's hackles rose and she growled softly.

I quickly caught up and patted my Hellcat. Kasha's deep growl sounded like distant thunder and didn't let up. Her red eyes bounced along the ruin, then she shook herself repeatedly before launching into the sky and hovering over us. She landed on one of the walls and paced the length, snarling.

"She doesn't like this place," Fane said and rubbed her upper arms with both palms. "Makes two of us. The atmosphere is… cold."

"Do you feel anyone around?" I asked.

Fane bent and flexed her toes on the foundation and screwed her lids shut for a few heartbeats. "No. This place is empty." She opened her eyes. "Curiously empty. There are no animals around either."

I sniffed the air, identifying the lingering scent of roasted meat. Faint, but there. "There have definitely been Demons around here often."

My Demon strolled through the ruin, checking out the nooks and crannies, letting her palm slide over the sandy bricks. Whenever she did, red dust trickled from the stone and softly rained down on the ground. The sight reminded me of something.

"I nearly forgot, I brought something along for you, or rather, it came along with me."

Fane pushed off from the wall and looked at me expectantly. "What?"

I dug into my pocket, feeling the tickling of sand grains against the pads of my fingers. When I pulled out a fist filled with the stuff, the rest twisted up my arm like vines. Fane's mouth opened in surprise and she jogged over.

I held out my fist and she cupped her palms together beneath it. "It nearly got me killed," I said. "It crawled up my leg as I was watching an Angel, she discovered me because of it."

The sand spiked and dropped into Fane's hands in one big blob. She smiled as the sand ran over her palms, her arms and up her shoulders. Quickly, it raced back down to her hands and she beamed at the stuff.

"Now, I can make you a new sword," she said happily.

Her simple joy at the living sand hit me square in the chest. Despite our rift, I felt like she should always look like this, happy and relaxed. In that very moment, the corners of her mouth dropped and her amber eyes found me. "Someone saw you?" The sand bristled and rustled as it wound up her arms and settled around her shoulders and neck like a cloudy stola.

"Yes, but I got away before she could tell someone." In a few words I told her what I had witnessed.

"That could have ended badly, Mihr." Her expressive face swayed between fear and anger. "I…" She looked down and nibbled at her lower lip. Right when she opened her mouth to say something, a bout of pressure resounded through the ruin.

With a yowl, Kasha sprang from the wall and bounded off in the direction of the canyon. The sand around Fane's shoulders drizzled to the floor where it stayed, its movement slowing down so much it was barely visible.

"Kasha!" I shouted after my cat, but a sudden stiffness gripped my limbs, then a shiver took hold of my entire body. Goosebumps raced across my skin and within a heartbeat, I felt arousal thrum through my body. My chest warmed beneath the necklace Gabriel had given us as the pendant twitched and trembled with magic. But any confusion about it wandered to the very back of my mind as my gaze snapped to Fane, who gasped loud when our eyes met.

She had the pendant in one hand, and let it fall when an unfathomable pull engulfed me, swept me up and erased everything but her.

Like magnets, we clashed within two steps. Her arms came around me, her fingers digging into the muscles of my back.

Her touch was of burning intensity and she groaned when our lips met as though we had no other choice. Our kiss was passionate and raw, as we devoured each other with acute desperation. My heart hammered with relief and marvel at holding her close, at feeling all of her against me, only a faint whisper at the back of my mind uttered warnings. I ignored the pesky insistence that this wasn't natural, and deepened the kiss.

Our tongues met with smooth and sliding abandon, then Fane sucked my lower lip into her mouth and ran her tongue over it.

I groaned, picked her up without breaking the kiss and thrust her up the closest wall, wedging my hips between her legs with a singeing urgency. Fane gasped and drove her heels into my butt, clasping my lower body to hers with her toned legs. Her fingernails scratched over my back, ripping into my shirt and through it until bites of pain bloomed on my skin. Exquisite pain.

My hands slid over her skin, sinking down her lower back and into her pants until I had both her cheeks in my palms. My Demon sighed and undulated against me, rubbing herself on my arousal. Our breath grew short between the hungry kisses and we began ripping off each other's clothes with total disregard to ever wearing any of them again.

Our groans and the ripping of fabric sounded through the empty ruin, and soon skin rested on skin. Burning, electrifying, maddening. All I saw and felt was her. Her heavy-lidded eyes, her soft lips, her smooth skin, her intoxicating scent of sin and secrets.

"This is madness," I managed to say between kisses.

"This is amazing," she answered.

When Fane pulled on my jeans, I felt the small voice perk up once more. *Unnatural.* The word floated through my mind softly, without any real gravity. Nonthreatening.

I grabbed hold of either side of her pants and ripped. They came apart, leaving her completely naked, her back perched against the wall, her long legs around me. She was perfection and I wanted nothing more than to get lost inside her. Especially after the fight we had. Confusion bubbled up. *What fight?* I couldn't remember for a second.

Unnatural. The fight? Out of nowhere, I remembered her anger, her words. Her accusations. It took all my willpower, but I pulled my lips from hers and palmed her face with both hands. "Fane?"

She tried breaching the distance and kiss me, but I held her head still. "Uhm?"

"Why are you angry with me?" I asked.

"Ang…ry? I'm not…" She frowned at me, her eyes swimming in and out of focus. "Angry. You are looking for a way out. An excuse to leave me."

"What?"

"What?" Fane's eyes fixated on mine. "Never fall for the good guy."

Unnatural. This time the word bounded off the edges of my mind stronger. Urgent. Like gears grabbing into one another, my mind returned to clarity. In that very moment I heard a whistling sound behind me, the swing of a blade.

I dodged, Fane still in my arms, twisting us both out of the way. A spear landed in the wall, right where our heads had been a split-second before. Setting Fane down, I turned, tugging her behind me to face who or whatever had attacked us.

My heart positively stopped when I saw two well-known faces. The Incubi who had killed Rapha stood in what was left of the doorframe, grinning and leering at us.

"Well, well, well… What have we here?" one of them asked.

Chapter Nine

Fane

The Surface, Damaraland

"Almost completely undressed," Horace said, his red eyes glinting with barely contained lust. "How convenient."

Valo nodded at his companion, both leering at Mihr. Within the space of a blink, every bit of that crazy arousal dropped from me. Horace and Valo, the Incubi who had brought Mihr to Hell. They were the Demon presence calling on the villagers to pick them off one by one. Both wore a collar made of Lilithium – the Devil's stone – meaning they had been blessed by an Angel, making it possible for them to be seen by Humans. And kill them.

All of it made sense now. How Gabriel was unable to stop his people from being drawn here, how he himself couldn't resist, how Mihr and I had nearly fucked each other senseless. Incubi power was strong, near irresistible, but since the attraction between Mihr and myself was crazy-high to begin with…

My Angel shook with tremors, as Horace closed in, blowing kisses at him. I felt the powerful spell he wove and snatched Mihr's hand. I tugged at him until he glanced at me.

"Focus on my touch."

Mihr grunted, his eyes trancelike and his foot rising to walk to Horace. Valo smiled as he pulled a dagger from his belt, ready to spring the trap his companion lay.

"Mihr, look at me," I urged.

He did, seeing me, making relief thunder through my chest. My Angel snarled, crouched down and gripped one of my whips that had fallen to the ground along with my pants. With a yell, he let it snap the air in a deafening crack, the tip slicing into Horace's cheek.

The Incubus stumbled back, smacking a hand to his face, his eyes darkening with malice. "Playtime is over, Angel," he rasped and grabbed the two daggers strapped to his hips.

Valo chose that moment to lunge at Mihr and I stomped the concrete with one foot, making the floor sink beneath him and my remaining whip spring up and into my hand. The connection to my weapon made it curl like a snake, while Valo tripped and stumbled, his focus shifting to me.

Mihr and Horace started circling each other and Valo grinned at me. "You sure you want to tango with me, little Ember? You will lose." His beautiful face beamed with excitement and I gripped my whip tighter.

"Oh, I love dancing, and no, I will not lose. But you will die."

The Incubus giggled and sprang at me, his dagger slashing through the air with a whistling sound. I snapped my whip and hit his blade, sending his aim off to one side as I dove away to the other. Catching my dodge in a roll, I jumped back on my feet and felt my arm being pulled up behind me by my whip. Something wet and hot hit my naked back and when I turned, I saw that the metal of my weapon was coated in black blood, resulting from a gash in Valo's chest.

The Incubus dabbed a hand on his wound and looked at his blood. He seemed shocked when he glanced from his bloody hand to me.

I smirked at him, letting my whip twirl. "Still want to dance?"

"I will rip you apart, Ember," he growled and barreled toward me.

Once more, I let my whip crack, this time opening the skin of his wrist, the wrist holding his dagger. Valo's weapon clattered to the concrete, but I didn't waste any time and let my whip circle his neck, then I pulled until he fell to his knees, grabbing the metal around his neck with both hands.

On the far side of the ruin, Mihr and Horace engaged in hand-to-hand combat – both their weapons lying on the floor as they punched, kicked and dodged each other.

The one second I looked for them was my mistake. Valo gripped the whip and pulled, making me lose my footing and sail forward. He wrenched the whip from my grip and sent his fist flying straight for my temple as I stumbled into him.

Bam! My head was knocked back, my vision swimming with tears and vertigo as I fell on my ass. I had no time to deal with the shrill ringing inside my head as a huge hand closed around my windpipe and picked me up. Valo glared at me, his face scrunched up in anger as he shook me like a wet puppy, his claws slicing through my skin on the sides of my neck.

"What now, Ember? With no connection to your element, you are exposed to mine." His angry face twisted into a gruesome grimace, a smile so evil it would have cooled my very soul – if I'd had one.

My face thrummed with pressure and my throat closed. I scratched and pulled at his hand, but he was a lot stronger than I. The panic grabbing hold of me aided in choking me even quicker. I shook with it, reliving that utter helplessness Lev had once subjected me to.

No breath breached Valo's grip and while I heard Mihr calling my name, it sounded as though he was far away. The world swam out of focus, making the twinge of movement behind Valo look like a trick of the light. It looked like a stream of clouds floating across the floor. Which was ludicrous, of course. But just as my heart fluttered with utter terror, I saw blackness enter from the edges of my vision like dark curtains and Valo raising the claws of his other hand, ready to slam them into my stomach and disembowel me. A soft prickling hit my fingers.

The angry cry of a thousand mouths. Outrage. Wrath. Fury. It laced through me like my own thoughts, while a solid weight settled around my fingers. The heavenly sand. Smooth, alive, and malleable. It listened to my every notion, spiked with echoes of my panic and twisted into something sharp and long.

Valo's face fell and my feet hit solid ground as his hand let go of me. My legs gave out and I landed on my knees, clawing at my throat, hacking and coughing to get much needed breath down my windpipe. Inches from me, Valo sank to his knees as well, my heavenly sand stuck in his chest like a bolt of lightning. I watched with a mix of horror and satisfaction, as the sand pulled together and widened his wound. Black blood flowed down his chest in rivulets. A crack sounded from within him, then he coughed out blood. His eyes rolled back and one last breath gurgled from him before he keeled over, face-planting into the foundation to my left.

A cry echoed through the ruin when Horace beheld his companions' demise. Tears burning in my eyes, I watched as he slammed his shoulder into Mihr like a rugby player, shoving him out of the way, running for me and Valo.

His expression made the blood in my veins freeze and I knew if he reached me, I would die. Mihr sprang up behind him, swiped Horace's dagger from the floor and flapped his gray wings to gain speed and catch up, but Horace was too close. Still fighting for breath, I did the only thing I could – I sank straight into the concrete beneath me.

Horace's claws scraped over the foundation above me, slicing into the material without reaching me. I shot up once he passed, infusing the ground at the soles of his feet with my power. He sank into the foundation to his ankles but his momentum carried his body further. I winced when both his legs broke with ugly cracks. Another yell tore from his chest but Mihr had reached him already.

"For Rapha," my Angel said and embedded the dagger into Horace's back to the hilt.

A grunt sounded from the Incubus, followed by a gurgling cough. Mihr snarled as he twisted the dagger and pulled it free. Poised above the Demon, he waited.

Horace reached for him, but Mihr easily warded off his feeble fingers with his free hand and watched grimly as the Incubus sank down. Slowly, the light vanished from his eyes.

Mihr blew out a breath and bent lower to slide Horace's lids closed. He got up, his back littered with claw marks, and turned to me. His chest rose and fell heavily when his eyes landed on me. He stumbled my way, then fell over. I caught him before he did the same move Valo had a few moments ago.

"The dead guy is poisonous," Mihr brabbled into the crook of my neck.

I gasped, my lungs still on fire, and turned him over to lie him down on his back. My Angel grunted, his movements getting very slow and stiff as he tried to sit up, then he just sank back and stopped moving all together.

Knowing how Sumu-Incubus venom worked, I tried to can my worry. Mihr would be out of it for a while, but it wasn't lethal, and the two Incubi were dead.

With trembling hands, I searched his body for wounds and quickly determined that he had none needing immediate attention. I made sure to not let my expression give away how relieved I was to have him in my arms alive. Stunned, but breathing.

Soon, the only things moving were his gray eyes, darting across my face and darkening when they stuck to the side of my face. The side that still throbbed from Valo's punch. I forced a soft smile to my face, stroked his sweaty forehead and reached for his shirt. Balling the tatters up, I made a pillow which I slid under his head. "Be right back," I said and gave his cheek another stroke, then stood to look for my clothes.

The ruin looked a bit worse for wear, the floor was splattered with blood, both black and gold, while the crumbling walls had been reduced to measly, hip-high half-walls. Red dust and chunks of stone lay strewn across everything. Me shifting and pulling at the foundation of things had given this place a serious makeover.

To calm my raging nerves, I spread out my power, feeling for my things. Hidden underneath a part of wall on the far side, I felt fabric. Very conscious of my surrounding, I walked over, feeling every step with absolute clarity.

Truth was, Mihr and I had been extremely lucky. My shaking fingers felt for the amulet Gabriel had given us, empty. There was no prickling of power left, as the Incubi magic had drained it. I let the pendant thump back against my chest and breathed out in a steady stream.

First things first. With one touch, I forced the bricks to change shape and rustle apart in heaps of sand. Then I dug out what was left of my shirt, hoodies and pants. I picked them up one by one. Mihr had done a bang-up job reducing them to tatters. Knotting together two hoodies, I fashioned myself a skirt. My shirt was ripped down the middle and I slipped it on, knotting it together in the front.

The strange yet familiar feel of the heavenly sand snuck up my right foot. I glanced down to see the cloudy-looking sand swirl up my leg, as though it wanted to cozy up to me. A trail of black blood marked the path it had taken from Valo's chest over to me. I watched as the swirling mass shook off the last of the blood – in a highly unsettling, casual kind of way – and reached out a hand.

It twirled around my fingers, smoothing into them and around my hand. "Thank you," I whispered. The thousand mouths rejoiced and their happy vibrations sent goosebumps up my arm. I marveled at the feel and wasn't sure whether I liked the connection and exchange, or if it was… unsettling. Feeling it close did calm me, and I decided to trust my instinct for the time being.

One thing was clear, the sand was exceptional. It reacted to each whim and thought, without delay. It took only a fraction of my power to make it coat my hand and arm like a glove. I twisted my hand to make my palm face up and thought 'sphere'. Within a second, the sand raced to form into a smokey ball, shrinking into the exact hardness I envisioned.

"Remarkable," I said and let go of it. "Stay close, ya hear?" It thrummed as it traveled up my arm to settle around my neck. I watched in surprise, as it coated the necklace and settled on top of it. Fusing with the metal, it reformed the necklace, dropping the pendant of bone and horn, shaping bits of itself into a teardrop – big as my thumb.

"Well, that should work," I mused. Semi-dense, it hung from my neck, right above my heart and a warm feeling radiated from it. Peace. A sense of belonging, and confidence trickled from it. The image of a satisfied and happy kitten came to mind. Speaking of kittens.

"Kasha!" I called, wondering where she had run off to. The power pulling at Mihr and myself must have spooked her. I didn't blame the Hellcat.

The question was, why hadn't she come back during the fight? I walked back to Mihr and crouched down next to him. His gaze was worried, searching the surrounding as far as he was able.

"We have to get you out of here," I said. I gathered my whips and looped them around my waist. Then I bent down and grabbed Mihrs wrists. With a grunt, I hoisted him up and half dragged, half carried him from the ruin. "Saints on a Sunday, why do you Angels have to be so heavy, Carol?"

A muffled sound answered, making me smile genuinely. He sounded well and truly pissed. Thank fuck I had no idea what he was trying to say.

"Kasha?" I called out again. "Kasha, where are you?"

By now, the sun stood high in the sky, beating down on me with merciless heat, making me sweat and pant as I dragged Mihr along. "Sure could use your help, Kash!" I hollered.

Another sound broke from Mihr and I turned to look at him, he grunted and looked to the left repeatedly.

"She's that way?" I asked.

He closed his eyes and let out an affirmative sound.

"Right, that way it is." I adjusted my grip on him and stumbled us in the indicated direction. "You know…" a heavy breath left me, "this has to stop. I can't keep lumping your huge ass around." I groaned under his deadweight. "It's… supposed to be the other… way… round, ya know? Shit on a shingle! Before this is over, I demand… to be… carried by you… for a change."

I stopped for a moment to gather my breath and strength. As my naked feet connected to the earth, I felt it once I stood still. Running paws, and twisting earth. The feeling I'd had walking over the circles was back. A scratch at the back of the mind, like sand beneath skin. Irritatingly familiar, yet unplaceable.

Something black bounded over a hill of rocks and I sighed with relief at seeing Kasha dash our way, just as the feeling broke free to reveal itself. Earth vanishing into nothingness, a circular patch of void. Leading to…

"No. Satan's fancy hoofhair. They found me." I sank down, rolling Mihr from my back and behind a rock to hide him, then I peered over the ridge and saw one of the circles open into a hole. A portal to Hell. My eyes widened and my breath hitched when I beheld who popped from it like a bunch of fucking Daisies.

Lord Ragon, my former owner and bane of my existence. He was followed by a man with red skin I didn't know, but judging by his skin he could be an Ember. An Ifrit warrior followed him, and… Jinx. The only person who – besides Lev – had been any kind of decent to me during my time in the eighth ring. Jinx, the former favorite of Lev. Jinx, the leader of the harem I had been sold into.

I ducked out of sight and looked at Mihr. "They found me, Angel. My former owner and three others." His gray eyes widened in shock, then glinted with unholy wrath.

"I can't let them get to you," I said. "Never."

That pissed off grunt-growl was back and made me smile. "Good thing you can't move, so even if the guy they brought is an Ember, he shouldn't be able to feel you if I distract him."

"Nghh," Mihr forced out.

"They know Kasha is here, and she will lead them to us." I chanced a glance over the ridge and glowered at Ragon, the Ifrit, Jinx and mystery-guy. The man pointed in the direction of Kasha, who closed in on us quickly.

I slid back down. "Shit." Closing my eyes, I felt the ground with my feet and hands. It was brittle, but would hold. "I'll hide you, till you can move again. The Devil knows who may come this way after the ruckus I'm about to cause. Can't have them find you."

"Nghho!" Mihr said.

"Can't hear you, love." I stuck my fingers into the sand and concentrated.

"Nho!" Sweat pearled from my Angels brow as his muscles shook and clenched with exertion. He only managed to reach out a hand to me, and even that had to have taken tremendous effort.

I slid my palm into his and squeezed. "I know. Were the roles reversed, trust me, I would shit a brick with anger. But they aren't and I can't let anything happen to you. I'll hide you, then distract them. Kasha can't outfly an Ifrit, not while carrying both of us. I'll protect her, I promise."

A feeble squeeze was all he managed, and another 'Nho'.

I palmed his cheek and brushed my thumb over his sweaty brow. Dear me, his gorgeous, angry face was nearly too much. It ripped into my heart and made my eyes burn with tears. If I lost this man, I would die. The prospect of never seeing him again made me tell him. "I'm sorry about what I said… I was scared. Scared you wouldn't make it back to Earth, scared you wanted to leave because you wanted to leave *me*. I'm not good enough for you, and deep down I think you know, that's why you have been pulling back. Building a wall." I sank my head down and pressed my forehead to his. "And you were right. There was no way we would ever have been able to keep our relationship physical. At least I can't."

Huffing out a breath, I pulled back and sniffed once. "I'll bury you out of sight, but don't worry, you will have enough air, and once you are able to move, you can just punch the ceiling I'll make and get out."

"Nho, Fah..."

"I know, love, I know. Listen. Once you are out, go to Gabriel and take him to Dax. Whatever happens, save Dax, okay? I'll try and..." Truly, I had no idea what my plan was after hiding Mihr. I bit my lower lip, unwound one of my whips and placed it next to him, then I dug both hands into the earth. "I'll see you soon, Bridget."

"Nho! Fayhhh..."

When I saw his face vanish beneath the red dirt, a tear slid down my cheek. I let it fall and hardened the ceiling above him, infusing it with hidden holes so he could breathe. Just then Kasha jumped over the ridge, panting heavily and sniffing the ground. When she started pawing the ceiling beneath which Mihr lay, I stopped her.

"We have to protect him, Kasha," I told her. "Keep them away."

Her front paw hovered in midair and she tilted her head to look at me inquisitively.

"We have to leave him and run, distract them." Once I pointed at the quartette heading for us, Kasha snarled. She placed her paw on the ground softly and growled, but stood still.

"Good girl. Now," I stood and turned toward the Demons coming for me, "let's give 'em something to chew on, shall we?"

I climbed onto the ridge and saw Ragon stop upon seeing me. "Fane!" he yelled. "This is the end of you, my sweet Ember."

"Neat," I yelled back, funneling my hand to my mouth. "You're gonna have to catch me first, though, you sideways-fucked, heap of shit." I grinned as his face clenched into an angry mask, one I could see, even across the distance. Mock-saluting, I jumped from the ridge and broke into a flat-out sprint.

Kasha's paws drummed the ground on my side and fear tempted me to spring onto her back and fly away. But I needed them to follow me. I needed them away from Mihr.

Punching at the fear I felt, I unrolled my whip and let it slide across the sand behind me. They were in for a surprise once they caught up. A big one.

Chapter Ten
Mihr

The Surface,

in a Fane-fashioned tunnel,

Damaraland

I kept still, listening to Fane goad her former Maester, then heard hers and Kasha's running feet. I would have given anything to be able to jump from this tunnel and face the piece of shit who thought he'd owned her. To annihilate him, like I had Rapha's killer. But I couldn't move a muscle. What I could do was utter muffled screams, but that would do no good. To my dismay, Fane was right – if someone found me in this condition, I was done for.

My heart racing, my ears straining and my breath heavy, I lay and listened, trying to make out whether or not Fane and Kasha escaped the Demons.

Within a minute – which felt like hours – silence blanketed me. At least there had been no screams or sounds of fighting. Maybe… maybe Kasha and Fane had flown off.

Trying hard to get my breathing and heart rate under control, I couldn't help doubt eating away at me. Scenarios and dark thoughts zapped through me like electric currents. Kasha killed, Fane dragged back to Hell… *Breathe*, I told myself. *Just breathe.*

To keep from spiraling I concentrated on inching my palm toward the whip Fane had placed next to my right upper leg. An arduous endeavor. My body felt like the stone-turned-sand around me. Immovable. Only by forcing every conscious thought to my hand, I was able to shift it closer. Slow, but steady.

Concentrating got harder, and soon pearls of perspiration tickled my temples, then my cheeks as they ran down my face. She had been afraid I wanted to leave her. Of not being good enough for me… I didn't understand. Fane was independence and confidence come to life. Had I done something to make her feel the way she did? I stilled completely when her words in the ruin shot through my brain, "Never fall for the good guy."

Now my heart sped up for a different reason. Was that the why of it? Had the nonchalant, playful Demon fallen for me? That couldn't be true, could it?

Before I was able ponder the possibility further, I heard soft rustling. The dragging of feet across the coarse sand. Tentative footsteps. Getting closer.

Cursing the Incubus and his poison to Hell and back, I waited. Maybe the person above would pass.

The steps halted right next to me and I held my breath. *Go on*, I though. *Come on, just keep going.*

Feet shifted, then a dull sound hit the ground. A knee? Was the person crouching?

Something scraped directly above my face, making grains of sand rain down on me. Light broke through a crack and fingers rounded the cracked edges, then pulled. More sand, more light, and an ageless face.

Gabriel.

The magic man pulled and dug until the ceiling was gone. Then he leaned back and raised a brow at me. "Didn't work out that well, did it?"

I garbled out a "no."

"Good thing I charmed the necklaces." He pointed at my chest where the pendant still rested. "Helped me find you."

I grunted as he reached for me, grabbing both my wrists and pulling. With a surprised gasp, he let me slump back. "Sho, you're a heavy one." He huffed out a breath, grabbed hold anew and tried again.

Cursing, hissing, and speaking in a foreign language infused with clicks and strange sounds, he managed to heave my torso out of the hole. Then he slipped inside himself and push-rolled the rest of me.

Unable to move, my face got caked with sand and I tasted dirt and small stones. Thankfully, Gabriel rolled me onto my back, his breath heavy.

The magic man placed a hand on my shoulder, right on one of the Incubus scratches. He mumbled in a completely different language now and I felt a chill spread into my flesh from the touch of his fingers. When he pulled back, he shook his head and gazed down at me.

"Lust-Demon. The poisonous kind. Good for me you went to find them. Are they still around? Is that why she hid you? Or did they leave you for later?"

There were many things I wanted to say. None of which would yield an answer to his questions.

He sighed, sat down next to me, and procured a few green twig-looking plants from one of his many bags. They were as thick as Fane's little finger and when Gabriel broke them in half, they oozed a milky-white goo.

"Melkbos," he explained. "Lethal to Humans and most animals, but it reacts with demonic poison and it will counter what got into your veins. This might be a bit irritating."

It wasn't irritating. The moment the white goo hit my wounds, they burned like Hellfire.

Gabriel watched me closely as he smeared the stuff into all the wounds he found. When I neither grunted, nor flinched, he nodded approvingly.

As the fire raced deeper into my scratches and made my entire body thrum with pain, I felt the stiffness receding. It was agonizing, but within a minute I could move my fingers, then my hands and arms. Soon, I sat up with a gasp.

"Incredible," I said.

Gabriel pursed his lips and got up, he dusted off his backside and said, "You have to wash it off now, or the pain will worsen."

"We have to find Fane first," I insisted. The connection I normally shared with Kasha was blurry and didn't give me any sense of direction. Not at all like it had before. It spiked my worry. "There are Demons after her, more dangerous than the ones we drove out for you."

His brows shot up, folding his forehead into an intricately wrinkled mess. "You got them?"

"Yes, we got them," I snapped. "But whatever we did made others appear." I indicated at the circle in the distance, from where the Demons had, no doubt, arrived.

"The fairy circles…" Gabriel whispered, his eyes big. "They *are* portals. I was right." A smile spread on his lips.

"We can debate anything and everything later," I urged. "Right now, we have to find Fane. She still has the necklace as well, can you tell me in which direction she is?"

Gabriel closed his eyes for a beat and uttered a word, then he bent down and picked up a handful of sand. Holding the fist before his face, he let the sand run from his fingers and blew into the stream. The grains slowed, curling to the ground in eerie swirls. The swirls changed color, from red to gun-powder gray-black. The way the grains landed looked like runes and strange symbols.

The magic man clapped his hands and studied the effects of his spell. "Ijo, I know in what direction she is."

Relief flooded me. "Then you can—"

"No. You go and wash off the Melkbos first. If not, you won't be able to help her. There is a windpomp in that direction." He pointed to a small hill speckled with dried bushes and clusters of red rocks.

I had no idea what a 'windpomp' was, but I also didn't care. "Gabriel, I need to know where she is. Now!"

"No chance." He met my glare with a relaxed ease that riled me up even further.

"She is in danger, they both are."

"Maybe. But if you want me to tell you, you go wash off first."

"Fine!" I yelled. "Over there?" I asked and he nodded once.

Without another word, I jumped and spread my wings, shooting off into the direction of the hill. After two wings flaps, I knew he'd been right. My wings burned and I kept losing altitude as they cramped in involuntary spasms. Speaking of which, the muscles of the rest of my body followed suit and I floundered quite a bit as I cleared the hill. Flying got harder by the second, and when I viewed a tall tower of metal, I landed in a stumbling run.

My antics made a group of antelopes dash away from a round, cemented watering hole situated in front of the tower.

Wind picked up, making the fan squeak to life until it rattled with the speed it turned. A soft, dull, repetitive *gah-gong* sound erupted and I jogged over, seeing that the turning made a rod pump up and down the length of the tower – which I assumed was the fabled 'windpomp' – and into the ground. Fresh water trickled from the rod and the metal pipe leading to the cemented hole gushed with a stream of clear freshness.

I held my hand to the water welling from the rod, not wanting to poison the watering hole, and began dabbing my wounds. Hasty as I was, the effect was immediate, the burn lessened, and the cramps subsided.

With each slice of relief, anger and fear grew like a counter-balance. I had to get to Fane. Now.

****

When I landed next to Gabriel, the magic man smirked. He held out the whip Fane had left with me and I grabbed it, looping it through my belt-holes and sticking the hilt into my pocket.

"Better?" he asked.

"Where are they, Gabriel?" Not only did I still not get any sense of direction, but the connection to Kasha felt like it lessened steadily. Did it mean something bad had happened?

The magic man consulted the symbols of sand once more. I squinted at them. They seemed to have changed since I left.

Gabriel sank onto his hunches and drew an arrow into the sand. "That way."

It was not the direction Fane and Kasha had fled in. "You sure?" I asked.

"Yes. She moved very fast for a time. Now she stopped."

"Will you come with me and help her?"

"No. The agreement was to take a look at the child when and if you rid us off the darkness. You have. He is my responsibility now. Debts must be paid. Always."

"Fine." I gave him the address – which he actually typed into a phone he unearthed from one of his pockets – and he winked with a cheeky smile at my surprise. "Technology, my friend, just cause we're in the middle of nowhere doesn't mean we don't have it." He stuck his phone back into a pocket. "It is far, but I will get there before you. *If* you get there. Good luck heavenly one. And if you ever see ti !khutse again – the Lord – you ask him…" he swallowed, his face solemn all of a sudden. "You ask him if me and others like me are truly damned. As is believed."

For a second, I let my gaze wander over him. "The Lord has no say in such matters. If you have a soul, you can decide for yourself. It depends on how you spend your life."

His face changed from solemn to worried. "Do you think I have a soul?"

I had to smile at his question, asked so innocently, so fearful. "You are half-Human, so I don't see why not. See you soon, Gabe. Or not. Please save Dax." With that, I shot into the sky, this time without pain or cramps. Gabriel sank back fast with each wingbeat, until he resembled an ant. Remembering his arrow, I sped off in that direction. All I could do was hope that Fane and Kasha had found a place to hide, or that they had been able to shake off the squadron of Demons chasing them.

I concentrated on the smidge of pull I had left of the connection to Kasha, but it fizzled slightly, then went dead. I dropped several feet before catching myself, the dread punching me without mercy. "Doesn't mean anything," I whispered into the wind. "Probably nothing."

Yet, as I strained my wings and raced on until I resembled a bullet in the sky, I felt the cold claws of panic scrape their way through me.

Chapter Eleven
Fane

The Surface,
somewhere between Kaokoveld and Damaraland,
Namibia

Time ticked away, counted in breaths and steps. It was all I focused on. Getting as many between myself and Mihr in his helpless state as possible. No matter what, I would not let them find him. He had lived through Hell once, there was no way he'd do so again on my watch.

While my bare feet smacked the sand, providing me with an accurate idea of how close Ragon, Jinx, the suspected Ember and the Ifrit were. Which was great, but meant that I felt them gaining pretty fast. Talons ripped over the earth and a second later I couldn't feel the Ifrit anymore. It had taken to the sky.

"It's time," I gasped at Kasha, then grabbed her mane and sprang onto her back mid-run. I landed a bit rough and a small growl immediately informed me of my clumsiness.

"Sorry, my sweet," I said, righting myself and clamping my legs to her strong body, right between her shoulders and wings. "It's my first time doing this maneuver." My hands free, I cracked the whip onto the ground, sending a wave of earth at the three who still followed us on foot. In that exact moment, Kasha jumped up. Her huge wings unfolded and each beat felt like being punched in the gut. Fuck rollercoasters, riding a Hellcat was ten times faster.

Turned out, not fast enough. Within moments of us taking to the air, I smelled it. The stench of fire and roast. Next came the flutter of flames in the wind, an almost snapping sound, mingling with angry hisses.

Kasha dove low and I felt the heat of something – most likely a claw – swipe the air where my head had just been.

Flattening myself to Kasha's back, I braved the onslaught of wind and speed a straight downward plummet brought along. Gripping my whip tightly, I held onto the Hellcat with the other hand for dear life. My entire being dropped out of my ass when she opened her wings and shot up.

"Holy shiiiit!" I yelled as the Ifrit zapped past us, continuing the plummet for a split-second longer. Then it was on our tail once more. Its black, fire-encrusted body moved with unbelievable speed. The smoke billowing from its wings stung my eyes and when its mouth opened in a snarl, heat and fire spewed from it.

To my utter horror, Kasha turned. The world went upside down and I heard growling, hissing, and yowling from above. My grip slipped precariously and went to shit the moment Kasha and the Ifrit actually clashed into each other.

Balls. This was going to hurt. Thankfully, Kasha had almost plummeted to the ground before, I still fell quite a ways. I fought my lids as my eyes watered in the cutting wind, staring at the fast-approaching sand. My whip curled and slashed, slicing into the ground of its own accord. *Thump.* My body felt like a sack of potatoes as I rolled over the ground with all the finesse of those very burlap encased vegetables. Breath got slammed from my lungs when I landed on my back, then kept on rolling and bouncing. My head swimming and my lungs collapsed, I finally came to a stop, spluttering like a steam-engine.

Every part of me thrummed with pain. Even that first sweet breath I took burned like Hell itself. Gasping and groaning, I pushed myself into a sitting position. *Can't stay here,* was all that rang through my mind. Feeling brittle and nauseous, I stumbled to my feet.

Where I had hit the ground originally, a crater had formed in what looked like a small dune. The tracks my body made, rolling down and to where I was now looked far apart. I had bounced along like a damned rubber-ball.

An ear splintering screech ripped through the sky above me and before my addled brain caught up with reality, my instincts already had. "Kasha!" I cried hoarsely, trying to glimpse her and the Ifrit.

"You can't help her, pet," a very annoyingly familiar voice said. I whirled around in the direction and saw Ragon, the strange, red-skinned, man and Jinx approach me from the right. A small consolation was a rip in Ragons pants, and red dust caking Jinx' leg. Looked like my sand-wave had given them a bit of a work-over. The unfamiliar man looked as good as new, renewing my suspicion that he was an Ember.

I flexed my fingers on the grip of my whip – which miraculously still lay in my hand – and stared Ragon down. "And no one can help you, Ragon. I am no longer bound to you, means I can rip out your heart, or throat, or…" I let my gaze dip a fraction, "other things."

"You are an Ember, Fane," he said, as though he were explaining it to me. "Your kind is weak, and if anyone dies today, it will be you." His black eyes glittered with anger, lust for revenge, and the same hunger they had always held when looking at me.

The man to his side twisted his lips into a sneer, but he didn't look at me. He obviously didn't take kindly to Ragon's description. He clearly was of my kind. Whether he could hold his own against me remained to be seen.

A roar echoed from above, this time not Kasha.

"Thank you for telling me what I am, I nearly forgot. Also, you I get," I pointed my whip at him, "you've always been a sore loser. But what are you doing here, Jinxy?" My stare wandered to her.

Lev's former favorite sighed heavily. "Revenge, dear. What else?" Deeply rooted and heavily nourished hatred shone from her face. "You took everything from me. My home, my Maester, my friends. Because of you, he is dead."

"Because of me? Have you been snorting lava? What in the nine circles would I have to do with his death?"

"All was good before you came…" She spat on the ground. "Before he plucked you from the third ring. An Ember. How disgraceful. He was meant for so much more. He deserved someone better."

"Like you?" I raised a brow, digging my feet into the ground deeper. No matter how hard her words hit me, I had to be vigilant and ready for an attack. I felt the makeup of the earth beneath me. It was old here. The blanket of marble told of a prehistoric lake. Bits of slate and ores of quartz wound along not far under my feet. The slate was useless to me – brittle and powdery, but the quartz and marble… Those I could use in a fight.

Snarls and roars sounded from Kasha and the Ifrit, so loud I was sure they'd be waking the Heavens themselves if it went on any longer.

"How dare you, Jinx? I made him happy. He loved me. He–"

"Yes, I remember you shaking and encasing yourself in stone because of him…" The Succubus huffed. "Grand love. Truly."

I had no answer to that, remembering that instance in my very bones. Never had I felt fear and betrayal as deeply. Not in all my over three hundred years.

"Enough," Ragon snarled. He had gone a peculiar shade of crimson, clearly not happy with not being the center of our attention. "Fane, you will come with us. Lucifer Himself wants to question you." A smile of pure evil spread on his thin lips. "He promised I could do with what remained of you as I pleased."

"Wow. The Devil Himself gave you domain over me? Congrats, pisspot, congrats." Focusing on the pockets of quartz beneath Jinx and Ragon, I watched my former Maester redden further. He was about to blow a major gasket. "I will die before I go back. That, I vow."

With a growl, he unsheathed his sword – a sword I recognized as Lev's – and took a stance, ready to pounce on me. "You aren't even worth the effort."

"Au contraire, peabrain, I seem to be very much worth considerable effort. What are you doing here otherwise?"

"You will submit to me," he yelled, spittle flying from his mouth. "Like you should always have. You are *mine*. And you will take me to the Angel who will bless me to walk this realm same as you." He pointed his blade at me. "And after I have killed him, we will spend eternity on Earth. Together." An alarming fanatic gleam crept into his eyes and I clicked my tongue.

"Mihr?" I forced out a giggle. "My Angel is very picky about blessing folk, and he will die before he'd consider blessing you. Or he'd just kill you, way more likely." I shrugged, watching a muscle in Ragon's jaw tick. "Did you know about this?" I asked Jinx. "Seems the naughty Lord wants out of Hell, as well."

Jinx eyed Ragon with disdain, clearly unimpressed with his lack of composure and regality. On his other side, the Ember looked less than impressed, as well.

Ragon huffed and puffed, unaware of how Jinx and the Ember stepped to the side, away from him. I slightly shifted my feet, adjusting my focus on the quartz to the new position of all three.

"You are mine," Ragon drawled once more, while another bout of noise from the sky blanketed the emptiness around us.

He shifted his weight, about to lunge at me, when my hair stood to attention. A ripple, a pulse of low pressure rumbled through me. Ragon stilled, and Jinx frantically looked around. They felt it, too. Another bout of whatever it was, rolled over us like soundless thunder, reverberating inside my chest as though it was a sound-body.

"What the…" Jinx breathed.

In that moment two things happened at once. Kasha and the Ifrit crashed into the same artificial dune my whip had helped me create, rolling away from each other upon impact, and a whistling sound rang through the following silence.

I didn't wait for anything else to transpire, but curled my whip on the ground and pulled at the quartz. The glittering shards shot from the sand like bullets, pelting Jinx, the Ember, and Ragon with calculated accuracy. It wouldn't hurt any of them seriously, but bought me precious seconds. As the quartz made sand and dust spray everywhere, I ran for Kasha. Using the earth beneath my feet to propel me, I sailed through the air like a dying swan and landed next to her. Throwing my body over hers, I grabbed my necklace and plowed my closed fist into the ground. We sank under, parts of the marble blanket and bits of quartz popping up around us in a circle. I added more as fast as I could, caging us in. Something hit the marble-quartz cage with the force of a small bus, sparks flew through the air, but my cage held. The Ifrit screeched, flapping its flaming wings aggressively. Then the sound of metal meeting metal broke through the screech. The Ifrit sped off, its talons digging into the dirt with urgency.

I felt them. More feet appearing on the earth, seemingly from nowhere. Clutching Kasha to me, I added rock and sand to our cage, until we had a solid dome around us.

Sounds and the feel of fighting reached us, but I didn't break focus until I was truly confident our cage would hold out for a while.

Beneath me, Kasha breathed heavily and I stroked her softly. "Good girl," I whispered into her mane. "You did so well. So well."

A small mewl answered me and I pulled back a little. Kasha's red eye blinked at me in the dim light and I beheld gashes, slices and burned skin on her entire body. Gingerly, I let my fingers glide over her fur, feeling for deeper wounds and – "Fuck!" My fingers found something hard and hot embedded right below her chest. Kasha jerked at my touch, accompanied by a whimpering mewl.

"I gotta get it out, love."

I thanked who or whatever had decided to show up and engage the quartette outside. While many feet danced around each other, letting metal clang and blood drench the sand, I coaxed Kasha to lie on her side, facing me.

"Be very still now," I said, softly gripping the piece embedded into her. The good thing about it being part of an Ifrit was that the wound would be cauterized and probably wouldn't bleed once I removed it. The downside was that it was going to hurt like a bitch.

I felt my skin blister and burn at the touch, yet I didn't flinch, but pulled. With a sickening, hissing, and slicing sound, it came out.

Kasha wailed, the sound piercing my heart. Luckily, no blood flowed from the wound and I let go of what looked like a piece of wingtip. Quickly, I dropped it, then scooped sand over it with a foot, dousing the heat.

With a sigh and blistered palms, I sank to my knees and leaned against the Hellcat a bit. My antics – even fueled by my whip and the heavenly sand – had left me exhausted. Pulling rock and quartz from the depth and forming it into a sphere the size of a carriage was no easy feat. Let alone if one did it as fast as I had.

"Ready to see what's going on?" I asked Kasha.

The Hellcat responded with a grunt and laying her huge head down, her breath even and deep.

I shrugged. "Fine, I'll take a look myself." Fighting the pain and cramps searing through my body, I placed my knuckles on the sphere-wall in the direction of the sounds and pulled at the quartz. Then I flattened and smoothed it to the point of it becoming a small window. My heart hammered in my throat and my pulse pounded through me like a drum. Sweat ran down my face as I blinked at the scene outside.

"Welp, seems like your fight really did wake the very Heavens," I told Kasha.

Contorted by the quartz, I saw the quartette engaged with two Angels.

"We are fucked, no matter who wins."

Chapter Twelve
Mihr

The Surface,
somewhere between Kaokoveld and Damaraland,
Namibia

Even if I had been mile high, I would not have missed them. In the silence – only accompanied by wind and the flapping of my own wings – I heard the fight long before I saw it. By which I mean I didn't see the fight I heard. At all. Even as I hovered above the sounds of metal, roars, and screams, there was nothing.

My mouth dry, my pulse erratic, I searched for Fane and Kasha, but couldn't find them. I dove even lower, shielding my eyes against the midday sun. Something invisible shifted around me, as though I entered an unseen barrier, and a sudden clarity washed over me.

Not only did I suddenly see six people fighting, Two Angels and four Demons, but my connection to Kasha was clear as day once more. She was close. Right beneath me.

I spied a half-sphere of rock, sitting smack-dab in the middle of a lonely dune and I couldn't hold back a smile. Fane. She had fashioned herself and Kasha a bunker.

A few paces away an Ifrit, fighting alongside what looked like a Demon Lord, sliced open a she-Angel from stem to stern while the Demon Lord held her down. Her screams rang in my ears, her wings trembling with pain and instinctually, I pulled Fane's whip free and sped down. With one crack, I circled the Ifrit's head. It hissed and snarled, I pulled and the hissing stopped as the metal cut through the fiery skin like a knife through butter.

The Demon's head dropped to the ground, the body followed.

I looped back up and flipped over, aiming my next attack at the Demon Lord. He could be the one who was after Fane – the one who had owned her. Wrath boiled up my stomach-walls when his arrogant sneer met me. He twirled his blade in one hand, then gripped it and took a stance, awaiting my attack.

Letting the whip whistle through the air, I sped toward him, a roar breaking from my chest. With a zing, the Demon deflected the whip, side-stepping the blow. A grim smile on his lips, he beckoned me to try again.

As I turned to meet his wish, I saw the other Angel fall to the claws of a magnificent Succubus, who proceeded to suck the Angel-blood from her fingers like he'd been a delicious meal.

She crouched, then launched herself into the air, right into my path. I swerved, dodging her wingless, but extremely fast attack. Her claws ripped into my jeans and pierced my leg, but the burn didn't deter me.

Again, the Demon Lord avoided my attack, but this time only by the skin of his teeth.

This was getting tiresome. I landed a few paces away and faced the two Demons.

"Big mistake, Angel," the Succubus said, biting her lower lip with a seductive grin. "Should have flapped off as soon as you pierced my shield."

I did a double take at her. A magic-wielding Succubus? One able to cast a shield of invisibility and disrupt soul-deep connections? That was rare. And only one Succubus I knew of had that kind of power.

"You are Jinx, the protector of Leviathan, son of Sathanas," I stated.

Her grin fell. "I was, before Fane came along and got my Maester killed."

Leviathan was dead? I'd had no idea. And whatever the rest of her words meant, I would have to unpack them later, as the Demon Lord lay a palm on her shoulder. "This one is mine, Jinx," he said. "Help Cecil get Fane out of her sphere."

The Succubus crinkled her nose, gave the man a disgusted side-eye, but she bowed her head, mumbled "yes, Maester," and turned from him. She strolled over to the ball of rock which looked like it was made from crystal or quartz, in front of which a Demon – apparently named Cecil – paced.

"She's mine," the Demon Lord informed me, a mean gleam entering his black eyes.

"Fane is free, thanks to me," I said.

That stopped him short. "You are the one? The Angel she refers to as hers?" His upper lip curled, revealing his fangs. "You won't be for long."

I had no time to wrap my head around the fact that Fane called me hers, as the guy dashed forward, letting his sword slash at me. At the last second, I turned and lifted my elbow, letting his face run straight into it. His nose cracked and he stumbled back, palming his bleeding nose.

He squinted at me and I smiled. "I thought you were serious, the way you doled out threats just now." I pulled up my right shoulder in a half-shrug. "Doesn't feel like it."

He swiped the black blood from his lips and sniffed. "You will die for that, Angel, right before you have blessed me. And I will keep her forever."

As my heart warred with my mind – one appalled at what he'd said and raging murderously, while the other dissected the way he moved and where best to embed his own sword – and I laughed. "Tell me, if you couldn't even control Fane when owning her, how are you planning to deal with a free woman? Got your affairs in order?"

He growled.

"If I don't kill you, she will. And I am planning to see your head roll, collecting dust, just like your Ifrit friend."

The Demon attacked. Enraged as he was, his movements were sloppy and with one crack of my whip, I opened the skin on his wrist, prompting him to let his sword fall with a yelp. Palming his wrist, he watched me closely. I snapped the whip again, but this time he was ready, and caught the tip with his good hand. I pulled both the whip and him toward me, wrapping the metal around him once he was within reach. He tried to wriggle free and punch his way out of my hold, but I ignored his efforts and forced him into a headlock. With a calm I didn't feel in the slightest, I circled the whip around his neck a few times, dodging his horns each time he jerked them at my face.

I pulled the whip tight and his claws ripped from where he'd embedded them into my arms to his throat. He grabbed at the whip, his claws slicing and pinging on the metal to no avail. The retching and coughing coming from him was music to my ears. For a moment the wish of prolonging his suffering flashed through me, but I flexed my fingers, ready to end him.

Shock slammed into me as a familiar sound split the air. Automatically, my gaze flew up and I cursed. A squadron of Angels appeared, their wings glinting in the sun like mirrors. If the shield of the Succubus worked on them too, I had little time. They'd soon enter it and see us.

The Demon Lord used my moment of distraction. He flipped his legs up and rocked forward, launching me over him. My grip on the whip lost, I simply rolled further when my back hit the ground, the movement committed to muscle-memory. Grabbing the sword he had dropped and using the momentum, I sprang up and ran. He wasn't important right now. Reaching Fane and Kasha was.

In a flat-out sprint, I let the unknown sword meet Cecil's neck, severing him and his thinking marble with one stroke. The Succubus spun around with a hiss, but fear and anger fueled me and she was too slow. Swinging the sword in a downward arc, I chopped through her upper leg, not daring to kill her and have her shield vanish.

Her scream nearly ruptured my eardrums and I shoved her out of my way. She dropped to her back and wailed at her stump, fingers flexed and face terrified.

I had no time to regret or feel sorry for her as I ploughed on and lifted the sword over my head, ready to hack at the ball of stone Fane and Kasha were in. We needed to leave. Right now.

But before I could execute any kind of blow, the rock splintered apart, revealing Fane, more pink than red, sweaty, and bruised, next to Kasha, who lay motionless behind her.

"Great timing, Claudia," Fane muttered through the Succubus' screams.

"My turn to schlepp you around for a change," I said. Then I tucked the sword into my belt, bent down and scooped up my girls. Kasha, big and heavy as she was, I hoisted over my shoulder, while I grabbed Fane around the waist and simply plucked her up, her back against my torso.

Fane grunted when I broke into another run, and strained my wings. Flapping them for all I was worth, we finally took off. Staying low, I headed back in the direction I had come from, confident that the Succubus' wails would draw the approaching Angels.

I didn't dare look back, but sped on as fast as I could, entering a dry riverbed and following its twist and turns until canyon walls surrounded us. Each wingbeat was hell, making me think there wouldn't be a next one. But there was. And another. Driving my body over the edge of its limits, I willed myself to go on.

After a few minutes that felt like hours, I spied a ledge leading to a cave and leaned into a sharp turn. My wings and back muscles rippled, feeling like they would unravel under the effort. With pain ringing in every part of my back, I landed inside the small cave.

Even as my body wanted to crumple into itself, I sat Fane down, and she slumped to the stony floor. Groaning, I bent down and lay Kasha on the ground, then fell to my knees beside her. I caught my fall with both hands and rolled on my back.

For a few seconds the cave was filled with the sound of my panting and a weird scraping noise. I turned my head and watched Fane crawl toward the opening. She reached out her palms and whimpered as she placed them on the stone, making the walls rumble. Dust and small rocks rained down on us while the entrance slowly closed.

Once darkness surrounded us, the scraping sounded again and finally Fane's fingers grabbed my leg. She pulled herself up my body and cursed when she lay next to me.

I pulled her closer, wrapping my arms around her. Her left hand slid over my chest and she pressed her face to my skin. Sniffling preceded tears running over my chest.

"Thank the stars, you are safe," she uttered, her voice heavy with exhaustion and tears.

"I could say the same. What happened to Kasha?" I extended one hand and drew it through her fur. A small mewl answered, followed by deep purring.

"She went wing to wing with the Ifrit. I removed part of the fire-Demon's wingtip from her chest. She did so well." Fane's hand met mine on Kasha's fur, and our fingers twined. "So very well."

"You both did," I rasped and kissed Fane's forehead. "But don't you ever leave me like that again."

"I can't promise that, love." Fane sniffed and snuggled closer, her words going drowsy. "If it would save you, I would reenter Hell itself."

My heart jumped at that, then hurt as it swelled with love for her. Listening to her even breathing and Kasha's purring, I lay in the darkness and felt more complete than I ever had. All I could hope for now was that we had gotten away unseen, and that Gabe was fast in finding Dax. As soon as I was able, we would be on our way back to see our boy.

Chapter Thirteen
Karina's Savior

The Surface,
Kaokoveld, Namibia

Agony laced through her entire body, culminating in her lower stomach and radiating out to her hips and chest area. Pounding. Dull. Covering her in waves of nausea.

Karina watched part of her entrails slide from her stomach cavity and dip into the sand. Like a surreal dream she saw it, felt it pull on her center, but didn't feel it. It was part of her, she should feel it!

Her lower lip trembled as she reached out a hand to scoop it back where it belonged. But it was covered in sand and her hand seemed to weigh a ton. Whatever part of her lay there, she couldn't reach it.

Tears pooled in her eyes and slid down her cheeks. Her breath got short and her body shook as she strained and groaned. Her blood-speckled hand groped nothing but air, then dropped into the burning-hot sand. Bile rose up her throat and for a moment Karina wondered where it came from, since she was disemboweled.

A shadow fell over her and Karina blinked, trying to see past her tears and the sliver of sun coating her face. Not even the pain – cooling her body and raging through every fiber of her being – had the effect the face above her did. It felt like the claws of the Ifrit ripped her apart anew.

"You let them get away," Shamal hissed down at her. "And look what happened to Thomas." He waved off to the side.

Karina rolled her head, the sand grinding audibly under the back of her head. "No," she croaked, more tears welling from her eyes as she beheld him and his dead stare looking up. "He – he must have followed me. I just… I just came to look. To see where he went, so I could warn you. So I could lead you to him." She looked at Shamal. "He was in Heaven."

His brows pulled together, creasing his forehead. "Who was?"

"That Angel. The one Michael was after. Mihr."

This time Shamal's brows shot up. "Mihr was here?"

The initial cold turned to a chill and made Karina's teeth chatter. Shamal fell in and out of focus, while her rattling breath came harder. Thomas… He shouldn't have been there. It should have been a simple recon mission. One to right her mistakes. But once she'd found Mihr and the Demons, Thomas, who had apparently followed her, had shot past her from above, diving into the fray. Thomas, the one she'd felt connected to, the one she had disobeyed Michael for.

As Karina felt the life draining from her and soak the desert sand around her, she still mourned their friendship, and whatever else they'd shared. Courageous, upstanding and – as it turned out – stupid. Of course, she'd joined the fight to help him. Now they both paid for his stupidity.

A sharp jab hit her shoulder and snapped Shamal into focus. He kicked her shoulder once more. "Focus, soldier. Mihr was here?" he hissed.

"Yes… he fought the Demons."

"Where is he?"

"Dunno. I followed him then smelled the Demons." Her lids slid shut slowly. "Demons fighting Demons... strange. We attacked and then Mihr was there."

"Which way did he go?"

Karina pointed to the left. "He carried a Demon and a Hellcat that way once you showed up."

With a huffing sound, Shamal's shadow vanished and Karina was hit with a load of sunshine. For a second, it warmed her, but even the sun couldn't stem the chill digging through her steadily.

"Bring him back home and bury him," Shamal instructed from a distance and Karina forced her lids open to see a young Angel pick up Thomas' lifeless body.

"The rest of us will go that way, fan out and search for the traitor and his Demon," the Archangel ordered.

One of the soldiers, a young woman called Cynthia, looked at Karina. "What about her? I could take her back up."

Shamal didn't even turn to look. "Leave her. Once we are done with our search and have found Mihr, we will take her body up."

"But she is alive, we can save her," Cynthia said.

"Did I stutter?" Shamal snapped.

Cynthia lowered her head. "No. We take her up when we come back."

"Exactly. Now let's go."

Wind and sand billowed over Karina as they took off, stinging on her face like needle pricks. They were leaving her to die. Real death. Like Thomas. Like Michael. For the first time since she'd woken as an Angel, she felt like calling out for her mother. Someone she only had a very vague memory of. No face, but a smell and a feeling of warmth and safety. Right now, she longed for her embrace, for her smell to envelope her, and for her safety to blanket her.

Karina stuttered out a breath and let her gaze roam over the red, barren landscape. The red rocks surrounding her had been scattered by the fight and some had bloody spots on them. Golden and black. In the distance, a huge mountain range loomed over everything. Blue, with ragged peaks.

Wind picked up, making the sparsely growing grass rustle in resonance. It tasted like heat and salt, and a wildness Karina had never experienced before.

As the life slowly drained from her and darkness entered her vision, she felt many things. Panic, betrayal, pain, anger, but also wonder and a strange sense of peace.

If she had to die, she might as well die in a place like this. Harshly beautiful and wide as the sky above it.

The sound of wings sliced through the peaceful quiet, then feet landed and jogged over, skidding to a stop at her side. Hands dug under her and picked her up.

Karina managed to open her heavy lids a fraction and saw Cynthia.

The she-Angel's lips were pressed into a grim line. "I can't do much for you, but maybe you'll survive."

Karina's center sank as Cynthia shot into the air and her consciousness flickered, close to giving up. What felt like hours, seconds, and minutes later all at once, Cynthia placed her in the cool shade of a tree. The sand was soft and fine. Thick and cool.

"Live, Karina," Cynthia whispered, then her steps receded.

Seconds later a shout sounded, followed by the running of many feet. Voices rose around her, speaking a strange language. Fingers nudged her but she was unable to open her eyes again.

Finally, her mind drifted off, leaving her with the impression of alien voices and soft touches.

'Not a bad way to go,' she thought to herself before plunging into nothingness.

Chapter Fourteen
Fane

The Surface, in a cave,
Namibia

I lay and listened to his breath, felt his heartbeat beneath my fingers and pressed my face to his skin. He was alive. He was okay. He'd come for us. Safety enveloped me and I was about to close my eyes when a thought hit me. I lifted my head.

"How? How did you get to us so fast? What about Horace's poison?"

Mihr hugged me a bit closer. "Gabriel found me. The necklaces he gave us also emit some kind of magical energy he can pinpoint. That's also how I found you, he told me what way to go. The poison... he countered it with another poison that gave me cramps from Hell, but I could wash that off without a problem. He should be on his way to Dax by now." My Angel turned his head, so his lips rested on my forehead. He pecked it with a soft kiss that had me closing my eyes involuntarily. Damn the nine rings, I was so far gone it was scary.

"We should wait until it's safe and we are healed, then head back home as soon as we can," Mihr said.

"Home? You see our little place as home?" My heart jumped.

"Of course I do. It has everything I need. Beaches, sea view, fog to hide Kasha in, friendly people, great food... Oh, and you are there, too." He chuckled, making my head bounce on his chest.

I playfully dug my nails into his pec. "Asshat."

He quieted down and palmed my face with his hands. In the darkness, all I could see was the glint of sparse light in his eyes. "Me wanting to stop both our kinds from harming this world further has nothing to do with not wanting to be with you. Please understand that. You are the best thing that has ever happened to me, and I can't imagine a life without you, Kasha, and our two Humans."

Did he mean what it sounded like? Tears lumped in my throat and I opened my mouth to answer, when

Mihr suddenly clamped a palm over my lips. An outraged grunt escaped me.

"Shhh," Mihr said, further angering me. "You can confess your undying love for me later, dear, right now you have to be quiet," he whispered.

That was it. I sank my teeth into his finger. Mihr's resulting jerk was very satisfying, but he didn't utter a sound. "Fane, stop biting me. There are Angels outside, searching for us," he breathed.

I opened my mouth and he took away his hand. "Why not lead with that, dingus?" I asked softly.

"Where would be the fun in that?" he asked.

Then we both went rigid in each other's arms when we heard them. Wingbeats.

A low growl started up behind us and we both tried calming Kasha, who struggled to get up and see what was threatening us. Mihr pulled her back down and whispered something to her I couldn't hear. Another growl, this time very quiet, answered.

The wingbeats grew softer, then louder once more. They zapped past our hiding spot again and again.

"They know we are here somewhere," I deduced.

"Yep, they can feel the pull of my blood," Mihr said.

"You're bleeding?" I sat up, cursing my cramping muscles as I went. "Is it bad? Why didn't you say anything?"

My Angel placed both palms on my shoulders to settle me. "It isn't bad, Fane. My wounds have closed already, but they can feel even a drop a mile away."

As if on cue, something big and heavy slammed against the wall I had erected. Just like it had back in my little marble-quartz cage. It had taken everything out of me to hold that cage steady under the other Ember's onslaught. He had been pretty powerful after all, and would have worn me out if Mihr hadn't decapitated him.

Speaking of which, Mihr was on his feet and pulled my aching body up to stand next to him. I felt Kasha's side slink past my hip as she faced the noise from outside.

Another boom rattled the cave, making dust and tiny rocks rain down on us. Thankfully, we were surrounded by granite and it would take them a while to break through. I had no illusions when it came to their success. Eventually, they would break through.

"I don't have much left to offer, in terms of steadying the barrier," I told Mihr.

He handed me something heavy and metallic. Lev's sword. The realization made it even heavier and I almost let it fall.

"Can you do something with that?" he asked. "To give me an edge in a fight?"

Sorrow was like a fist grabbing hold of my heart. This sword was almost as legendary as he had been himself. Then Mihr's words penetrated my skull. "In a fight?"

"Well, it's gonna come to one. You said yourself you won't be able to hold them off."

I cradled the weapon, letting my fingers slide over the blade and tapped a nail to it, making it sing. It truly was sublime. No irregularities, no brittleness and perfectly balanced. I frowned. There was something strange about it, though. An echo, a feeling… Like a lingering taste. Sharp, a bit foul – dangerous. Skimming my fingers over it, I pinpointed the feeling. It ran down the exact middle of the blade. Fine as a hair, almost not there. Lilithium. The dead metal. How? There was no Ember alive or dead who could work it. How was it part of this sword? And in such a small amount? It made no sense, yet intrigued as well as disgusted me. Lilithium had one Master and only one. Him. Lucifer. The Fallen One. Legend had it that the impact of his unholy fall had burned the Earth and scalded the stone on his plummet to Hell, creating Lilithium. His element. The only reason why a sword would have part of it was Him.

As if being burned, I let the weapon clatter to the floor. I stared at the spot it had hit and stepped back.

"Fane? Fane, what's wrong?" Mihr asked, accompanied by another loud boom.

A crack forming at the entrance let a sliver of light into the cave and I saw him bend over to pick up the sword.

"Don't!" I said, terror making my voice pitch over.

Mihr looked at me over his shoulder with a raised brow. "Why? What's wrong?"

"The Devil Himself made that sword, or part of it. Don't touch it, Mihr."

My Angel looked down at the blade, then back up at me, then at the steadily crumbling entrance. His face hardened and he snatched the sword from the ground.

"We don't have a choice," he rumbled, weighing it in one hand.

I stared. "It is cursed. There is no telling what kind of effect it will have on you, but I am sure it will harm you."

"It didn't harm Leviathan. He had it for ages and killed countless of my kind with it." Mihr glowered at the sword. "Did you know he was dead? Your former Maester told me."

Sadness, pain, and guilt twisted my chest. "Lev was a Demon. His powers would have been amplified with that sword, although I can imagine there was a price. Maybe pain, maybe life-force. You are an Angel, Samantha, I can't say what it will cost you to wield it."

His gaze met mine and I had to flee it by letting mine drop to the floor. "As for his death… I knew. He died in my arms."

My revelation was met with silence. Silence broken apart by the continuous smashes from outside. I knew they would break through at any moment now, but I couldn't meet his eyes. I had no idea what I would see and it scared me. *Fascinating*. This close to imminent danger and what I was concerned with was him. And what he made of my past.

"We have to get ready. They are almost through," Mihr said. He kept his voice carefully level, but I was still afraid. Mostly because he said nothing about Lev and I had no idea what went on in his head.

I nodded and took a stance, pressing my naked feet flat on the granite to work my powers on it. Or what was left of them anyway. My whips had been casualties of the last battle and I felt vulnerable without them.

While I debated on how best to ward off the Angels – singling out loose rocks strewn across the cave – a sudden tug on my neck distracted me. I looked at my necklace and saw the pendant swarmed by the living sand lifting off my chest and bouncing back down. I reached up and the sand detached from the pendant, dropped into my hand and sang to my skin. The thousand mouths chattered with urgency, before swarming over my fingers and floating to the floor. The swath of sand snaked through the cave and circled a piece of wall on the far side. A huff escaped me when I walked over and felt what the sand was trying to convey. The wall was thin and behind it, a crevice led deeper into the stone. A crack I could widen, even in this condition. Especially if the sand helped me.

"Agatha, would you be so kind as to hit this part of wall with that cursed sword?" I asked Mihr, a smidge of hope dancing in my belly. Maybe we were getting out of this one.

"What? Why?" Mihr walked up to me and scrutinized the wall, still circled by the living sand.

I rapped my knuckles against it eliciting a hollow sound. "Cause of that. I can widen the crack behind this wall and maybe we can escape."

"We won't have room to fight though," Mihr interjected.

"No. But if they follow, I can smash them with pretty little effort."

A muscle clenched in his jaw, worry written plainly on his features.

"You'd have to trust me," I said.

Mihr let out a long breath, then raised the sword and hacked at the wall. The thin layer of rock cracked and burst with his swing, spraying cool dust and pieces of granite everywhere.

With a satisfied grunt, I reached for the sand and it coated my fingers in the blink of an eye. I clapped my hands and *voila*, two palms filled with sticky, happily buzzing sand.

Punching my hands into the revealed crack, I opened it wider, so even Kasha would fit through. Widening the crack was not hard, but even with the sand as an amplifier and my enthusiasm, my body reminded me of its limits fast. I had to widen, then walk, crouch, or squeeze myself forward, then widen again. Once the jagged and torn rock sliced into my skin, I knew it would soon be game over. Normally, my skin and stone had a symbiotic relationship with each other. The fact that rock would rip and pierce it, meant my powers waned. In all honesty, if the sand wasn't along for the ride, I would have maybe been able to burrow us into the rock as long as I was myself. Which was not all that long.

A huge boom, followed by a reverberating crack behind us, told me they were through.

"Hurry, Fane," Mihr urged.

"Calm your tits," I snapped, concentrating on their steps. Two sets of feet, then three, then four, stomped through the cave. Voices echoed from the walls, shouts bounded through our tunnel, then I felt them approach. They didn't enter, but piled up in front of our getaway aisle.

"Come on, you feathered fiends," I whispered, ready to use the last of my power to smash the stone around them together, should they follow us.

A small prick on my right palm made me focus on the sand in my fingers. Following its lead, I skimmed along the stone to my right. Another crack, this one leading into a tunnel, one that was naturally wide enough. Boulders stacked on boulders, leaving space in between. An idea zinged through my head.

"They can sense your blood?" I asked Mihr.

"Yes. But what does that have to do with–"

"Get rid of anything they might feel," I told him.

Close to me as he was, I felt him rustle around, before the naked skin of his chest touched the back of my arms, sending a shiver up my back and down my front.

"Anything else?" he rasped, dropping fabric to the floor.

"N-no, you're good," I stammered.

"I know," he rasped close to my ear.

Just as I went weak in the knees, a commotion in front of our escape tunnel broke out.

"You go in first, have you seen the hand marks in the stone? The Demon formed this tunnel. What else do you think she's capable of?" a female voice asked.

"I don't care," a deep male voice answered. "Someone is going in, preferably before that thing has burrowed her way out somewhere else."

"Thing? I'll show him what kind of thing he's messing with," I grated. "Hey, fucktard," I yelled. "Afraid of a little Demon? Come get me, you big wuss!"

Someone was shoved into the tunnel and I smiled despite the pain shooting down my spine and branching into my back, legs, and shoulders as I opened our way into the natural tunnel. I turned and grabbed hold of Mihr's upper arm. He looked down at me, and our skin touching, combined with the confusion in his pale-gray eyes, zapped through me like lightning. How his eyes managed to hold me like a physical touch – even in a situation like this was beyond me, but there was no time to ponder it now. I pushed him into the tunnel and despite his confusion, he allowed me to. Kasha followed her Angel as soon as he was through and I wiggled myself right into the crack, waiting for the Angel creeping up my widened tunnel.

It was a shame that they weren't followed and the rest just waited to see what was going to happen, but a small part of me didn't mind it so much. A small part that was happy my actions would mean the death of only one.

"Mihr, get ready to catch me and hold me upright," I whispered and waved him closer.

He stepped behind me, circling me with both arms until his torso was fused to my back and his hot breath fanned over my neck. "Ready."

Using the sand and forcing my power to flow from me, I ruptured certain points of stone in the tunnel, making it collapse in a deafening rumble. The Angel inside the tunnel screamed. I felt the poor bugger getting crushed under the stone and stepped back into Mihr.

Quickly, I closed the gap I had made over the rumbling collapse, then my legs strained as my body struggled with exhaustion. *Too much*, I thought, feeling my muscles spasm and cramp. *Too much.*

Huge hands caught me and lifted me up, cradling me to a rock-hard, naked chest. Even as I forced my lips to remain shut when all I wanted to do was scream under the onslaught of pain, I felt his presence envelope me like a safety blanket. Tears ran down my cheeks and dripped onto his skin as he carried me away from the still rumbling and crashing stone I had caused.

Chapter Fifteen
Mihr
The Surface,
Kaokoveld, Namibia

I felt dazed as I carried a whimpering Fane through a row of spaces, tunnels, and caves, created by roundish boulders stacked together. Here and there patches of sunlight hit the ground, lighting up our surroundings so I could actually see. Kasha led us through the maze and I followed her swishing tail as though it was the guiding shine of a lighthouse.

I had killed countless Demons and – recently – some Angels, but this had to be the first Fane had ever ended. Even knowing how hypocritical it was, I had no idea how to feel about it. I also didn't know how to feel about the fact that Leviathan had been the one Fane had loved. The one who had hurt her. *Great*, now anger was part of my confusion. This day kept getting better by the second. It took me a few minutes to realize what Fane had actually done back there. There had been no fight, only one death – if I had heard it correctly.

"You are a devious genius," I told Fane, who snuggled closer, her lips thin as she pressed them together.

"T-tell me about it," she mumbled weakly. I smiled down, still a bit confused as to how I felt in general and specifically toward Fane.

Ahead of us, Kasha squeezed her huge body through a surprisingly small nook and jumped down and out of sight. I stuck my head through and saw a spacious cave, with two openings leading back outside.

"We can hide in there until you are better," I said, hoisting Fane up.

She groaned, but crawled through the hole. Her weight shifted through and when her legs suddenly pointed up and accelerated, I grabbed her ankles and lowered her slowly into the cave.

I had a bit more problems than Kasha and Fane in fitting through the tight space. My shoulders were too wide and scraped along the sharp granite. Luckily the stone could not pierce my skin, so blood was not part of the ordeal, but it took me a considerable amount of effort and time to get inside.

Finally, I sank down next to Fane, feeling dirty and sweaty. She had her lids closed but leaned against me and let her head drop onto my upper arm. "You did good," she murmured. "Thank you for trusting me."

"I trust your powers and your way of thinking."

Her head shifted slightly. "Not me?"

I thought about it. Did I? Even after what she told me about being with Leviathan? After her killing an Angel? "I trust you," I said.

Her grunt vibrated up my arm. "That answer took a bit long."

"Because I'm confused."

"Anything I can help you with, Serena?"

Kasha, who had been busy sneaking around the cave, sniffing the stonewalls and the small bones lying strewn around, meandered back to us and flopped down on my other side. Purring, she placed her head in my lap and closed her red eyes as soon as I began scratching her behind her ears and around her horns.

"Don't think so, no," I finally said. "It's something I have to work out for myself."

Fane sighed and slid a palm over my leg until her hand hit mine and she laced our fingers. "You *can* trust me, you know," she said.

"I know."

"Good."

I frowned and drew circles on the back of her hand with my thumb. "You don't want to know what's bothering me?"

"Nope. Don't need to. You said you have to figure it out and I can't help. If you're ready, you'll tell me."

I was at a loss for words. Fane – once again – showed more understanding and patience than any of my peers ever would.

"I hope we get back to Dax and Cam soon," Fane murmured. "Do you think Gabriel found them already?"

"He did say he'd be there long before us, so yeah." I squeezed her hand once. "Do you think we can move soon? The other Angels will be looking for us."

My Demon puffed out a long breath. "I guess so. But how will we even get past them if they're still around? Do we have to wait them out?"

"I don't think that will work," I said. "They will put up sentinels and keep watch over the entire place. For as long as they need to."

"So, what do we do?"

Wasn't that the question? "We need a distraction."

"Hmm." Fane lifted her head. "I think I could manage something. But in order for me to do that, I'll need to fully rest." She dug her naked toes into the grainy sand and played with the necklace Gabriel had given her. It looked different now. The heavenly sand I had brought her nestled around the pendant, forming and reforming in strange patterns. Some of the grains ran over her fingers and a soft, tired smile grew on her luscious lips.

She looked so vulnerable and beautiful sitting there, holding my hand and playing with her sand, that my heart lost a beat and grew heavy. Yes, she was many things I used to abhor. A Demon, a hedonist, a little self-centered, and filled to the brim with a passion for life. Yet, she cared, she saved me without thinking about it. She had done so over and over. She might be the Demon and I the Angel, but did I actually deserve her? The things I had said to her, thought about her... I knew she would see past it if she ever felt the same as I did, but could I?

She let out a small sigh, her breath tickling my bare chest and a tremor went through me. My body reacted to her in a way it had never done for another. Even now, here, in this cave, I wanted her. I suspected dimly, that I always would. And still, my heart throbbed with heaviness... with love. In that moment I knew I was lost to her. Screw Heaven, Hell, and everything in between – she was the one I would die for. But what would happen if she knew?

Fear grabbed hold of me. I couldn't ask her how she felt. I didn't dare to. Even if many of her words and actions indicated she might feel something similar toward me. She had told me she was afraid of me leaving because she thought she wasn't good enough for me. Still... in regards to relationships I pegged Fane as fickle.

"I should be out there, fighting them," I said.

"Not with that sword, you're not," Fane said, nodding at Leviathan's blade in my belt. Another topic I was wary of, but as I felt anger spiked with jealousy rage inside my lower belly, I couldn't contain it any longer. "So… you and the Demon Prince himself."

Fane looked at me. "Yes. Him and me. It was short lived and ended in his death, so you don't need to worry."

"Who says I worry?"

She giggled. "The jumping muscle in your jaw. Not to mention the murderous intensity of your eyes." Fane pulled my hand into her lap and added her other hand to the mix. She scooted closer, so her side pressed against mine. "Soft, hot, jealous Angel," she purred. One palm sneakily slid onto my naked stomach and up the ridges of my abs, to settle on my right pec.

To distract myself and mask my breath getting short, I asked, "You think I'm jealous?"

A small laugh tumbled from her mouth, then she pressed a kiss on my upper arm. "I know you are. I mean let's face it – I am irresistible." Her hand slid over to my other pec, then up as she let her fingers dance over my collarbone. "And we are alone, in a cave, with nothing to do, but wait."

I groaned in answer and began reaching for her, when a soft growl sounded from my lap. We both looked down and snorted out a laugh when Kasha opened one lid to glare at us.

"Okay, maybe not all alone," Fane conceded. "I'll be good," she promised and placed her wandering hand back on mine.

"Pity," I said. "But I think it's better. You do need to get your strength up anyway."

My skin felt like it was on fire from her sly caresses and all I wanted to do was pull her onto my lap and lose myself in her. The way she crossed her legs and sighed, while squeezing my hand, I bet she felt much the same.

"Being good sucks," she said.

"Agreed."

For a few minutes, we sat in tense silence, with unsaid words and unfulfilled wants between us.

"Party-pooper," Fane said to Kasha, before she rested her head on my shoulder once more, either to get ahold of herself or to truly rest. Perhaps it was a bit of both.

The heavy feeling between us didn't last though, as Fane's head rose from my shoulder with alarming suddenness. She closed her eyes and dug her toes deeper into the sand. Then Kasha lifted her head as well to stare at one of the openings leading outside.

"Something is happening out there." Fane tilted her head to the side, looking deep in concentration. "I feel the ground opening... At the circles. Portals. More Demons are coming."

I sprang up and pulled her with me. We both peered out of our cave but there was nothing to be seen. Then something huge and feathery zapped over us and vanished around the nose of the canyon ahead. An Angel. Another one followed immediately, then three more. Noise erupted from that direction. The sound of battle.

Fane and I looked at one another. "You wanted a distraction she said. *Presto*. Let's skedaddle."

"Agreed. Again," I said and grinned. I picked her up and she wound arms and legs around me, clinging to me like a koala to a tree.

"Fane, a little more up," I grunted. "If you don't want to be impaled while we fly."

She burrowed her face into the crook of my neck and wiggled against my crotch. "Yes, please."

I groaned, grabbed her butt, and hoisted her up further. "Another time, naughty Demon. Let's get home first. Kasha, up!"

The three of us shot from the cave, and took the opposite direction along the canyon, away from the fight. We raced through the winding riverbed until I was sure it was safe, then we climbed higher into the sky. As fast as we could, Kasha and I flew toward the coast. The landscape beneath us was breathtaking, even as we fled God only knew what kind of battle. We flew through an ever-changing treasury of mountains, bushland, and spectacular rock formations that were a sight to behold. The land passing beneath us was speckled with herds of antelopes, the one or other group of apes, and even a small herd of elephants that made their way down the same riverbed we followed. Like huge gray boulders, they moved silently and cautious, heading for a bunch of gnarly, thorny trees.

We hovered to look at them for a minute or so, captivated by their presence. But when Kasha tried to approach them – no doubt to make new friends – I called her and we flew on.

At the first taste of sea, brought along by a chilly wind, I felt like coming home. A strange notion. Deeply satisfying and exciting. Heavy and warm.

It was almost sundown and no mist in sight, so we stayed high up until we circled our house.

"You think Gabriel is there?" Fane asked, squinting down and into the wind.

"I hope he took a look at Dax already if he is," I said.

I told Kasha to wait and spiraled down. The wind got stronger the closer to the Earth we got and soon I noticed it had emptied the already sparsely used sidewalks completely. I whistled and Kasha dove down, sailed past us and landed on the terrace leading to my bedroom. With Fane still wrapped around me, I sank lower until my feet hit the tiled ground. Instead of letting go, she snuggled a bit closer and kissed the crook of my neck with a loud smack. "Thanks for the lift." She slid down, winked, and pulled open the glass door.

I chuckled and wiped away her intentionally sloppy kiss, before following her and Kasha inside.

Once inside, the first thing we heard was noise. Camille's voice was shrill and loud, while a deeper and way more leveled one answered.

Fane looked at me. "Gabe," we both said at the same time and dashed from the room and up the stairs to Dax's room.

The shouting got louder with each step. We burst into the room, coming up against a view that stopped my heart for a second.

Chapter Sixteen

Fane

The Surface,

a coastal Namibian city

Dax floated. Dressed in nothing but underpants, his body riddled with deep cuts and his skin clammy with beads of sweat, he hovered in the air horizontally. Beneath him, Cam jumped up to snatch his leg, her eyes wet with tears. She screamed and shouted, while Gabriel, shirtless and wearing that ridiculously small loincloth, tried to calm her and stop her from touching Dax.

The whole room smelled like rotten flesh, dried blood and old sweat. It made a cold shiver creep down my back and yet I knew with absolute certainty, if Cam touched Dax now, something horrible was about to happen. There was no way to describe how I knew, but it was a grueling truth, pounding through every cell of my body.

I ran straight for Cam and hugged her to me, clamping my arms around hers to keep her from reaching.

My friend hugged me back and yelled my ear off, her nails digging into my skin with a ferocity that almost made me feel pain. I couldn't understand what she was screaming, only a few words were clear enough and not raked with sobs.

Gabriel threw me a tired but thankful nod before he waved his hand to indicate we should stand back a little.

The moment I tried to tug Cam away from underneath her son, she attempted to rip herself from me.

I palmed her face. "Look at me, Cam," I said in a level and calm voice. "Gabe is here to help. He promised. Now, we have to let him."

Cam's lips quivered and tears ran down her face in streams. "B-but… Dax started floating the moment he came into the room," she pointed at Gabe. "What is he doing to my boy?"

Gabriel held up his hands. "The magic he seems to have tapped into is demonic – going by the smell – and my presence threatens it. No one can touch him in this state, as the magic inside Daxter would protect him. I can calm it. But I need you to step back and let me do my work."

Cam's face scrunched up with pain and fear, her green eyes searching my face for advice. A feeling of utter helplessness hit me. She trusted me with the life of her child. "You better get him down, magic man," I said and walked us back to Mihr and Kasha, my arm firmly around my friend.

"I will," Gabriel said and pulled a shimmering powder from one of his pouches. He walked around beneath Dax, sprinkling the powder around intermittently, while glancing up and down. Once his powder was apparently distributed to his satisfaction, he added an assortment of rocks, small bones, and horn. If I wasn't mistaken, it looked like Demon-horn, and my naked feet felt the unmistakable smoothness of rose quartz.

Next to me, Cam followed his every move with rapt attention, tears running down her cheeks the entire time. Mihr laced his fingers with mine, his hand shaky and clammy with sweat. Even behind us, Kasha stood, uttering small, inquisitive sounds that told of her nervousness. All of us hated being unable to do anything but watch.

Gabriel – chanting low in a language that was both familiar, yet unknown to me – circled his powder, rocks and horn with carefully placed steps. His voice grew and fell like the current of a stream, following a specific path. The words came quicker and a gasp sounded from Dax.

Next to me, Cam whimpered and grabbed my free hand, still resting on her shoulder. She squeezed with all her Human might and I swallowed at the lump of fear clogging up my throat.

Our boy arched his back, sweat dripping from his body, the drops sizzled when they hit the powder. Then blood oozed from his countless cuts and I nearly ran for him. A split-second glance from Gabe stopped me and I grunted, wanting nothing more than to close my eyes at the surreal sight.

Soon, Cam and I sobbed uncontrollably and Mihr pulled us both into his arms. We stood, a knot of terrified limbs and laced fingers – unable to help our Dax as he contorted, bled, and trembled in mid-air. It got worse when he screamed. I didn't recognize his voice. It was echoey and deep... very different from its normal cadence.

Pressing my lids shut – I was sure I wouldn't be able to stomach it otherwise – I hid my face against Mihr's chest and bit down on my lower lip until I tasted blood.

There was no telling how much time passed, but eventually, Mihr tapped my shoulder to get my attention.

I turned my head and blinked. The raw and deep screams tapered out and Dax's cuts were no longer black and rotting, but red as they should be. His voice broke through in high-pitched lilts for a few moments, but were soon overshadowed by that echoey sound once more.

Gabriel continued to chant and circle, throwing his hands up and waving them around. A series of hissing and spitting sounds alternated with the chants and I saw his naked back glistening with sweat. His muscles strained as if he was lifting, or pulling on something extremely heavy, his face scrunched up in a mix of concentration and pain.

Gabriel suddenly went rigid, but his body was still taut as a wire. Then he stumbled back as if something keeping him connected had been ripped apart.

The light in the room flickered, followed by the bulb popping and shorting out. The few seconds it took for my eyes to accommodate the sudden change, seemed like forever, but once they did, I nearly sank to my knees with relief.

Gabriel was flat on his ass, busy with sitting up, as Dax sank down slowly. The sweat and blood dropping from Dax, still hissed and sizzled on the powder, now making little sparks of blue light and smoke erupt from the ground and up to him.

Cam and I surged forward, Mihr and Kasha hot on our heels. The four of us crossed the room, but we refrained from touching Dax as he hovered lower.

Gabriel stood, dusted off his behind and nodded at us. I wanted to turn from him and hug Dax to me with all I was worth, but something in the magic man's face made a cold shiver scamper down my back. Something wasn't right.

Dax sank into Cam's arms, who caught him and pulled him to her chest, cradling him like he was a babe. She cooed sweet nothings to him, crying all the while.

Mihr, Kasha, and I crowded them, all watching Dax with bated breath. His lids stayed shut.

Cam softly shook her son. "Dax? Baby? Wake up. Please wake up." Her voice was thin and cracked a few times.

"I am sorry, madam," Gabe said. "But he will not wake now."

"What do you mean?" Mihr asked. "You said you could fix him."

"No. I said I'd take a look at him. I have." Gabriel said, his lips thin. "Lay him down on the bed and I'll explain what I found."

Cam's lower lip trembled and a bout of new tears threatened to spill down her cheeks, but she did as Gabriel asked.

We all gathered around his bed and when I reached out to hold his hand, I was shocked at how hot it was. It felt beyond feverish.

"So, tell us," Mihr demanded. "What is wrong with our boy?"

Gabriel wiped off the sweat from his face and scanned us with tired eyes. "To understand what is wrong with him, you have to understand the basics and origins of magic. There are different types and different sources."

"What do you mean?" Cam asked. "Isn't magic, magic?"

Gabriel shook his head. "Heavenly magic is different from hellish magic, and Humans have another type entirely. Depending on who – or what – you are, you use your type of magic. I, as a half-being, could theoretically use both Human and Demonic spells, but as I have never met my hellish parent and am not in Hell, I have only learned how to use earthly magic. Dax found a very peculiar book," he pointed at the tome on Dax's nightstand. "It was written by a Human sorcerer, but contains spells in a very old demonic dialect. So old, in fact, it has similarities to the old heavenly language."

"That's the one we couldn't read?" I asked, remembering Dax asking me and Mihr about particular passages.

Gabriel narrowed his eyes. "There are few left who can, if I am not mistaken. But more on that later. A Human can use the magic intended for their kind if they have an affinity for it. It is basically an energy exchange. You draw on the energy around you or your own and fuel your spells with it, if you have nothing, the magic will take what it needs from you. Demonic spells work differently. A tithe is needed for them to work. A sacrifice," he added at Cam's blank face.

Knowing bits about demonic magic I nodded. "The sorcerers I know use animals and slaves. Sometimes rare artifacts work as well... And there are those who use pieces of soul. For the big spells."

"Right," Gabe said. He sighed deeply and looked down at Dax. "The boy used human magic without knowing how to pay for it, so it took what was owed from him directly. He will have had small cuts, shallow and easily healed. Constant magical strain will have demanded constant payment."

Guilt zinged through me at the thought of Dax suffering from summoning me to Earth. Then he had erected the shield around this house. A constant strain. Had I known...

"Something changed though," Gabriel said. "According to the magic he is exposed to now – which is demonic – he found a way to read and perform the demonic incantations." The half-Demon fled Cam's inquiring gaze. "From what I can tell, he combined some of the human spells to make a new one. What resulted was a powerful inquiring spell. He asked for knowledge. It must have worked, because the very last incantation is demonic. I can't say exactly which one he tried, but the energy it elicits is devious and evil, almost like it has a mind of its own. It is not ordinary, as far as I can tell." He finally looked at Cam. "The spell will have taken from him what was owed, just like his human ones have. But he is not a Demon."

"What do you mean by that?" I asked, a terrible thought bouncing around in my mind.

"Daxter has performed magic not meant for his kind – without knowing how to direct the energy exchange. No matter if what he tried worked or not, it took a part of him."

Cam looked from me to Gabriel, then back to me. "Wh-what? I don't understand."

"How much did it take?" I asked.

Gabriel said nothing for a while, he just looked at me. "All of him. As far as I can tell, his soul is linked to Hell now."

My best friend went rigid, then tremors ran over her. Mihr uttered a curse far too foul for his usual self and I almost forgot to breathe. Cam stroked over her son's arm. Again and again. "B-but he is here. My b-boy his h-here."

"His body is still connected to his soul, but the connection is fragile and will break eventually. The energy protecting him from me is trying to infuse him."

"Are you saying it is trying to take over his body?" Mihr asked, his brows pulled together. "Magic has no mind, it can't inhabit a body."

"Of course it can," Gabriel said. "It normally doesn't, sticking to objects, rather than organic material. But that does not mean it can't." He pointed at my necklace, surrounded by my heavenly sand. "The sand is magic. And whatever radiates from your weapon," Gabe glanced at the sword in Mihr's belt, "is very similar to what infuses the boy."

I closed a fist around the pendant, feeling the sand rejoice at my touch and attention. There was a mind pulsating in my fingers. Very different from mine, but there was clear intent behind it. "So, you're saying that magic is alive?"

"Magic is energy. Everything around us is made of energy. Magic is the balancing weave connecting everything. Give and take, yin and yang, if you will. We, who can wield that energy, will force it out of its natural state, and that costs a price. Different realms have different rules of life and therefore magic."

"What does that mean regarding Dax?" Mihr rumbled. "How do we get him back and... whatever, or whoever, wants to take him over out?"

Gabriel slowly shook his head. "I don't really know. I slowed the process of the magic, but was unable to pull the boy back. Something is anchoring him."

The sand in my hand still pulsated softly. "You said the energy holding Dax is similar to Mihr's weapon?" I asked.

"The signature is weak, but yes," Gabriel answered.

I shot from my seat next to Dax and held a hand out to Mihr. He pulled the sword from his belt and handed it over. The moment my skin touched it, I felt like retching, the Lilithium making my stomach convulse. I dug my fingers into the metal, heating it, then ripped the sword in two, right down the middle.

Both Gabriel and Mihr gasped. "Why would you rip my sword apart?" Mihr said.

I gagged as I pulled the sliver of Lilithium from one half of the blade with two fingers. The feeling was one of utter disgust and weakness as I held it out to Gabriel. "Similar, or the same?" I asked him, my stomach lurching.

My Angel blinked at me, then the Lilithium, and Gabriel drew a pinch of powder from his pouch and sprinkled it over the dead stone. It hissed and sizzled just like Dax's blood and sweat had.

The half-Demon stared at me. "The same."

I nodded once, then pressed my lids shut. Drawing a huge breath through my nostrils, I crumbled up the vile thing with both fists. As fast as possible, I wound the metal of the sword around it, shielding it from view and my skin. Bile rose up my throat and by the time I was done, I had almost ruined the floor.

Cam, Gabriel and Mihr talked during my efforts, but I had no idea what they discussed. All I could hear was the pulsing of my heartbeat in my ears and the rushing of my own blood. Sulfur and ash, I hated the stuff. Dropping a neat and perfectly rounded metal-sphere from my fingers onto Dax's desk, I sucked in breath after breath. Slowly, my mind quieted and my heart stopped racing.

"Fane? Fane?" Cam's voice pierced the pulsing and rushing and I looked at her. Her pale green stare was pleading. "What was that?"

"Lilithium," I said. "Dead metal. It is said that Lucifer Himself created it while falling from Heaven and through Earth to Hell." Only now did I feel the tug on my necklace and felt for it. The pendant with the sand had wandered to the back of my neck and pulled against my neck. Once I touched the sand, I felt it clearly. Fear, coupled with wrath. The sand felt much like me about the Lilithium.

Gabriel walked past me and picked up the sphere. He weighed it in one palm and gazed at Dax thoughtfully. "Do you know where to find this in Hell?" he asked me.

"Partly," I said. "Most of it is in the ninth ring, beneath Lucifers castle. Why?"

"At the very least, it is somehow used to hold the boy. Maybe it is even the source of the magic infusing him."

"Didn't you say that magic is the 'weave that balances energy' or some such bullshit?" I asked.

"Human magic is, yes. It originates from life. Demonic magic is different, I only know what it demands. When it comes to heavenly magic?" He shrugged. "No idea at all."

"So, you're saying Dax is tethered and being overtaken by Lilithium?" The thought alone had me gagging once more.

"It could be, or it used to hold his soul, as I stated before," Gabriel said. He watched as Cam sobbed, holding her son's hand while stroking his head with her free palm. He drew his shoulders back, seemingly coming to a decision. "Whatever the case may be, he is close to this Lilithium stuff. If you get me into Hell, I could pinpoint where the boy's soul is anchored."

"Are you serious?" I gaped at him.

"Deadly."

"No one is going to Hell," Mihr said.

"Screw that, I don't even know how," I said. "I just escaped it. And I highly doubt that Mihr can fly into the ground."

"And if I, or we, discovered a way?" Gabriel asked.

Decidedly ignoring Mihr's glare, I stared at Dax. "If it means we can save him, yes. I would take you there."

Chapter Seventeen
Mihr

The Surface,
a coastal Namibian city

"No one is going to Hell," I repeated, feeling like a broken record, because apparently, I was being ignored. Cam, Gabriel, and Fane all spoke at once, throwing around ideas and scenarios, while anger and panic bubbled up my stomach-walls like acid. Kasha grunted at my side, feeling my unease. She gave a little flap of her huge wings, nearly throwing Gabriel off balance with the resulting gust of wind. Then she growled. Loud and deep.

Within a split second everyone was quiet and looking at us. "No one is going to Hell," I said. "It is way too dangerous."

When my eyes met Cam's, I felt guilt close around my heart like a fist. "Even if this theory turns out to be true, and his soul is beneath Lucifer's castle, we would have to travel through nine rings without being made. And then? Even if we manage, which I doubt, how are we going to free Dax? Fane can't work Lilithium, right?" My Demon nodded. "And Gabriel has no – or limited – knowledge about demonic magic."

"We have to save Dax," Cam said.

"Of course we do," I answered. "But we can't just burst into Hell half-assed. We'll be dead and Dax's body will be overtaken by…" I waved at the sphere in Gabriel's hand. "Plus, not only are there Angels and Demons after us, but from what things look like, Demons will soon roam the Earth uninhibited, while Heaven builds a secret army with stolen souls. We have to plan our next steps carefully, or all could be lost."

Fane grunted. "How much time does Dax have, magic man?"

"As long as I am with him, I can regulate the hold the magic has over him. Once we leave, I'd say a day. Maybe," Gabriel mused.

"Then we damned well find a way to save him fast," Cam said. "And once inside Hell, we need to get out as fast as we can."

"Someone should stay here and look after Dax," I said to Cam, who glowered at me.

"He is right, Cam," Fane said. "It's too dangerous for a Human to enter Hell."

"I should just sit and wait? And trust that you will save my boy?"

"Camille, Fane and I love him, you know that. And we will do anything and everything we can to get him back."

Cam crossed her arms and sniffed, her eyes red and puffy. "I know. I just... I'm supposed to protect him, I'm his mother."

"He will need you to call him back, to find his way," Gabe said. "Once we lift whatever anchors him, he will need more than the frail connection he still has to his body. He will need you calling him, guiding him." The half-Demon nodded at Cam, their gazes connecting a tad too long for my liking.

The half-Demon's words did seem to have an effect though, as Cam's shoulders sagged. "I'll do anything to get him back."

Gabriel placed a palm on her shoulder softly. "Ijo, and I will show you how to call him."

My Demon scrutinized Gabriel, then his palm on Cam's shoulder. "Say, isn't your debt to us paid? You said you'd take a look at the boy and see if you could help. You have done that. Why offer to find his soul in Hell?"

Gabriel smiled and pulled back his hand. "I have spent my life researching all the spells I came across. I traveled the world for years, until I came back here, back home to where the circles are. I always knew they would one day lead me to my kind. And now I have the opportunity to go to Hell? I will take it." He strolled over to Dax's nightstand and swiped up the tome. "Now I'll try to find the spell he made up, so I can read the demonic incantations. I'm sure it'll help figuring out which spell is responsible for this whole mess. And what he was trying to do."

****

"I don't like the way he beams at the tome," I rumbled, standing in the hallway to Dax's room with Fane and Kasha.

"I don't like the way he looks at Cam," Fane said.

I chuckled and she glanced at me, her amber eyes glowing very subtly. "I don't think she minds, Demon." Jerking my chin up, I indicated at Cam, who sat beside Gabe, holding Dax's hand firmly in her own. The Human's lips trembled into a very brief smile when Gabe looked up from the book, they nodded at one another then just sat together. The half-Demon reading and Cam glancing over his shoulder at what Gabe was reading now and then.

"Pish posh, Cam has other things to worry about right now," Fane said, a crease appearing between her brows. "Speaking of which, we should think of a strategy. Or on how to get into Hell in the first place."

I let her ramble on, counting things that came to her brilliant mind on her fingers. My heart stopped for a beat, then went heavy and bouncy at the same time. A contradiction. Just like my Demon herself. And my feelings for her. Something hit me out of left field, blindsiding me with a memory that had been blurry. Now it stood out, clear as day.

Her veins painted in a fiery orange, visibly burning beneath her skin, her agitated and scared expression as she looked down at me. Her shaky hands on my face and arms. The way her voice had shaken along with them. Telling me to stay put, because she needed to keep me safe. Saying that I'd been right, there was no way our relationship could stay physical. Not for her.

I couldn't believe I'd nearly forgotten her saying it. But I had been scared for her, unable to defend her, stunned by Incubus venom. And she had buried me in a hole while saying it, so one could forgive my lapse in memory.

A strange feeling formed a lump in my throat and I swallowed repeatedly to get rid of it. No matter how scared I was of her ridicule – before we went to save Dax – I had to know.

"I think I could work out how the portals function… Now that I know what they are. But I'd have to go back to the circles, and then what? What if it actually works and we're in Hell? We have to think of a way to conceal us, especially the further in we get. Or–"

I grabbed hold of both her arms and turned her to face me. "Yes. We need to talk about all of it. But first, you and me are going to have a chat."

Fane opened and closed her mouth like a fish on dry land, her expression outraged. She glanced from me, into the room, and back again.

"I know. But Gabe will take a while and Dax is safe for now. We have time for this." I bent lower, bringing my face very close to hers. "We need this."

With that said, I snatched her hand, told Kasha to 'stay' and pulled Fane with me. As I heard her footsteps speed up to keep up with me, her hand still in mine, I smirked when no word of protest came from her.

We barged into my room and I closed the door behind us. Fane let go of my hand and stepped back until she hit the bed. Slowly, she sank down on it to sit at the foot, seemingly very interested in the carpet floor.

I sighed and leaned against the door. Nervousness riddling my insides until they felt queasy. *Get a grip, man*, I told myself. *You're over seven hundred years old. Stop acting like a stupid youngling.* It was no use, my throat seemed to have clamped shut and I was at a loss for words for a few seconds.

Fane – uncharacteristically quiet herself – stroked the duvet to her sides and then cleared her throat. "W-what did you want to talk about?"

Was that fear in her voice? It couldn't be. Seeing and hearing her being as worked up as I was, gave me a surge of confidence. "Did you mean it?"

My Demon looked up to meet my face, a confused expression on her features.

"Back when you buried me. You said this relationship isn't just physical for you. Did you mean that?"

Fane blew out a stream of air and I saw the wheels in her head turning. For a split-second, a shadow of the cheek she normally hid behind flashed over her face and I nearly cursed, but then it was gone and she tilted up her head and looked straight at me. It was the strangest thing, for the first time since knowing her, she looked bare. Stripped down to her very essence. She could give herself over completely when we had sex, she never did the same in conversation. There was always something she hid behind. Her snark, her sass, or her need to shock me with vulgarity. Right now, there was none of it. For some inexplicable reason I knew whatever she was about to say was the truth.

"I meant it."

A knot loosened in my chest and I felt like I could take flight without my wings. "I want us to be on the same page," I said.

"Meaning what?" Fane placed both hands into her lap and nibbled at her bottom lip. "Did you – did you mean what you said in the cave? That you wanting to leave had nothing to do with me? That you saw this as home and you wanted to stay?"

"Of course I did."

She knotted her fingers. "Then... what does 'the same page' mean, Kate?"

I smirked and pushed my back off the door to walk across the room. "I think 'fucking each other to death' as you once so eloquently put it, will no longer work."

Fane jumped. "What? Why? No sex? W–"

This time, I actually chuckled. Standing right in front of her, I reached out to cup her chin. Then I sank to my hunches so we were on the same level. "Of course there will be sex," I said, and laughed at Fane's relieved expression.

"Stop scaring me, you ass!" she snapped.

"My wonderfully complex Demon, what I'm trying to say is that I want to be with you."

"Well, you're screwing that up, Angel." She recoiled. "What do you mean 'be with me'? Like now? Is this some sort of weird, angelic sex-suggestion? Do all of your people do this when you want to get laid? Seems exhausting." She fled my gaze. "Also, this is kind of a weird time, but you could just ask next time, or tell me what you want."

"Fane! Shut up!"

My Ember stared at me.

"I'm trying to tell you that I love you. And I want to be with you forever. If you'll have me."

Fane blinked. "Love... Saints on a Sunday, Bridget, of course I'll have your holy ass." She launched off the bed and into my arms, effectively tackling us both to the carpet. Her lips found mine without effort. The kiss was not filled with passion or teasing, but honest and hard.

It surprised me but I quickly got with the program and hugged her to me, deepening the kiss. When she pulled back and we both gasped for air, I saw tears running down her face.

"I love you too." She sank down, kissing me again. "By all that is rock and metal, I love you, Mihr."

The way she rasped my name against my lips ignited a fire inside me that singed me down to my marrow. All consuming, my love and passion for her spread out and through me.

She was mine. Sliding my hands down her back and up the little skirt she had fashioned from her hoodies, I got ready to show her just what that meant.

This time was different, it wasn't fast and heady like the other times, but slow and intensive.

I saw the love she felt mirrored in her eyes, her abandon shining in her veins, and I let her see what I felt. Without a wall to hide anything, I gave myself to her. Trusting her with my heart.

It didn't matter who she'd loved before me, or where she came from, I loved her. And every part of her life had brought her closer to me, to us. Yes, she was mine, just like I was hers.

Our gazes connected, we made love. I watched her fly apart beneath me, rasping my name in a guttural voice and she saw my extasy mixing in with hers.

Clinging to each other like we were the only thing left on this Earth to hold onto, we became one. Truly.

Chapter Eighteen
Fane

The Surface,
a coastal Namibian city

There was nothing I could compare to what I felt. Because it was unknown. I knew what love was, but I had never known the depth of trust and truth before. No matter how certainly I knew Lev had loved me, he had never truly supplied me with the sense of safety Mihr did. My Angel gave me the knowledge – just by conveying it with his gray eyes – that he'd take care of my stupid heart. With him, it was safe. Just like I was.

He loves me, I though, delirious with happiness. *This gorgeous, angelic, upstanding man loves me*. No matter how much I told it to myself and how clearly I saw it in his eyes, it took a bit for me to wrap my head around it being a fact.

I lay beneath him, my breath heavy, my heart pounding like mad and my skin slick with sweat. Radiating with the afterglow of being loved, body and mind, I could do nothing but stare at him in wonder. Mihr swiped at an auburn strand sticking to my forehead with a thumb. His gray eyes searched my face, his fingers stroked over my cheeks, my brows, and lips. He dipped down to kiss me softly. Sweetly. And I nearly started crying. What the Hell? Would anyone have told me that a sweet kiss from an Angel would do funny things to my stomach and spur my heartrate to new heights, I would have laughed.

"You have to stop that," I choked out.

Mihr pushed himself up on his elbows and frowned down. "What exactly?"

"Kiss me like that. It's my undoing."

He grinned deviously and bent down to do it again. This time a tear ran down my cheek and when he loomed over me, he smiled softly while wiping it away.

"I created a monster," I said.

"It's not that bad, Demon. You'll get used to it."

"If we live long enough," I said. "Speaking of which – and I can't believe I'm saying this in the position I am in – we have to get up and discuss a plan. Let's shower, get dressed and see how far Gabe is with the book. Maybe he found something."

Mihr pouted. "Party-pooper."

I shook my head. "Seriously. I created a monster."

He laughed, but disentangled his body from mine and stood. My Angel reached for me and pulled me to a stand as though he were righting a feather. "Yeah, the past has definitely been the wrong way round. From now on, I demand being the one getting injured, stunned, or tortured, so you can carry me. It seems to be no problem for you." I gathered what fabric lay strew across the room and tossed it into the bin.

Mihr's gaze followed me, a relaxed expression laced with cheek resting on his face. "Might I remind you, that I *did* carry you from the last battle?"

Picking up a stray sock and tossing it, I raised a brow. "Not to mention Kasha. Which is exactly my point. We would have been fucked if I had to get the two of you to safety."

"You could consider taking up weightlifting," he said.

I clutched my chest. "Was that a joke? Di-did Mihr the Stoic just make a joke?"

My Angel threw a shirt at me he had just picked up. "You are an idiot."

"At you service, Mandy." I bowed mockingly and when I straightened, my gaze wandered up his delicious body and I had to clench my fists and bite my lip to stop myself from groping him. No doubt that would lead to more groping, and… stuff. Still, the way he half leaned, half sat on the bed, all of him on display for my hungry eyes, it was tempting. He noticed me staring and leaned back on his arms, making his shoulders bulge and his abs clench.

"Nghh," was the only thing I was able to utter.

"What does 'nghh' mean, love?" Mihr asked.

When I looked at his face, his gray eyes gleamed with naughtiness and a certain amount of heat that almost had my knees knocking together in weakness.

I tilted my head to the side. "Didn't you know? 'Nghh' is universally known as a synonym for: I plan to lick every inch of you at the earliest opportunity."

His brows shot up and in the corner of my eye I saw him twitch. Success.

"I don't believe anyone has told me that, no," he said.

I shrugged. "Well, clearly you heavenly types don't know everything." I winked at him and started walking toward the bathroom.

He shook his head, chuckling as he stood. When he gave me his back, reaching for something on the bed I nearly stumbled. That fine, *fine* ass…

"One of these days, I will remember to do it," I declared

"Do what?"

"Bite your ass."

I sauntered on, closed the door on his completely derailed face and cackled while stepping into the shower. Despite facing the unavoidable fact that we looked for a way to get into Hell, to save Dax's soul, I felt my heart bounce with a sweet weightlessness. I knew it wouldn't last once we left his room, but for the remainder of my shower I smiled into the spray like an idiot. Curious that such a stupid thing could make me this giddy, or maybe it was because of the severity of our situation. All I knew was that I felt more alive than I ever had before. Electrified and wide awake. If our trip into

Hell happened and we got caught? I'd make the most of the time I had left with my Angel.

****

"I'm not confident about this at all," Mihr said half an hour later. His index finger followed the line I had drawn on a piece of printing paper. "Even if our initial plan works and we get the distraction we aim for… How well do you even know the ninth ring?"

I blew a breath from puffed out cheeks and grimaced at my – admittedly – bad drawing of Lucifer's castle and the surrounding landscape. "I uh… I went there once. With Lev. To the feast of the Fallen." The memory sliced into me like a blade. On that particular night our relationship had started. I swallowed and raised my head. Mihr's face had turned glum and angry.

Even as the painful memory of Lev rebounded through my ribcage, I felt a weird flick of joy at Mihr's reaction. Strange.

"And you think having been there once is enough?" His voice had gone hard.

"No, I don't think it's enough, Angel." I glared at him. "But it's all I fucking have."

Mihr heaved out a sigh. "I know, sorry. It's just... This is madness, Fane." He placed his fists on the kitchen counter we were standing in front of. "We don't know if this is the right place. Do we have a way of telling where Dax is tethered?"

My stomach sank. "I have no idea. But that is where most of the Lilithium is, so it would make sense." I played with the necklace and felt the sand soothingly caress my fingers. "Wait a minute... You said Gabe put a spell on these through which he could find us?" I held up the necklace.

"I know what you are thinking and I don't believe it will be that easy," Gabriel said from behind us. We both spun to face the half-Demon. He came down the last few stairs and joined us in the open kitchen. "I could try and rework the spell and make it search for the boy... But his body is here." He tapped an index finger to his lower lip, deep in thought.

"Did you find anything?" Mihr asked.

"Hm? Oh, yes. Yes, I found the spell the boy combined, the exact incantation. I am wary of trying it though, mainly because it is worded quite unusually."

"Meaning?" Cam asked, who emerged from upstairs. She looked like a shell of her former self and I immediately felt bad. Even while glad Mihr and I had cleared the air and... made love, I couldn't help feeling guilty for stealing bits of joy and happiness where I could in a time like this. It seemed unfair.

"There is no telling what your son's demand for knowledge will manifest in me. The spell is worded... wrong." Gabe scratched his head, seemingly confused. "But it obviously worked, so..." He spread his hands in a helpless gesture.

"What do mean with 'wrong'?" Mihr asked.

"There aren't many people with magical abilities who can write or combine spells. Some try, but they almost never work. I don't have the talent to invent spells." He glanced at Cam. "Your boy does. Apparently. But there are rules that apply to the wording and order of actions. Daxter had no idea, I think he just did what felt right to him."

"But it worked," I said.

Gabe gave me long look. "That is what worries me. It shouldn't have. The way it is worded is very clear, but I have no idea what he actually did. There are actions and words he added, and I have no idea where they come from or why he added them. There is no way of knowing or understanding what the spell will eventually do if I use it. Also, I have no idea how much energy it will take."

"You would need it to read the demonic incantations and see which one he used, right?" Cam asked.

The magic-man nodded.

"Is there someone else who can figure it out? Someone we can ask?"

"I'm afraid not. No one we could reach easily, at least."

"Can you use it on someone else, like me?" Cam asked.

"Absolutely not!" Gabriel snapped, his face incredulous. When he met Cam's gaze, his expression softened. "The magic would destroy you. You are not built to use it, dear. No, no. I will try it."

The next half hour was filled with Gabriel rearranging the living room. He ordered Mihr and me to clear the couches and the coffee table, so he would have room. Cam was sent to Dax's room, to look for the supplies Gabe would need. The magic man was sure our boy had a hidden stash of ingredients somewhere.

After the living area was cleared, Gabriel paced the length and width of it. He dug into one of his pouches and unearthed a piece of coal with which he started drawing onto the floor. Black symbols soon covered the gray tiles, the scraping of the coal eliciting a weird feeling in my naked feet. Almost like a powdery tickle.

A warm hand grabbed mine and I leaned against Mihr who stood next to me.

"We'll need to make a lot more preparations. Weapons, a way to hide, a way into Hell…" he rumbled.

"Yes, we do." With my free hand, I touched the sand on my necklace. I didn't want to use it for weapons, it felt like it belonged on my skin. It had crawled – for lack of a better word – there by itself. But my Angel was right – we did need weapons. My whips lay somewhere in the Koakoveld, near a battle ground of unknown proportions. I wondered briefly whether Jinx and Ragon had escaped the Angels, then decided I didn't care. What I was curious about was the battle that had drawn the Angels away from us. How many Demons had emerged to occupy them? Had it been Ragon's men?

The thing was, my whips had been the perfect weapons and their loss was hard. I would be able to fashion Mihr a great sword from Lev's old one. Without the Lilithium. But that still left me short.

My nerves flared as I watched Gabe continue his preparations. If this worked, we would probably go to Hell. Like really. Up until now, I had been able to compartmentalize that fact, but seemingly no more. The thought sent a shudder through my body and left me chilled to the bone. I had waited long to escape, only to go back now. My breath grew short as stark fear snaked up my stomach to wrap around my chest. My breath hitched and for a moment I felt like running. Cursing myself a second later for my cowardice, I knew there was no way around it. If Dax needed me, I'd knock on old Lu's door to get him back – quite literally, if my assumptions were right. Before my stupid panic reached its peak, I heard footsteps from above.

I snuggled closer to Mihr, then squeezed his hand. His presence was grounding and comfortable. Like a warming fire. I allowed myself to bask in the safety he brought and rested my head against his chest. But soon, fear for him and what would be done to him in Hell ghosted through my inner eye. The memory of him in that cell in the Deep, spread-eagled, naked and tortured, came to mind. Back then, the picture hadn't fazed me. He had been a means to an end. Now... now, I felt true pain at thinking back. He should not come along, Hell was too dangerous for a creature like him. Come to think of it, I would happily go all by my lonesome self, but I knew I'd have a hard time arguing that wish.

I breathed out and cleared my throat to make sure none of my inner ruminations could be heard in my voice. "I'm gonna go check on Cam," I said.

My Angel hugged me to him. "Good idea."

I left the safety of his arms, feeling chilly as soon as I had, but quickly, I traversed the living room and jogged up the stairs. It did not matter how fast I was – my thoughts and fears bobbed up and down next to me like helium balloons fastened to my wrists. I grimaced and tried ignoring them as best I could.

Walking past Dax's room, I saw Kasha standing watch over him like a black statue. Her red eyes flashed up at me for a second, her body tensing to spring. When she recognized me, she calmed and meowed softly.

"That's my girl. You keep watch, Kasha," I said and carried on down the hallway. From the sounds of it, Cam was further ahead, in the small storage room to the left.

I found my friend between boxes, mops, an old microwave, and a vacuum cleaner. Dust-moths hung in her curls and she was busy ripping open a box. She sensed or heard me and turned, swiping at a dusty strand of hair. "I can't find anything," she said, waving at the boxes. "There is nothing."

Leaden guilt dropped into my gut as I watched my usually strong friend's despair. It was partly my fault. Dax had used magic for a year to summon me, then to portal us around, then to protect us. We shouldn't have asked it of him.

"Don't do that," Cam said.

"Do what?"

She sighed and flopped down on a box, which compressed to half its size beneath her ass. "Feel guilty. I can see it on your face. Don't."

"I'm sorry. Can't help it." I stepped closer and picked at the dust-moths in her hair. "We shouldn't have stayed with you," I said. "I am sorry we did. If Dax hadn't tried to shield me from my enemies... Mihr was right, the two of us should have gone looking for our kind. To thwart their plans. What was I thinking? Staying with you–"

"Fane. Your guilt trip isn't bringing my boy back." She glanced up, her green eyes looking tired and strained. "And you damned-well know that we wouldn't have allowed you to leave us. We are family, you red fiend." She let her head sink again and leaned her forehead against my belly. I drew my fingers through her hair and massaged her scalp. She sniffled and I tasted my own tears coming.

"I will never forgive myself if we fail," Cam said, looping both arms around my upper legs and hugging me closer while twisting her face to the side. "We can't fail, Fane."

I cradled her head and stroked over her cheeks, tears now running down my own. "We won't."

The panic happily clawing at my insides didn't let up, but it could screw itself, I was ready to get our boy back. No matter what.

"Let's turn this place upside down," I suggested. "I'm sure Dax had his hiding spots."

Chapter Nineteen

Mihr

The Surface,
a coastal Namibian city

When I watched Fane leave to check on Cam, I wanted nothing more than to follow. She might have thought I hadn't noticed her shiver, or how her grip on my hand had grown desperately hard. My Demon was scared. I did not blame her. While I didn't want to enter that foul place again, it didn't frighten me. What did was her going, or Dax suffering and losing his soul in those cursed depths.

"Fane said you are one the Fallen?" Gabriel asked as he crouched at the edge of his drawings and filled in details. "How did that happen?"

I didn't know whether I wanted to tell this halfling of my so-called shame. Had I found him pre-Fane, I would have killed him. But my Demon was right,

I should stop judging as much. Gabriel had helped me when I was stunned and he was about to try a spell he was clearly wary of, just to help a boy he didn't even know. While his motives were… questionable, as he did it to enter Hell and had told us so, I felt like he did deserve a bit of my trust.

"The two Incubi who terrorized the village you protect dragged me to Hell. Funnily enough, I met them at this very coast."

"Yes, I do believe the fairy circles are portals to the depth and most of Hell's kind comes up through them. It makes sense, as it is in the middle of nowhere and unlikely for there to be Humans around." His ageless face flickered, hinting at pitch-black skin underneath. I wondered why he would keep up a charm to hide, since we all knew what he was.

"They managed to capture you–"

I snorted. "They were not alone, and my charge, Rapha decided not to heed my warning and attacked. Once I decimated the rest of the Demons apart from the Incubi, they had grabbed Rapha already…" The memory still inspired both anger and guilt. "I tried to save him, but that one Incubus poisoned me, and they killed him in front of my eyes." Thank the Lord I had finally gotten my revenge. It did little to dampen the anger or the guilt, though. Revenge seldomly turned to a feeling of righteousness. But knowing those two had gotten what they deserved, helped.

Gabe looked a little struck and was careful to not raise his eyes at me. "Well, all I was going to ask is why would them capturing you and bringing you to Hell make you a Fallen? Surely ti !khutse wouldn't count that as an act you could have controlled?"

"No, but the heavenly Father does tend to dislike it when one of his Angels bless Hellspawn."

The halflings eyes snapped to mine. "When Fane said that you were a 'blesser of Hellspawn,' I thought she was joking."

I smirked and crossed my arms. "How do you think she is able to walk your realm? And Kasha? They were both tied to the depths by their bonds to the Devil. No one escapes or leaves without the Prince of Darkness knowing and condoning it. Fane freed me and demanded to be blessed so we both could leave. I did. That makes me a Fallen."

Gabriel blinked, his fingers holding the charcoal, hovering over his drawing.

"But killing an Archangel didn't help my case any further," I muttered. "Even if he deserved it." The memory of Michael dying at my hands left me empty and devastated. Still. And for the hundredth time I asked myself 'why?' Why had had he felt the need to go against what was right? Why had he not listened to me? And why, by all that was divine, had he gone about stealing souls? I clearly hadn't known him at all. Or rather, the young Angel I had befriended during our early years, had drastically changed. What happened? And why had I not noticed?

Those questions made a sour taste settle on my tongue, mainly because I knew I'd most likely never get the answers to my questions. Dead people had the tendency of not giving reasons for their former behavior.

A loud crash from above interrupted my dark train of thought and our conversation. We both jumped and rushed toward the stairs, when a shout came from somewhere upstairs.

"All is good," Cam yelled. "That was just Fane, digging for concrete under the floorboards."

The half-Demon and I exchanged a look. "Does this sort of thing happen a lot?" he asked.

I shrugged and sauntered back into the living room. "I live with a Demon, a Hellcat and two Humans, nothing around here is normal."

****

The women returned from the first floor not much later, carrying a box each.

"Found the stash," Fane trilled, her voice a little too shrill. When our eyes met, I knew that she was trying hard to mask her nervousness and fear. It made something primal and exceptionally powerful thunder through me. For a very short moment, I wondered what it was, but when the urge to snatch my Demon and hide her from all harm coming her way grew near unbearable, I knew. Protectiveness.

I had spent hundreds of years protecting my kind and Humans from ilk, but it had been my duty, my life. This was different. This was an acute need. A compulsory feel so strong that it took considerable effort on my behalf to quash it. The vastness of my urge scared me a little and I knew one thing – Fane would have to come away unscathed – or I was going to lose my shit.

"Great," Gabe beamed and momentarily opened the box in Cam's hands. He fished out a couple of things with a wide smile and then turned to Fane to do the same. When he had gathered all he needed, the half-Demon walked back to his drawing and sank to his hunches. Carefully, he placed the stuff in his arms on the floor.

Small crystals, bundles of herbs, pieces of bone, small pouches with unknown contents, and what looked like sticks, were neatly lined up. Gabe lifted one of the pouches, opened it and stuck his nose inside to smell. He tilted his head from side to side in a 'this will do' kind of fashion and picked up the next one.

The three of us stood and beheld his actions.

"Can we help?" Cam asked after a while of this going on. She dropped the box she held onto the dining table. Fane followed suit and also regarded Gabe with a questioning expression. When she tried to smile, I saw how the corners of her mouth trembled before she forced her lips into the desired shape.

"No," Gabriel said curtly. "This needs to be done right. It will take a while."

I raised a brow and pulled up one shoulder. "Anyone want something to drink, or eat?" I asked.

"Yes, please," Cam said and followed me when I headed for the kitchen.

Both women sat down on the stools at the kitchen island while I opened the fridge and got out an assortment of goods. I fished three glasses from a cabinet, topped Fane's with rosé, Cam's and mine with white wine. Then I proceeded to cook a huge omelet. It was one of the things Dax had taught me during our last two weeks here. And he'd said I did a decent job.

Silence hung around us, thick and heavy, while I worked. It was strange. I felt I needed to say many things, but right then wasn't the moment for it.

Cam gave me a tired and thankful smile when I placed the plate in front of her. I reciprocated in kind and went to give Fane hers. My Demon reached for me and held my wrist. She pulled me around the kitchen island and next to her stool. Her face still only reached my shoulder and she hugged me to her sitting form. "Thank you," she uttered.

I slid one hand under her chin and tilted it up, so she looked at me. I searched her face and for a moment she seemed like she would pull away, but then she met my stare head-on. Stark fear greeted me, along with guilt and sadness.

"I'll be okay," she said. "Promise."

I bent down and kissed her. When I pulled away, her expression was lighter and the sight warmed my heart. She hugged me once more, then let go to start eating. Cam ogled us with rounded eyes, but quickly grabbed her fork and gulfed down a mouthful.

I rounded the island and dug into my own food. Fane never openly touched me in front of Cam or Dax, and for her to reach for me like that either meant she was comfortable in our relationship, or she was so scared that she needed the contact. I decided to believe the former.

In the exact moment I set down my fork, a silent buzz went through the room, making the hair on my arms stand. I straightened and glanced into the living room. Fane and Cam had felt it as well, as they swiveled around on their stools to do the same.

A green hue shone from the tiles, lighting up the runes and symbols Gabe had drawn earlier. He sat smack-dab in the middle of his artwork, floating above the ground by a hand's-breadth. His eyes closed, his coat of fur billowing around him, while his countless necklaces hovered and floated around his face like little snakes.

We scrambled past the kitchen counter and halted at the top step, leading down into the lowered living room.

The half-Demon opened his eyes and mouth, both shining in the same eerie green his drawing did. A deep and rasping growl sounded through the room. It was so deep that I only heard the words hidden in it after a few heartbeats.

Gabe chanted in that rattling growl while bobbing up and down softly. Next, he began to turn horizontally in midair. Slow at first, then speeding up. Soon, he was naught but a blurry figure, his features swimming in and out of focus. All while the tone and depth of the chant got louder.

We jumped back when a loud crack reverberated through the room and the tiles Gabe had drawn on seemed to crack along the painted lines. Even more green light broke from the cracks, until it grew to a blinding intensity.

What felt like heated wind and a strange pressure hit us and we were nearly blown back. Fane grabbed my and Cam's hands and we stood together, trembling under the onslaught of magic before us.

For a second, a thought raced through my head. *When would Dax have done something like this without us noticing?* Then I remembered a day last week, when he had asked to go play in the desert with Kasha. He had begged incessantly until Cam had loaded both of them in the pickup and driven so far into no man's land that she was sure no one could see them. According to her, they had frolicked through the dunes and vanished for an hour while she read the new book Fane had gotten her.

Clever boy. I glared at the ceiling where I felt Kasha. And she had watched over him. I felt betrayed in a way that she had not alerted me, but Kasha and Dax had a strong bond. Seemed like it was strong enough for her to keep his secrets.

The howling wind and rattling, growling chant got stronger and the whole room shone, making it impossible to see Gabe, or even look in his direction.

It seemed to have reached its peak as a crescendo of light, noise, and pressure rolled over us, bringing us to our knees. Then, it was gone.

I blinked at the very normal looking living room. All it missed was the furniture. The tiles – which I had thought destroyed – sat neatly and as unmarred as they had been before.

Gabriel stood and dusted off his leopard-cape carefully. He huffed out a breath and turned toward us.

"Holy shit," Cam uttered and I was very much on board with that curse. Gabriel looked different. His ageless face, formerly a deep brown, was now black as pitch. His eyes as green as the magic he had used, burning in his skull like little lanterns. He had two circular scars on his temples, right at his hair line. They looked like burns and I surmised they had to have been his horns. Someone had burned his horns down, stopping them from growing. It had to have been done when he was young, or it wouldn't have worked.

He held up a palm and twisted it in front of his face. His other hand flew to his necklaces and fingered one that had gone black as soot. Gabriel pulled it off and regarded it with a mix of anger and horror. Then he glanced at us, shame plain on his face.

Chapter Twenty
Fane

The Surface,

a coastal Namibian city

He was a beauty. When I saw his true form, I couldn't help gawking. 'Holy shit,' was exactly right. Not that he had been unattractive before, unsettling, but still kinda hot, but now… I was a sucker for glowing eyes and from the look of Cam's awestruck stare, we had that in common.

"Ijo… uhm… So, this is me," Gabriel stuttered. "I know it's a bit much. I–"

"Wow. I mean, wow!" I clapped my hands together once. "You've been holding out on us, handsome." I winked and pranced down the steps, having registered his shock and shame when he'd noticed. Without missing a beat, I placed a hand on his shoulder, to show him I didn't care about his changed appearance. He shrank back a little, almost ducking when I reached out and my suspicion was cemented. Gabriel had been taught to hide and hate his true appearance. Probably by a caretaker or parent, possibly the same cunt who had burned down his horns.

"Did it work?" Cam asked, also coming closer.

Gabe's eyes darted from me to her, to Mihr and back to Cam. "Y-you don't mind my appearance?"

My friend frowned. "Why? What's wrong with it?"

The half-Demon worried his lower lip. "It is appalling."

Cam waved him off. "My best friend is red, and has a penchant to catch fire, burning off her clothes. You? You look amazing. Even hotter than before."

Before Gabe had time to digest her comment, Mihr stomped our way. "She asked if it worked. Did it?"

"I-I think so," Gabe said. He jogged to where he had placed the grimoire on the dining table and opened it. With an excited mien, he rustled through the pages. "Ijo. Oh, yes, I see. This is… it is all clearing up." The half-Demon's hands tightened on the book and he brought it closer to his face, nearly hitting the pages with his nose.

"H-he did what? Why? I don't understand…"

"What is it?" Cam asked, fear vibrating in her voice.

Gabriel let the tome sink and looked up when cam stood right before him. "Your boy… he… He tried to close the portals of both Heaven and Hell."

"What?" thundered Mihr. "How did he… What?!"

Even I was at a loss for words. Why would Dax… then it hit me. Of course! "He tried to protect us!" I said. "He wanted us to be safe. He knew our kinds would never stop hunting us, or influence Human souls. Closing our realms from one another would stop the war, at least the part fought on Earth. Hell and Heaven would have to find a way to enter each other's realms without crossing through ours. This one would be closed. Dax, you genius."

A strangled sound came from Mihr. "I don't know about genius… He is currently lying upstairs with his soul in Hell, so obviously something went wrong."

Gabriel snorted. "You can say that again. He did the very same he did on the knowledge spell. He wrote his own. This time, in the old language." He tipped a finger to one of the pages. "This isn't demonic as I first thought." His face lit up with a radiant smile. "This is the original dialect, the one spoken in Heaven, before Lucifer fell. Before Earth existed."

"Uhm… I don't want to sound like an idiot," I said. "But if this is a heavenly language, then why is the spell demonic and why is Dax's soul currently being kidnapped, or held, or… whatevered by Lilithium?"

"Because even while understanding the language and inventing his spell, Dax is still Human. He isn't made for this type of magic. Oh, and according to this passage here…" Gabe squinted at the writing. "The part that opens Heaven up to Earth is demonic, just as the part that opens Hell is divine."

"That is – interesting news, but what does that have to do with anything?" Mihr asked.

"No idea," Gabe said and frowned. "I do know it is important though."

"Aren't you supposed to know things now?" Cam asked.

"I do. Which is how I know it's important, but I'm not a bleddy clairvoyant all of a sudden."

"None of this really matters," I interrupted the two, who by now glared at each other. "Is there a way to find Dax's soul in Hell or not? Also, do you know how to open the portals now?"

Gabriel pointed at me. "Can be worked on and yes, I have a plan. Your idea before was good, but I didn't know how it would work. Your necklace… if I add part of the Lilithium to it, it should be able to pierce the veil to Hell and make the boy visible to me if I change the spell to sense him. And we get into Hell through the fairy circles. Simple."

"I don't think putting Lilithium anywhere near Dax is a good idea. And simple? I have felt the circles and know of no way to open them," I said.

"The Lilithium is connected the boy already, using one of your necklaces on him will show me the way more clearly, as his body still has that small tether to his soul. And opening a portal is much simpler than I thought." He grinned like a schoolboy. "All we need is for one of them to open, then I can keep it that way for as long as is needed."

"I can probably make them open – one, provided they're still searching for me," I said. "But then what? We fight the Demons coming to get me?"

"No, we hide and let others fight them," Mihr said.

****

The preparations turned out not to take long at all. I made a sword for Mihr, this time fusing just a few grains of heavenly sand to the metal and stripping it completely of the Lilithium. Though I loathed to part with even a few grains of my new acquisition, it made all the difference. I knew from the moment I heard the finished weapon sing in my fingers, that it was exceptional and would fit Mihr like nothing else. And because of the sand aiding me, the whole deal took me a fraction of the usual time.

"Does it have commands?" Mihr asked, weighing it with a satisfied expression.

"The ones your former blade had. Arken, to burn through metal and bone, Seyrich, to harden for a powerful strike, and Fang, to light up with Hellfire. But that only works when you are riding Kasha."

Mihr's brows nearly popped off his face the way they shot up. "Hellfire? That is new."

"Nope. Your former one had it too, but we never came around to me explaining the commands."

Arken, Seyrich, Fang..." Mihr mumbled softly. "Hellfire will come in handy in regards to the plan."

I felt weird, sitting on the floor of Dax's room, watching my Angel handle a blade made of Lev's sword. But before I was able to define what I felt, my attention shifted to Gabriel, who had charmed Mihr's necklace, using straps of leather to attach the Lilithium. It looked wrong, and it felt wrong. The creeping nausea it inspired was vile and I forced myself to be still while the half-Demon placed the necklace around Dax's neck.

Kasha growled softly while Gabe did it and he nervously glanced at her every two seconds or so. Cam stood at their side and stroked Kasha to calm her, she herself didn't look it, though.

"I'm still not cool with Dax wearing that thing," I voiced.

"It will not harm him," Gabe said. "It doesn't want to hurt this body. Look."

I clambered to my feet and sped to the bed. The Lilithium smoothed over Dax's scrawny and waxen chest, as if it were languidly caressing his skin. Flat and net-like, it soon covered his whole chest.

"What is it doing?" I asked.

"Protecting him," the magic man said. He pointed his finger at Dax's chest and tried touching him. The net-like swath of Lilitium lashed at his fingers lightning-quick and he pulled back.

"Hmmpf. I'm still not convinced."

Cam stroked her son's hair. "I'll stay with him and keep watch. If the stuff does anything to him, I'll rip the necklace off."

I instantly felt better, not just because I knew she'd do what she said, but because my friend had decided to stay here.

"Are you sure?" Mihr asked.

"I am. Whatever use would I be in Hell? It would scare the ever-loving shit out of me and I can't fight like you," she looked at Mihr, "or have powers like you," her eyes wandered to me. "I belong by his side, to call him back if he gets lost. You just… You find him, okay? Find him and free him."

"I promise," I said. "Whatever it takes, he will be free."

We went over the plan once more, before readying for departure. It felt like my bones buzzed with fear, excitement, and determination. The plan Mihr and I had come up with was bold, bordering on unhinged, but – if timed right – I was sure it would work. Saints on stakes, Hell and Heaven were in for a surprise.

****

"Now I know why you got to Cam and Dax so fast," I slurred, trying to find my footing. Not unlike Dax's portal from America to Germany and then to here, Gabriel was able to open what he called a 'rip in space,' through which we tumbled. From the coast, right back to the desolate waste of the western Damaraland.

It was early morning and I basked in the feel of the sheer vastness around and beneath me, while trying to get my stomach in order. I liked none of the portal, rip, beaming shit.

Mihr looked a bit pale and he bent over, his hands on his knees, gasping for air. Mildly smiling at the both of us, Gabriel walked from the tear like he did this kind of thing daily. Heck, I had no idea, it could be that he did.

To hide my discomfort and to ground myself, I crouched and stuck both hands into the sand. It felt elating being this connected to my surrounding. A small part of me tried to feel for my whips, but came up empty.

Behind us, Kasha snorted and sneezed, then threw herself down and rolled herself on the ground. Dust billowed around her and hit us when she sprang back to her feet, shook out her fur and flapped her wings.

"Ugh. Stop that, you overgrown weirdo," I snapped, biting on grains of sand.

"Hey, we all deal with this traveling part differently," Mihr said. "Don't listen to the mean, red woman, darling," he cooed at his Hellcat.

Shaking her mane, Kasha traipsed over to him and nearly knocked him from his shoes, the way she smashed her head to his chest.

I would have laughed at the sound Mihr made as a result, but I was too busy keeping the omelet from earlier down.

"You guys done?" Gabe asked. He picked at his leopard-cape and started walking.

I reached out a hand for my Angel and he took it. Together, Mihr, Kasha, and I followed the half-Demon through this spectacular place.

It didn't take long to reach the circles, and just like before, I felt the malice under my feet. And again, it made my skin crawl.

"This is where we leave you," Mihr said.

Gabriel pulled a band of leather from one of his pouches and laced it around Mihr's right wrist. "Remember, one tug means you are in place, then we begin. Once we feel them coming, you'll feel this." The magic man twisted a similar band on his wrist and I watched as Mihr's tightened visibly.

"We will hide in my cave," Gabe continued. "Once you get back, just fly straight into that boulder," he pointed at the one camouflaging the tunnel leading to his cave. "We go together from there."

My insides roiled with nervousness. I did not want him to go.

"Right," my Angel said. He grabbed hold of me and I clawed him to me as if I were drowning. Palming his magnificent face with both hands, I kissed him over and over again. Feeling a desperation I had not known before. If anything happened to him… I would simply cease to exist.

He returned my kiss with equal force, his strong arms squeezing me tight, nearly crushing me. I loved the feel of him so firmly pressed to me, and never wanted to be parted from him again, but we had to. Too soon, he disentangled himself from me.

"I love you, Nancy" I said, pulling him in for a last kiss. His lips on mine were fire and heat, paired with anxiety.

"I know you do," he teased. "I love you. Keep your head down until I get back, okay?"

Kasha pranced on the spot and I snatched her horns to pull her face to me. I kissed her between her beautiful, red eyes. "You take care of him, ya hear? Give those feathered fiends a taste of Hell."

She grunted and licked across my entire face, then pressed her purring face to mine. I rubbed her wet kiss off on her fur and stepped back.

With one elegant jump, Mihr was astride his beast and while my heart spasmed painfully, they shot into the sky and were soon out of sight.

"Time to go to work, magic man," I said, my voice a little thin. "We have lives to destroy, and one to save."

He chuckled as we headed for his cave. "No matter how this ends, Fane, I am glad you came looking for me."

"Likewise, my good sir, likewise."

Chapter Twenty-One
Mihr

The Surface,

in the air above Southern Angola

The plan was reckless. Of course it was, Fane had thought up half of it. She had not liked the part of me and Kasha flying up to the Heavens, however. I was not happy to have left her behind. And with her drumming up those out for her blood. But here we were.

A swath of vertical white became visible in the distance. The entrance to Heaven. I kept my distance and twisted the leather band on my wrist. Then I held my breath.

Kasha, feeling my inner turmoil, mewled and nearly rolled in mid-air to look at me. I leaned forward so I practically lay on my belly and hugged her around the neck. "All is good, my beauty. Now we wait for Fane to do her thing." It couldn't have taken more than a few minutes, but it felt like hours had passed without something happening. I repeatedly grabbed hold of my sword grip, while keeping an eye on the wristband, afraid I'd miss the signal. I was so nervous, that when the signal came, I nearly jumped out of my skin, and my wings snapped from my back and opened.

Kasha tread air and floundered to keep us upright. A disgruntled growl vibrated from her enormous chest.

"Sorry, love, won't happen again." I patted her between the horns, then unsheathed my blade. "It's showtime. Fang," I barked and nearly dropped my sword, when indeed, it lit up with singeing Hellfire. Huffing out a breath, I twisted it, then bent lower on my Hellcat. "Let's give them something to look at."

Kasha shot forward, directly at the tear in the sky and when we got closer, I made out four shapes, hovering around the swath of vertical cloud. Sentinels.

My Hellcat roared, galloping through the air like the Hellspawn she was. The shapes stilled and became more visible with each of Kasha's wingbeats.

One of them vanished momentarily in the cloud, no doubt calling for backup. Just as I wanted.

We sped closer and I brandished my burning sword, mixing a war cry with Kasha's roar.

The remaining three Angels unsheathed their swords and barreled toward us. When we nearly reached them, I cried out 'roll' and my beast flipped over in a somersault, catapulting me from her back and straight at my kind. The sword flickered out, but clashed with and severed the one a she-Angel aimed at me. She gasped and stared at her hilt when Kasha slammed into her, rolling through the air in a tumble of screaming feathers and fur.

I opened my wings and spiraled around another Angel, and with two swipes, he was incapacitated and fell down.

As my sword zinged against the metal of the last Angel, something moved in the cloud beyond. I grinned when I beheld them coming. Shamal, and his consorts. A whole damned battalion. If I was not mistaken, they were the ones he and Michael had stolen and trained. For a second, I felt bad, they had not wished for this, but I knew one thing, these Angels would chase after me, into Hell itself if need be.

I decapitated my last opponent, whistled for Kasha, who threw away what was left of her prey like a ragdoll, her muzzle and claws golden with blood, and we both dove down.

Screaming and roaring, the battalion of Angels followed.

****

Fane

The Surface, Gabe's cave

"The plan is solid," Gabriel said.

"Huh?" I sat on the floor of his cave, cross-legged, digging my feet deep into the fine sand, while staring into the next cave-wall and nibbling on the nail of my index finger.

The magic man dropped down on one of the small boulders that were the perfect height to double as seats. "He will be okay," he added when I looked at him without truly seeing.

"Yeah... I know. I'm just..." I sucked in a lungful of air, trying to dim the rampaging fear galloping through me like a bunch of Helhests. "We have no idea who or what I'll be calling from Hell. It does kind of unnerve me, you know? And regarding Mihr, I don't worry, I know he'll be fine. He can look after himself. I just don't like him flying up to that place. What if they catch him? What if he and Kasha aren't fast enough?"

"So, you do worry for your Angel?" A small smile played around the corners of Gabe's lips.

I pulled the finger from my face. "Of course I worry, who said I didn't?"

The half-Demon chuckled, his glowing green eyes blinking through the semi-darkness. "You, Fane."

"Oh," I said, grinning at Gabe sheepishly. "Seems I did. I don't want to worry, maybe that is why."

"You care deeply for him, so it makes sense. But are you certain you can live with an Angel? They are so very different."

I raised a brow at him. "You are a halfling, and you are asking this question?"

"True. It is why I ask. My father was a simple man, who succumbed to a Succubus. She had been summoned by a magic user in my father's village. Back then magic was a big part of my people and summonings happened more often than they do now.

"I think my mother should have killed him – not to mention me, but she left him alive and placed me in front of my father's home one night. He tried raising me. But he hated every moment of it. It got especially bad when he joined the church and found God. His hate grew proportional to my suffering." Absentmindedly his palm slid to his temples and over the scars where his horns should have been. Then he dropped his hand and glanced at me. "Our kinds don't mix well. There is too much hate, too much prejudice. You must know it can't work."

"I understand what you are saying, and yeah, Mihr can be a judgmental sack of idiocy, but we sorted it out. And besides, if we both don't care, who else is there whose opinion I need to worry about?"

"You are blasphemers, in the eyes of both your worlds. You will be forever hunted for choosing to be together."

I snorted. "We will, but not only because of that. I stole Lu's newest toy from Hell and escaped, Mihr killed an Archangel. I think those facts trump our little romance, don't you?"

"That might be. It's just... unusual for your kinds to get along and even..."

"Love each other? No, it is not. We are just people, Gabe. I don't love Mihr despite or because he is and Angel. I love him because he is a good man, and he has my back, no matter what. I know of no Demon who I would trust as much."

Gabriel opened his mouth to say something, when he dropped his head and lifted his arm. The leather band on it twitched visibly. "It is time," he said.

I cracked my knuckles and stood, sand raining down my shorts and legs. "Good." With my innards trembling, but my mind set, I walked to the wall closest to the fairy circles outside.

Placing both palms to the rock, I felt it warm to my touch. "Ready, Gabe?" I asked.

"Ready."

"Here goes." I formed fists, drew them back and rammed them into the stone, right behind the crumbling slate lay the vein of ore I had singled out upon entering the cave. I stuck my fingers into it, melting it as they sank deeper. Once I had made a hole big enough for Kasha, I pulled my hands free and held a palm under my pendant. The heavenly sand dropped into my fingers and happily buzzed. Clapping my hands together, I thought of gloves. *Presto!* The sand covered both my hands in a thin veil, fused to my skin like gloves. As I flexed and clenched my hands, the sand stayed glued to me. With a smirk, I rammed my closed fists into the ore-vein.

Power exploded from me and the sand and, with an ear-splintering boom, the tunnel opened before us. "Not bad," I said, not feeling the slightest bit exhausted. I walked into the tunnel and to the very edge of where my power had opened it to slam my fists into the ore and stone once more. It was like having a wrecking ball for hands, the stone and ore parted beneath my power almost willingly. Amazing. As I dug further – happy as a mole shoveling its way into a cavity filled with worms – stone, dust and crumbs of earth flew around me. Deeper and deeper I went, until I felt the malice radiating from the circles. It went deep. Round cylinders of nothingness, reaching into the unknown depths. It went so far that I couldn't feel where, or even if, they ended.

I still pushed on further, making as much noise as possible. If any Ember was looking for me, they had to be seriously useless if they didn't pick up on this.

When I was only a hands-breath away from one of the tunnels, I stopped. Reaching out, I placed my palm on the wall, shivering when I felt nothing. It was akin to standing on a cliff, knowing the drop was deadly. Only that I had no idea if there was a drop, or if it ended.

A little winded, I scraped the floor with my naked feet. There. Something shifted under me.

My hands pinched and tickled and I looked at the gloves of heavenly sand. The thousand tiny mouths rejoiced, and a feeling of... kinship vibrated in my hands. That couldn't be. But it was. Something heavy and very much alive raced up the cylinders of nothingness. Many somethings.

"They are coming, Gabe," I yelled back through the tunnel. I pressed my entire body to the wall, feeling. "Living sand. No, Something else..." I screwed my eyes shut to blend out everything else. Breathing, feeling, listening to my element. This time, the cylinder right at my fingertips sent up something. When it passed me, energy zapped through me, a reservoir of untamed, wild, chaotic, power. A tempest of life, ever changing shape, but I could feel it. I knew it. Like I knew any kind of stone. It was a lump of heavenly ore, zinging past me and opening the way to Hell.

Too stunned to do anything, I felt the sand on my hands pass through the remaining piece of wall and embed themselves into the ore. I was sure I could hear them rejoice with a 'whee' when they were carried up and away.

There was no time for me to wrap my head around what had just happened, or what my discovery meant, as the part of the floor where I stood dropped out from under my ass. I landed in a hole, up to my chest, resulting in an undignified 'umpf' leaving my lips. The granite around me drew tighter, encasing me. I knew right away that this was the work of another Ember and got ready to fight.

"Fane!" Gabriel called.

He stumbled along the tunnel, heading for me.

"No, get back, Gabe," I hollered, but he didn't stop. My eyes trained on him, I didn't notice the hole opening over my head. Someone dropped down and vile darkness clamped around my neck. I gagged and felt the heaviness of the Lilithium collar drop onto my shoulders. My power was cut from me and the granite smashed against my body, nearly squashing me.

Gabriel stared in shock and the figure who had dropped from the fucking ceiling, threw a fistful of slate at him. I screamed when the stone cut into the magic man, making his very dark-red blood flow.

****

Mihr

Side by side, Kasha and I were fast, both of us racing across the sky at mind-boggling speeds. I still had the feeling that the Angels steadily gained on us. It unnerved me only slightly, as my initial worry had been for us to pace ourselves as not to lose them.

The ground flew past us way below and yet, I was anxious it wasn't quick enough. What if the Demons found Fane and Gabriel before I arrived? What if something went wrong and I just unloaded a whole battalion of pissed-off Angels on our little group.

Kasha – seemingly sensing my worries – mewled once, then pawed the air playfully. It brought a smile to my face despite everything. In the rising sun, she looked magnificent, her black fur shining and her twisting horns glinting like polished stone. I felt our connection thrum deep within me, like a wire leading to my center, and I couldn't believe there had been a time when I had thought of her as a liability. Or even as dreaded Hellspawn. She was my beast, my warrior, and I loved her with all my heart.

In that exact moment she let her tongue loll out, so it flapped in the wind, making her look slightly stupid. I laughed, then dove down, recognizing the mountain formation beneath us.

A tug went through the band on my wrist, then another, and another. My pulse quickened and dread slid into my throat. What was that? Had something gone wrong?

I beat my wings once, then smoothed them to my body, shooting toward the ground like a bullet. Kasha mimicked me, and together we plummeted.

Soon, I saw it. Shapes, like ants protecting their hill, swarmed the ground. My breath short, I cursed heartily when I saw that they were hundreds. How?

Black holes covered the sand like Swiss cheese, and still Demons clambered from them, adding to their numbers by the second.

"Lord have mercy on us all," I whispered, still barreling straight for them.

From behind I heard shrieks and roars, alerting the Demons below to our arrival. "Those damn idiots," I grumbled. "So much for the element of surprise."

The Demons who were able to fly shot from the ground and came at us, then a horn sounded from way above, one of my kind's. It signaled acute danger and called for the designated ones to get backup.

For a small moment, I felt drawn back to the times of great battles, when our own numbers had still been enough and both born Angels and born Demons had fought on desolate places around this realm. The feeling was the same, and with a bit of imagination, I could tell myself I was amongst my allies, attacking the Hellspawn army before us. Things had been so simple back then. Black and white. Good and evil. Now… I had no idea who was good and who bad, if such a thing even existed. But when Kasha let out a roar that thundered across the land, I knew that it didn't matter to me anymore. I needed no side, I had found my purpose. Something I had done on my own. I had people in my life I loved, who cared for me the way I cared for them. And somewhere down there was the Demon I loved. If I had to go through the entire army facing me to reach her, I would.

An Ifrit flew up to meet me, leaving a trail of smoke in his wake. I didn't open my wings, but only rolled to the side and aimed my sword. Cleaving the Demon in two, from top to bottom took little to no effort, but in a split second, I was up against the next.

Kasha and I weaved through the oncoming masses, dealing damage as we went. Black acidic blood soon burned on my skin, but I hardly felt it. All that mattered was to get to Fane.

Soon, the first Angels clashed with the Demons in mid-air. The noise was deafening, a mix of metallic clangs, screams, roars, and snapping wings. I knew it intimately.

The good thing was, that for both parties, I was nothing more than another opponent now, not someone to be followed. And I used that fact to swerve right, heading in the direction of the hill underneath which Fane and Gabriel should be waiting. Bit by bit, we traversed from the middle of the Demon onslaught to the outer side. Still coming up against foes left and right, but in the whole commotion, some Angels mistook me for an ally and many a Demon did the same mistake when it came to Kasha. It was an advantage I hadn't thought about before.

The tricky part would be to – one, get to the ground alive, and two, get into the cave unseen. Because no matter how many foes we faced and defeated, the earth beneath was filled with Hellspawn waiting for us.

I hacked at a Gargoyle, using Arken to burn through his stony skin. He petrified the moment I severed his head from his torso and fell to the ground as solid marble. Around me, a whole gaggle of them popped up, surrounding me and moving in. I beat my wings and let my blade sing, while Kasha nabbed one of the Demons from behind, her huge maw closing over an entire head.

She shook the marble-turned fiend, then let him crash into one of his brethren. In a miraculous coincidence, the stony wing of the dead Demon hit the one snarling at me right in the temple and I could watch him lose consciousness. Both Gargoyles dropped out of sight, leaving only three to face us.

We made quick work of two and then flanked the last one, who managed to ram his spear into my lower belly, slicing me open like a thanksgiving turkey. Kasha snarled and positively ripped him to stony shreds after that. Once done, she hovered under me and I gladly sank onto her back, holding a palm to my bleeding wound. I solidly pushed the worry about it being a wound inflicted by a Gargoyle to the back of my mind. There was no time to concern myself with what it meant.

I looked around, seeing that apparently, we had drifted off even further during that last fight and at the moment, no one was coming for us. This was our chance!

With a nudge to our connection, I told Kasha in which direction to go and she did so without hesitation.

We dropped lower, and right when we were about to reach the ground, Kasha opened her wings and raced through the air, only a few feet over the sand. Lucky for us, the battalion of Angels met the Demons who couldn't fly, so we slipped off undetected.

"That one," I said to my beast and pointed past her face, at the boulder Gabe had shown me.

My Hellcat dove into the rock with the trust of a child, knowing it would be caught by its father. It felt like entering a curtain of water, then it was gone. Darkness greeted us on the other side of the mirage and it took me a few seconds to adjust from the sunlight outside.

Kasha's paws met the sand, but she carried on along the tunnel in a bounding gallop, that nearly threw me off her back.

Soon, the tunnel opened into a large cave, Gabe's home. It was empty.

Kasha stopped short and audibly sniffed the air. I slid off her back, still holding my wound, the stinging pain, radiating from it forgotten as I searched the cave. "Fane? Gabriel? Where are you guys?"

We were supposed to sneak out from here through a Fane-made tunnel, leading to one of the portals. I stumbled along the entire cave, from wall to wall, searching for a hole, a crack, something. The dread from before clogged up my chest and while my heart hammered like a drum, I couldn't get enough air into my lungs.

A small mewl from Kasha had me speeding to her side. She tapped what looked like a roundish boulder, but her paw went straight through it. Right in front of it, black blood soaked the earth. I stuck my head inside and saw a figure lying in a tunnel. Quickly, I grabbed hold and pulled. A groaning Gabriel came into view, his torso littered with cuts.

"What happened, Gabe? Where is Fane?" I asked, panic puncturing me.

"In Hell. She…"

"So, this is where you snuck off to," an icy voice said behind me.

I spun round, coming to face Shamal and four other Angels. Kasha crouched low at my side, her rumbling growl echoing off the walls, nearly making the cave shake.

"Oh my, you found a pet," Shamal said, glaring at my Hellcat. "I think I will mount this one. Humans have that strange practice and lately, I have taken a shine to it."

"You have taken a shine to many things lately," I said. "None of them good."

My eyes darted across the Angels facing me, and I knew there was little to no chance of us winning. No matter how exceptional Kasha was, I wouldn't sentence her to death because of my wound.

"Go," I told her. "Take Gabe and go. Find Fane."

My beast tilted her head and snarled. I nudged the connection to her. She growled. I nudged once more and she hissed, but with a yowl, she turned from me and walked toward the boulder.

I heard a body being dragged through soft sand behind me and unsheathed my sword. I would give her and the magic man as much time as I could.

Chapter Twenty-Two
Fane

Hell, the first ring

This sucks donkey balls, I thought as I was led through the alleys of the mansions I knew, right on the edge of the Waste. None of the Demons around me were people I recognized and they'd had the audacity to gag me and place a sack over my head, so I couldn't see. Not that it mattered, I felt the different stone types with my naked feet and knew exactly where I was. Even with my power sapped, I knew the makeup of the ground I was walking on and where what type of stone was. And it wasn't like I was going to scream and alert everyone to my presence.

Come to think of it, my kidnappers tread softly and we stopped often. This looked like a secret mission. I wondered who was at the head of this little operation. Too elegant for Ragon, and he would have wanted to do it himself. But who else – despite Lucifer Himself – would have an interest in me? Maeve? No, this was not my former roommate's style.

My gut twisted and clenched as we snuck on to Satan knew where while above, Gabe was wounded and Mihr and Kasha headed for a very much Faneless cave. The Lilitium around my neck made my rate of discomfort shoot through the non-existent roof of this shithole. Which meant I was irritable as fuck, worried and pissed off, not to mention nauseated. How was I supposed to free Dax while collared, gagged, and kidnapped? "Fuff yew, hitfaffes," I grumbled through my gag.

This resulted in a "shhh" and a slap to the back of my head. *Pissants.*

Then my feet hit black marble. It was the type of stone my former Maester, Rhys, had loved using. He had been my owner before Lev and Ragon. An Incubus I had served for over a decade. For a few moments, my memories were drawn to that time in my life. It seemed like eons ago that I had shaped statues of Rhys, then got the news that he would sell me to pay for a feast that would secure him domain over the third ring. Lev had bought me at that feast.

This floor… it felt very similar to the one I had shaped for Rhys back in the day, but I shook the notion off. What would he be doing in the first ring? And why would he have me napped and brought to him?

The sound of hinges holding a large metal door squeaked, giving me hives. Someone needed to adjust that. I was prodded to move on and stumbled up a few steps and through the noisy door. Looking at my feet, I saw the Demons around me, mirrored in the spotlessly polished marble. Candles cast a dim light around us and every few feet we passed the iron stands of those candle holders.

The trip inside the mansion didn't take long and eventually, I was manhandled into a chair, my hands fastened to the armrests by iron bands to keep me in place. The musty bag was lifted from my head and I came to face my head napper.

He stood, a wide grin on his pretty face, wearing only very short shorts and an outrageous pair of flaming-red heels. His light-gray skin – as always – set off his emerald eyes perfectly.

"Fane, darling, how I missed you," my former Maester cried. He waved a hand and the gag was taken from me.

"Rhys," I rasped. "What the Hell?" I pulled at the bands on my wrists, who were tightly infused into the stone I was sitting on. "Why am I here? And why are you here? What is going on?"

It could have been worse. I guessed. My former Maester had always been fair, if a bit over the top. He liked shiny new things and I had been able to make him countless of those. He had valued me highly, but I was a bit unnerved by the collar and bands.

"My dearest, I have saved you, of course." Rhys flopped down on the broad armrest of my chair, his butt squishing my left arm. He reached out and clasped my chin with a palm, twisting my face left and right to scrutinize me. "Ragon, Maeve, Jinx, even Sathanas is out for your blood. When you made a ruckus upstairs, a whole army went to capture you."

"An army?"

"Yes, my sweet. Why, when Satan himself decrees someone found, they will be." His smiled and winked. "You have been quite naughty, darling. What were you thinking? Springing an Angel from the Deep and fleeing good old home?" He clicked his tongue and rolled his eyes. "It was a scan-dal." He drew out the last word as if he was tasting it.

I managed a small shrug. "Dunno, I didn't feel like being raped by Ragon nightly, so when I saw an out, I went for it."

Rhys threw his head back and laughed, his pearly-white fangs glinting in the candlelight. "Sweetheart, you crack me up. Always the prude. You never wanted to be in my harem either, remember?"

"Well, I wouldn't call not wanting being raped prudish, but okay. And you never minded not having me be one of your lovers. Thanks for that, by the way."

Rhys stroked his thumb over my cheek, then drew me even closer. "I don't like taking what isn't offered. Never have." He kissed me on the forehead and let my chin go.

"So will you tell me why you 'saved' me?" I made air quotes with my fingers.

"I am appalled, Fane. I did save you. Why? Because we share a bout of fun and memorable history together." He beamed at me and I felt his strew – the powers of seduction Incubi could conjure at will – slip over me. I shook my head to free myself of its grasp.

"Then why am I collared, not to mention bound?"

"Tsk, tsk, so you wouldn't hurt your saviors." He waved his hand around, indicating at a pair of Demons who stepped forth. They looked identical, safe for the fact that one was a woman and one a man. Both had red skin and a subtle glow to their veins.

"These are my new Embers. Twins!" Rhys gushed, jumping from my armrest and prancing around his Embers. "Aren't they gorgeous? I wager they are even better than you, love."

I tilted my head. "Cute. But no one is better than me. Take off this collar and I'll prove it."

Rhys almost howled in delight. "Didn't I tell you she was a riot? Wasn't I right?"

The twins bowed their heads once, no decipherable expression on their faces. "Yes, Maester."

Rhys calmed down and sighed. "Brilliant, but boring. Oh, Fane, I missed our banter. The only thing I ever get out of these two is – Yes, Maester, no Maester… Ugh. No sense of humor. None."

"That might be because they are your slaves, Rhys," I said.

"Never stopped you, Fane."

I slumped in my chair. "Let's cut the crap. I know you. You are not sentimental, but you have a sense for business. Either someone is paying a hefty sum for me, or you want to be the one giving me to Satan, to rise in his graces. Which is it?"

"My sly Ember. Never could fool you, could I?" Rhys sauntered to my chair, swaying his hips in an almost hypnotic way. "I will not give you to Satan even though I was tempted at one point, but that would mean thwarting my initial plan. No, you, my dear have been bad for business. Not only does the Prince of Darkness now regulate the ones going to the Surface even more, he collars them so they can stay longer, and even kill people. Messy. No." He shook himself. "As a result the business I had on the Surface has suffered immensely." The Incubus raised both arms and twirled around. "The first ring? I ruled the third one, baby, before you and your Angel escaped. I was well on my way to the fourth, but you had to go ahead and kill my business partner."

I frowned. "I didn't kill anyone. What are you even talking about?"

Rhys grabbed hold of a chair, made of granite, and spun it around like it weighed nothing. He gracefully sat down and crossed his long, toned legs. "Do you know how Angels are made, Fane?"

I stared at him, a terrible notion taking hold of me.

"The souls of the worthy ascend and are asked how they want to continue. Paradise, or holy battle against our kind. As you can imagine, not many choose battle. But the feathered fiends need new meat for the grinder, or we'll simply overrun them one day." The Incubus placed an elbow on the top leg and leaned his chin on his fist. "Now, this war has gone on long enough and I made a proposition to an Angel I knew. Did you know that some of the mighty Archangels have a dirty side? Yes." He nodded with a deviant smirk. "And they can fuck, but I don't need to tell you, do I?" My former Maester winked at me. "I'm pretty sure free will and a hot Angel will only allow for so much time to pass before the boning starts."

I squeezed down on my armrests, sure I would have ripped the chair to bits had I not been collared.

Rhys smiled when he saw my anger. "But I digress. You see, the souls travel through the portals closest to where they die, but if you open secret passages, no one will know some of them go astray." Rhys clapped his hands, beaming with excitement. "Genius, right? All I needed to do, was supply a few Angels with Lilithium and *bam!* they were able to steal souls."

"You... you helped Michael steal souls?" I gaped at him, the notion settling in my gut like a shard of ice.

"Yes. In return he would have invaded Hell when the time was right, slaughtered all the boring ones and Satan, and I would have ruled." He pouted. "Now my secret part-time lover is dead, Lucifer is more paranoid than ever, and my new business partner has no taste when it comes to sex. All. Because. Of. You. You, my dear, have gone and screwed shit up. Royally."

"Hey, I would have been all for you sitting on Lu's throne, seriously. But you can't force innocent souls to a battle they never wanted, that's wrong."

"It is what our kind has done for millennia."

"And it's wrong!"

Rhys chuckled. "Dearest Fane. You have gone soft. Don't tell me you care about those unfortunate people."

Did I? If I thought about it, they were like me. None of them ever had a choice to say no. They lived, fought, and served a war none of them understood or wanted. What did it matter that I didn't know them? They were me, only, they had no way out. "You fucking bet your sweet ass I care," I rumbled. "But I have better stuff to do than to sit here and listen to your delusions of grandeur. No one beats Lucifer. He will smack all your asses three ways till Sunday. And you will regret plotting against him. This is bound to fail, Rhys, you must see that. Even if not, why capture me? I can't help you."

"Au contraire, ma *chère*, you will help me a great deal."

"How? What do you want from me?" I yelled, pulling at my wrists.

My former Maester gave me a look I had never seen from him before. His face lost all charm and cheek, leaving behind a regal mask of indifference. His emerald eyes laced into mine, grabbing all of my attention. Maybe because I knew him only as playful and boisterous, but the sight chilled me to my core.

"You are here, because of this." He gestured to someone behind me and the Sprite who had once auctioned me off, flew past me, carrying a silver platter in his stubby, little arms. His back covered what was on it when he hovered over to Rhys and I couldn't see. He placed the platter in my former Maesters lap and then buzzed to hover by his side. I gasped when I saw my whips.

"You made these?" Rhys picked up one and let the slim metal glide through his slender fingers.

"Yes, what of it?"

He handed it to one of the Ember twins. "Break it," he ordered.

The woman took the whip into both hands and… nothing. Her face scrunched up, her hands and arms started to shake, her breathing came in bursts, but nothing happened. The whip stayed exactly the way it was.

"I don't… I don't get it. Wha–"

"My Embers tell me they sense a material inside your weapons, something holding them together they can't control." Rhys pointed the hilt of my second whip at me. "You can, though." He grinned and curled the whip back onto the tray.

The living sand. Other Embers couldn't use it?

"You see, Fane, the reason why no one has been able to defeat Lucifer is simple. He controls Lilithium. And, as you are currently experiencing, none of us can fight its power. Now for an experiment."

Rhys tugged the whip from the woman. "You can stop now, Agatha." She let go, visibly relieved. Then my former Maester threw the whip into my lap. The moment the metal made contact with my skin, I felt the joyous welcome of it. It recognized me instantly and snaked up my torso, bristling at the collar around my neck. With tiny pings, it lashed out against the Lilithium, then proceeded to tug at it. When nothing worked, it slid down to my left hand and sliced apart the iron band. Quickly, I grabbed the hilt, feeling better instantly. Collar or not, I understood my whip, and it me.

"Hm... Pity," Rhys said. "I thought it would maybe take care of the collar. Whelp, no matter, you being able to control this means you can control the material that opens the way to Earth. We'll need a big opening. Soon."

"The only thing I will open, is you," I snarled, snapping the whip. Rhys was way too far for me to hit him and he smirked indulgently. But when the tip flicked back, it severed my other bind. Rhys' smile fell from his face when I stood, took a step and flicked my wrist. The tip of my whip ensnared the weapon still lying on the tray, whisking it my way. I caught it with my free hand and my weapons coiled around me like snakes.

"Giving me one of these? Big mistake," I said, feeling my own lips spread with a grin.

"You wanna play, Fane-baby? Let's play." Rhys vaulted backwards over his chair. "Agatha, Aaron. Get her."

Chapter Twenty-Three
Kasha's Excursion

Hell, the Ascend

She was careful as she glided down, spiral by spiral, balancing the man on her back. His weight shifted from side to side, nearly making him fall off a few times. Her heart was heavy but her warrior had given her an order, even if it was stupid and meant leaving him behind. This one she had to keep safe, and she had to find *her*. The red one she loved.

Kasha sniffed the moist, hot and heavy air, searching for Fane's scent. She had been busy drifting up and down this huge tunnel, sniffing and looking. Around them, countless Demons either flew up, or used the stairs winding up the large circle around them. It was hard finding Fane's scent in all the odors floating around her. Something dropped onto them, rustling and soft. Kasha sneezed a couple of times as sand tickled her nose. She swiped a paw over her face and it came away with gray sand. The fine grains raced from her paw, up her front leg and settled around her shoulders, deeply into her fur. She swiped and snapped around a few times, but it was gone. A grumpy yowl boomed from her chest, testimony of her discomfort. She couldn't shake herself, or the man would fall off, so she gnashed her fangs and continued sniffing the air.

After minutes, a whiff from below carried up something. *There.* It was faint, but Kasha was fine with faint. She spread her wings and followed the trail.

On her back, the man grunted and hugged her with both arms, steadying himself. Finally, she could speed up a bit.

"What... where are we?" he slurred. "Ti !khutse!" he yelled, his hands digging into her fur.

Kasha growled, and he softened his grip.

"Askies, Kasha. I nearly lost my breakfast just now. Is this Hell? What am I doing here? With you?" he asked.

Since he was done sleeping and also done pinching her with his hands, she carried on her hunt and followed the scent further down.

"Wait. We are looking for the boy, right? You have to take me down, so I can cast my spell and read it." The man waved his hand in front of her face, then pointed down.

Kasha grunted. She had no time for whatever it was he wanted, she needed to find her friend. Ignoring his incessant chattering, she dogged Fane's scent of rock-dust and fire.

They dove lower, to where the stone turned to clouds, lightning, and thunder. Kasha sniffed hard, then dove inside.

"What are you…? No, no! Aikona! Stop, don't go in thereee…!" Gabriel's words got lost, ripped away by the wind and storm around them.

Memories from this place erupted within Kasha. Called forth by the electricity tensing up the air, the sound of thunder and lightning forking through the clouds. She had come this way before, with her warrior, and the one she searched now. She had been small and weak back then, fighting grimaces made of fire. Shaking her enormous head to clear those pictures, she let out a growl and shot straight ahead. The wind pounded against her body, trying to throw her off course, but she persisted and with the suddenness of a light switched on, they were through.

The storm parted and Kasha glided through the hot, moist air over the Lake of Despair. It smelled like rotten eggs and old socks. Kasha sneezed and bounded up and down to find her faint trail.

The man on her back made strange sounds as she looped and flitted around, his fingers digging into her mane from time to time. Eventually, he sank down against her neck, hugging her close, breathing hard.

A mewl escaped Kasha when she found that special scent of rock dust and fire, and she dashed on, determined to find her charge as soon as possible.

"Please, go down," the man slurred, patting her weakly.

But Kasha sped on, across the mountains and over the Waste they went, straight into the first ring. She hovered over large buildings, sniffing here, rounding one there. Fane's scent led her deeper into the thicket of mansions, until she repeatedly circled one specific house. It was huge and black – like many of the others – and the trail ended here.

Just as Kasha determined on how to get inside – front door or window – one side of the house exploded into dust and rubble. With a roar she charged for that part, knowing things often crumbled around her friend and she was surely at the center of it.

The domed ceiling cracked open like and egg and beneath a group of people fought Fane.

A maelstrom of crushed stone – heating up and reddening – separated the Ember from the rest. She slashed at oncoming people with two silver whips, slicing into muscle and flesh. Her feet were planted on a ledge, the maelstrom getting closer and closer. Kasha beheld two similarly red-skinned people, who had sunken to their knees side by side. Their feet and hands were buried in the stone-floor, their skin gleaming with veins of fire. The ground around their hands and feet glowed, reaching out and mixing with the glow of the twisting earth widening toward Fane.

"Fane!" the man from her back called. "Up here."

The Ember glanced up in surprise, then a grin split her face. She pointed at the two crouching people. "Get them, Kash!"

With a snarl, Kasha dove down, her right paw connected with a head, ripping the male from the stone and sending him flying. He hit the halfway intact wall behind him with an audible crunch, then sank down, not moving. The result was immediate. The maelstrom lost its momentum, backing away from Fane.

Kasha beat her wings to snatch up her friend, when pain laced through her right wing. She growled and twisted in mid-air, seeing a gray, winged man holding part of her wing and raising his sword to slice it off.

Kasha pulled the wing – and the man – closer, then snapped it open and down. His grinning face turned to surprise, then horror, as he was flung off and punched into the maelstrom.

He screamed and flapped his wings, but the moving ground twisted around him and pulled him under.

Kasha roared her victory, then glided over Fane, reaching out a paw. The Ember jumped, grabbing hold. Kasha looked down and cradled her friend to her chest.

"Satan's blue balls, am I glad to see you, Kash," she said, snuggling closer.

Kasha licked over her entire head once, happy to have found her charge.

"Pfft. Ugh! Stop, you giant slobbermouth," Fane squealed, then laughed. "Now quick, we need to make ourselves scarce." She indicated to fly in a certain direction and Kasha was all too happy to leave this place. Her wing hurt as she flew away, but there were Demons hot on her tail, so she raced ahead.

It was time to find her warrior.

Chapter Twenty-Four
Mihr

The Surface, Gabriel's cave

Wounds inflicted by Gargoyles had an unpleasant effect. They didn't hurt as much, but hardened the flesh in and outside of the wound, stiffening and slowing the recipient. In this case, me. The discomfort of hardening skin pulled at my abdomen, feeling like mud cracking underneath midday sun. Already, swinging my sword wasn't as smooth as I was used to.

Ignoring the feeling, I faced off Shamal and his stolen warriors.

"Get him," Shamal roared, his face pulled into a mask of hate.

The four Angels to his sides gripped their swords tighter and advanced as one. I knew I had to be fast to even make an impact, so I covered the distance to them, whispering "arken" as I went, feeling magical heat promptly radiating from my blade. Swift and precise, I attacked. As my sword sang through the weapon of a huge man, who blanched and stumbled back, staring at what was left of his sword, I pushed at the pity and guilt roiling through me.

These men and women hadn't chosen to fight, and they definitely hadn't chosen to die permanently.

The soft rustle of sand behind me had me twisting, blocking, and slicing through the blade of a she-Angel who had snuck up. She, too, was flabbergasted as the blade part of her weapon melted and fell off when meeting mine.

The other two faltered, glancing back at Shamal for guidance.

"You have a choice," I told them, masking my steadily creeping exhaustion as best I could. "You can stay and die, or you can run and live."

"Nobody is running!" Shamal ordered. "End this sorry excuse of a Fallen!"

When their faces hardened and the two I had disarmed pulled daggers from their side-holsters, I resigned to the sad fact that I would have to act. There was no time and the risk too big.

"So be it," I mumbled and swung my blade.

Two of them attacked together, trying to flank me, but with two strikes, both their swords were reduced to smoldering metal. Something sharp pierced the skin on my lower back, right above my kidneys. I spread my wings and knocked back the she-Angel who had – yet again – managed to sneak around me.

My wings hit her in the chest and she flew back, hitting the cave wall behind her with a dull thud. I yelled swinging my blade, beheading the oncoming Angel, not even watching as he sank into a heap and his daggers fell from his hands.

I grabbed the next Angel by the throat, ignoring his punches and kicks to my sternum, and slammed him – head-first – into one of the sitting-boulders. The crunch of bone and the warm spray of blood hitting my face didn't slow me. I let go of his lifeless body and turned, letting my sword cut through the air in an upward arc. It met clothes, skin, bone and feathers, slicing through it with no effort at all.

The Angel I had just parted from bottom to top, grabbed at the large wound on his chest, then looked at me with shock and horror, before his eyes dimmed and he practically crumbled into the sand.

Heaving and sweating, I faced Shamal, pulling the dagger of the she-Angel from my back. The sound was wet and squishy. I twirled the dagger in my fingers, hearing the she-Angel moan and shuffle where she had hit the wall.

"You shouldn't have brought them," I told Shamal, who blinked at the carnage. "And you should not have stolen their souls to fight a good-for-nothing war."

"Wh-what is he talking about?" the she-Angel mumbled as she pushed herself up, then she gasped as she saw her fallen comrades.

Shamal licked his lips, glanced at my sword and then at my face. "Nothing, Cynthia, he will say anything to save his own skin and confuse you."

I smiled, feeling the stunning sensation of the Gargoyle-wound spread further. "Save my skin? Who will kill me? She?" I pointed Cynthia's dagger at her. "You?" I switched to point at Shamal. "You let your pawns die – your stolen pawns – just cause you're afraid to face me yourself."

Shamal glared at me. "I am not afraid." He pulled his sword from his back and took a stance, his eyes flashing to black – the same color as his wings. "You killed Michael. Now you die."

I let out a shaky breath, my strength fizzling out of me by the second. With a flick of my wrist, I let the dagger fly at Shamal, who swatted it away with ease, but I had bounded across the distance between us and was up against him before he was fully ready to face me. My blade cut into his lower arm as he tried to ward me off, and the moment my weapon hit bone, it jarred through the blade, cracking, but not severing. I saw that my sword was back to normal, the spell seemingly fizzling out too.

Shamal pulled his arm back, a grin on his face. He twirled his blade in one hand and the started hacking at me. "Seems," *clang,* "your weapon," another swipe, "has lost its," metal slicing into my upper arm, "unholy magic."

He stepped up, bringing his hateful face close to mine. "Now it's only me and you."

Sweat and blood ran down my body, my muscles ached, my wounds burned, and the pure lethargy the Gargoyle-wound brought on hovered close to the surface of my mind. This needed to end, now.

Something crashed into Shamal, tackling him to the ground. Two bodies rolled across the cave-floor, making sand and dust fly everywhere.

Shamal growled and swiped his blade up, eliciting a gasp. He scrambled back leaving Cynthia crouching, her hand on her stomach. Golden blood seeped through her fingers.

"What on Earth were you thinking? Stupid bitch!" Shamal yelled and got up. He trudged toward her, bringing his sword up.

The she-Angel opened her mouth, golden blood welling from her lips. "He said you stole us. Why would he say that?"

Shamal's gaze turned murderous and he propelled himself forward with his wings.

I made a split-second decision and jumped between them. Sliding in front of Cynthia on my knees, I brought my blade up.

Shamal didn't miss a beat as he shot forward like a bullet, his sword aiming straight at me. When I adjusted my sword to the trajectory of Shamals swipe, the Gargoyle-wound sent a cramp through me and I curled in on myself, my blade hitting the sand next to me.

Shamal's foot sent it flying, just as his sword sank into the crook between my shoulder and neck. This was it. I lifted my head to see him bearing down, bringing his whole weight into the swing to cleave my head off my shoulders.

Time seemed to slow to a crawl. I felt the tug on my skin from the metal as if from far away. The sounds around me muted to a muffled mix of indistinguishable nonsense and I knew that no matter what I did, it would be too late. The time it took for me to blink was enough to send a thought through me. Gleaming. Whole. And hopeful. Wherever Fane was, I hoped Kasha had found her and I hoped they would be able to find Dax and bring him home. Together, they stood a chance. Maybe it was all they needed. I was flooded by my love for them all, happy to have made it this long. Long enough to know them.

My body was thrown to the side by a wave of pressure, my neck ripped free of Shamal's blade. I bounced across the floor and landed on my back, close to the magical boulder Gabe had conjured up. It happened so fast that I hadn't been able to retract my wings. I felt my right one breaking under my own weight, but the pain barely breached the surface of my consciousness.

Light exploded around us as rock, dust, and sand rained down. The ceiling of the cave opened, revealing a picture I hadn't seen in a long time. The sky was filled with wings. Demons and Angels fought and dashed around.

Hundreds, thousands. I hadn't witnessed these numbers fight in forever. A horn sounded, light and brassy. It was the horn of the Archangels. I saw Gabriel, Raphael, Uriel, and Jophiel hover above us, their three-paired wings whisking up sand around me.

No doubt it had been them who had parted the slate-hill we were in.

"Kill all Demons and all Unpure," Gabriel roared. "We charge Hell today!"

Shamal sped past me, racing toward the fairy circles. I turned on my side and watched as he dove into one of the portals head-first.

An angry shout bellowed over my head and I managed to use the commotion to slide into the boulder, effectively hiding myself.

Cynthia, who crawled out from underneath two flat slates, stared up in shock. I cursed. If they saw her, she was dead. She, and those like her were meant by Unpure.

"Cynthia," I whisper yelled. "Quick, over here."

She continued staring.

I grunted and crouched, my right wing dangling from its broken joint painfully. Popping my head from the magical hiding place, I called to her again.

This time, she frowned and her gaze found me. She stared at my head for a moment, then staggered to her feet.

Jophiel saw her and dove down.

"Run!" I urged her.

Cynthia broke into a limping jog, holding her wound as she went. Her wings flapped behind her, trying to add speed. But she wasn't fast enough.

"Down!" I yelled and she dropped to the floor without question, Jophiel's sword whistling over her head. She had landed close, so I grabbed her wrists and pulled her body through the soft sand.

Above us, Jophiel twisted in the air, readying for another attack. His face flushed with rage when he recognized me. "You!" he cried, his pure-white wings vibrating with anger.

I continued pulling Cynthia into the Fane-made tunnel and vanished alongside her from his view.

Holding each-other up, we stumbled along the tunnel. After two steps, my foot hit something hard and I nearly laughed when I saw my sword. Swiping it off the floor made my whole body ache, but I felt instant relief when my hand clasped the hilt of my weapon.

Quickly, we hobbled further, hearing crashing and rumbling behind us.

"Go, go, go," I whispered, and Cynthia sped up her steps.

"Who are they?" she asked, fear stark in her voice.

"Archangels. And they will kill you if they get you."

Her wide, blue eyes met mine, right before we stepped into nothingness and fell. My right wings fluttered in the air, useless as I tumbled down, head over ass. It was dark and a feeling of utter emptiness spread through my chest. I knew this smell, I knew this heat.

A circle of light grew closer and I fell from it, right into Hell's Ascend. Two hands grabbed me from behind, under my arms and around my chest. A lithe, yet hard, body pressed into mine and pressure punched into my gut when my fall slowed.

"What now?" Cynthia cried next to my ear, as she flapped her brown wings, keeping us both airborne.

Demons, alerted to our presence, started roaring, growling and heading for us, and I pointed down. "That way!"

Cynthia pulled her wings to the sides and we dropped. Straight into Hell.

Chapter Twenty-Five
Fane

Hell, the first ring

As happy as I was – to one, see Kasha, and two, have her fling Rhys into a maelstrom of rocks, crushing him – I kept wondering one thing, dangling from the Hellcat's paws. Where the fuck was Mihr? And also, where were we going? I had showed Kasha a direction but as of a few minutes ago, she completely ignored my questions and pointing.

"Gabe?" I yelled and seconds later his face appeared over Kasha's shoulder. He looked a bit worse for wear. Part of his face was bruised and scraped open, and judging by his expression, he was either constipated or in pain.

"Do you know where we are going?" I asked.

He shrugged and crouched lower, dodging a ball of fire thrown at his head. "Etse!" He flattened himself against Kasha's back. "No idea, but I hope we get there fast."

Right. As if dangling over the mansions of the first ring, collared and barely having escaped being churned into dust wasn't enough, a squadron of pissed off Demons followed us. Kasha wasn't as fast as usual, her left wing had a huge hole in its webbing – courtesy of Rhys, the twat – and she had to lump both me and Gabe around, while outflying the aforementioned squadron of Hellspawn.

Things looked grim and not at all survivable. When Kasha flew over the Waste, heading for the Sea of Despair, I started tugging at her mane. "Where are we going, love? We still have to find Dax. We can't leave yet." She ignored me. "Kasha, stop. We can't leave." A small snarl flew out the corner of her snout and she patted my stomach – where her huge paw held me – softly. It felt like being punched by a fully grown Angel.

Kasha growled once, which was all the warning we got, before twisting into a horizontal spin, evading as flurries of rocks and fire hurled at us. I heard Gabe screaming and felt a wail fight its way out of my chest, while my stomach was busy deciding what could go and what could stay. Apparently, everything would go.

As if I had timed it, I nearly emptied my belly on a Gargoyle, swooping up underneath us. Somehow, I managed to keep my throat shut and snapped my whip at him instead. He snarled when the metal sliced open his face and he fell back, screeching and swiping at his skin.

My stomach plummeted when Kasha shot up, narrowly clearing the mountain range at the edge of the Waste. The very same Maeve and I had once lived in.

I pulled up my legs when we zinged over the Sea of Despair, so close that I could smell the acid and sulfur right underneath me. "Please don't let me fall, Kash," I begged, holding onto her paws for dear life.

She let out a mewl and climbed higher, as rock-missiles and fireballs hit the water to our sides, making the poisonous water spray everywhere. The drops hitting me, immediately burned like little specks of fire and I rubbed at my arms furiously. It only helped spread the sensation. Great. "Higher, please," I shouted and Kasha obeyed.

We closed in on the storm, leading to the Ascend, when the clouds parted and something shot from them, straight at us.

I blinked. Those were wings. And not the kind you found down here – unless they were nailed to a wall, or put up for decorations. That was an Angel, and a pretty fat one too. When it came closer, I saw that it were two Angels, one carrying another. My heart stopped short. I'd know those gray feathers anywhere.

"Mihr!" I roared.

His gaze caught mine and I couldn't help the grin widening on my face. No matter when, or how, he had found an angelic taxi, he was alive, coming our way.

The smile lasted for about two seconds. Behind him and the one carrying him, countless other Angels popped from the storm. At their front – the fabled Archangels of legend. Their six wings were huge and magnificent, their size incredible. To say they were awe-inspiring didn't fit. Their presence was overwhelming, blasting into me with the force of a desert storm.

I heard a horn blasting and the Angels answered it with booming war cries all around. How the fuck had they gotten in?

"Shit," Gabe mumbled from above me. "The spell is still in effect."

"What do you mean?" I asked.

"When the first Demons came up, I fashioned a spell. Kind of like propping a door open with a brick."

"The portals are open?" I asked.

"For as long as I am down here and don't pull the figurative brick out, yes."

"That's not good," I mumbled.

Still, Kasha was racing toward her warrior and his carrier to us. By now, I saw that it was a she, beautiful but pale as death. Her copper-red hair tangled in the wind, dark rings underlined her strikingly blue eyes and her legs were covered in golden blood. Either she, or Mihr, or both of them, were bleeding like a fountain.

We needed to get out of this situation as fast as possible. "Down!" I said and pointed to the ground and back. Kasha dropped and Mihr managed to get his new friend to do the same.

Two Angels followed them, while the Demons on our tail now faced the Angel-filled sky. Hisses and roars echoed over the Sea of Despair, answered by wails and horns from deep within the rings. A deafening rumble reverberated through everything, making my teeth chatter and my innards freeze with fear. For a moment, there was silence. Heavy. Scary. Absolute. Then it was like Hell itself came alive. Even from this far away, I saw how the Waste seemed to move. A wave of Demons – those that could fly – took to the air, while the black sand was overrun by what looked like ants, but were thousands of my kin. Hell was breached. And it would rise up and fight.

Lucky us.

I squeezed Kasha's paws and felt her grip around me tighten, then I pointed past the ridge of the mountain we had crossed before, only further down one side. "That way, love. We'll try and hide in the canyon."

She rumbled lowly and we were off. I craned my neck to look behind us and saw that Mihr and the she-Angel followed us, and still two Angels followed them. I bit down on my lower lip and hoped that we would be able to shake them in the canyon, because one of them was huge. With six wings. And wearing a very pissed off expression.

We headed for the Waste, only to glide into the canyon behind it. The wind drafting from the lava river made Kasha nearly hit a wall and I urged her to go lower. So low that the heat of the lava nearly burned off my toes, but like this she could follow the twists and turns more easily, as opposed to up top, where the wind was extreme.

Following the river, I kept a lookout for the opening I had made back when fleeing with Kasha and Mihr. Maybe we could hide from the two Angels, and any Demons who might still be on our tails.

I unclenched one of my hands from Kasha's paw and fiddled out one of my whips from where I had looped them around me. Something slid from Kasha's neck to my own and I nearly dropped my weapon. Thousand tiny mouths. Passing the numbness of the collar and stroking over my skin. A sense of happiness and recognition hit me and I tried to see what I knew was there. The heavenly sand.

"Sulfur and ash, how did you get here?" I squeaked. There was no answer, but bristling when the sand slid past the collar, swatting it with a soft *ping*, to travel down my right arm and settle around my wrist.

Looking like a cloudy armbrace – the kind archers wear – the sand clung to me and swirled lazily. Leaden sleepiness pulsed from the mass and I shook my head to stop the sensation from travelling to me. I definitely didn't feel like sleeping right now.

"Good of you to show, captain runaway. Had fun with your… whatever that was up top?" When thinking about the larger body of the same material – what I had felt as ore – queasiness churned in my gut. If it was what I thought it was, how did it get there? And what exactly was it?

Either way, I had no time to ponder it now as I continued searching the canyon walls for that elusive opening. Finally, I spotted the crack I had created so long ago. It felt like ages, when it had only been a few weeks. I snorted. Strange how your life could fundamentally change in such a short time.

"There," I tugged at Kasha's mane until her head faced the crack and I was sure she saw it. A small snarl was all the answer I needed. Once more, I craned my neck to see how closely Mihr and his followers were. Mihr and the she-Angel were right behind us, copying our maneuver. I couldn't see the other two. I was about to sigh in relief, when Mihr pressed his lips together and raised an index finger. Looking up, I beheld the two fiends floating straight above us.

"Nuts." In that moment, we entered the darkness of the underground maze leading to the Deep. I was dropped and my feet stung with the impact. Catching my fall with bended knees, I stood before Mihr and his air-taxi entered and Kasha landed.

Immediately, I ran for him. Tears brimmed my lids as I wrapped my arms around him and smelled, felt, and touched him. His chest heaved and sank, his heart hammering like it was about to pop from its cavity. But I sank into him when his arms came around me and his hands squeezed me as tight as mine him.

He kissed the top of my head and drew his fingers through my hair again and again. "You are safe," he rumbled.

"Ditto," I said with a teary voice. Kasha stuck her huge head between ours, a monumental purr vibrating through us. Mihr laughed and pried one hand from me to stroke her and hug her. "You found her. Good job, my girl."

She mewled and bumped his head with the crown of her own. Her red eyes blinked in the semi-dark, conveying the utter love she had for him. My heart swelled painfully at the sight, I could relate.

With herculean effort, I stepped back and unwound myself from him. "We gotta hide," I said, glancing at the opening. Any moment now, the Angels would burst into these tunnels.

Taking my Angel's palm firmly into mine, I pulled him with me, leading our convoy down the tunnel. I sniffed and wiped at my tears, then cursed when I realized I still couldn't feel the stone. My senses to them were completely muted and cut off. I grumbled and yanked at the despicable collar, retching when my skin connected with it. Vile thing.

We came to a fork and I was torn about what way to take. Without my powers I was blind to dangers and had no way of knowing if we ran into a dead-end or a creature who didn't want to be run into.

"Kash, which way?" I asked. I heard her sniffing loudly, then she slunk past me. In the darkness I couldn't see shit, so I grabbed hold of her tail, following her into the unknown.

"Where are we going?" the she-Angel asked, she sounded drowsy and weak.

"No idea," Gabriel said, who shuffled back to steady her and help her along.

With every step, Mihr leaned on me more and more, while Gabe and the she-Angel fell back. We needed to rest and gather our strength. Get our bearings and plan the next steps. But we couldn't. Not as long as the two Angels were leaving a trail of blood to follow and we creeped along like snails.

"Satan's fucking crown jewels," I griped, tugging at the collar once more.

"What is it, Fay?" Mihr slurred.

"This fucking collar. I wish I could *see*…"

His hands reached for my neck and patted around, finding the Lilithium. His big body seemed to shake at my side, a sizzling sound and the smell of burning flesh reached me, but he added his other hand nonetheless.

"Mihr, what are you–"

Crunch.

"Did you just…?"

Pling.

"No one collars my woman," Mihr said, then I grunted when he nearly collapsed. I drew one of his arms around my shoulders.

Frantically, I patted my – now free – neck. He had broken the collar in two. *In two*. "Fucking Hell. You are such a show-off." The result of his efforts was immediate though. I felt the stone at my feet. It was like breathing the air from above for the first time. Sweet relief and power surged through me as I felt the tunnel again. There was no stopping the smirk taking up space on my lips as I closed my eyes and let go of Kasha's tail.

The sheer activity of claws, feet and hooves moving through the maze was amazing. They all had one destination – Outside. It was a miracle, or thanks to Kasha's nose, that we hadn't run into any of them yet. Now feeling, I led my little group past and around creatures, searching for a nook, a small cave I could seal off.

Stopping short, to let a herd of hooved creatures empty their liar, I determined the vacated cave would do nicely for a quick resting place.

Once I felt that they had all left, I rounded the corner and let my group file inside. Propping Mihr to the wall on my side, I then closed the stone behind us. Sweet, sweet volcanic stone. It closed like a curtain, listening to me without fail.

The thing was, my feet felt the approaching booted feet of two people. Had to be the Angels. "Shit." I turned from the stone. "They can sense your blood, right?" I asked Mihr.

He grunted, leaning against the wall next to me. "Yup."

"Aha. I see you have turned into a cowboy in my absence. Any plans?" I heard ripping fabric and a second later a swath of drenched cloth was handed to me. Breathing in, I ratcheted up my inner fire and slowly my veins shimmered in the dark. Mihr held out his shirt for me, then pulled it back to dab at his back.

"Nice, but what about her?" I asked and gestured at the she-Angel. Gabe was busy helping her to sit down. When she looked up and saw me, she swallowed and her face twisted into a frightened mask. "Demon," she rasped.

"No shit, this is Hell, sweetheart. What did you think you'd run into? Crocodiles?"

She didn't answer but shrank away from Gabe when she saw his dark skin and horns.

"Didn't you notice when you followed us?" I asked.

The she-Angel shook her head. "I just did what he said. I followed the black cat."

Kasha, sitting at Mihr's right like a sphinx, licked over her flews.

The she-Angel ogled her as though seeing her for the first time. "She is a Demon as well?"

"Saints on a Sunday, I can't with this one," I told Mihr.

"She saved my life," he simply said.

I gave the frightened person a once over. "Okay, we can keep her, but she is bleeding like mad, we have to clean the wound and somehow stop her from leaking, or that pissed-off guy with six wings will hammer down this cave."

"Jophiel," Mihr said. "He followed us since we fell down your tunnel."

"You know how to pick em, don't you?" I glanced at my Angel, motioned for him to turn his back to me and took a look at his wound. It was closing and had stopped bleeding. The one on his belly was not bleeding at all, but looked... weird. I'd have to ask him what it was later.

"Gabe, can you help her in any way?" I asked.

The magic man sank onto his hunches and reached for the she-Angel. "Where are you hurt–"

"Get away from me, creature," she yelled.

"Cynthia, he is a friend," Mihr said. "He won't hurt you."

"But he..." she swallowed, looking from Mihr, to Gabe, to me and back to my Angel. "I don't understand. Why would you consort with Hellspawn? I knew Shamal wasn't telling us everything and he made us leave one of our own to die, so when you said we were stolen... I wanted to know. But this... I don't understand."

Mihr pushed off the wall and staggered over to where Cynthia cowered. "I will explain, but right now, you need to let us help you so your bleeding will stop. Otherwise, all of us are done for."

She licked her lips nervously, but didn't ward off Gabe when he crouched down next to her again. I had to hand it to Gabe, he was fast. The magic man drew a circle around Cynthia's blood-slick armor and spoke a few soft words, the drenched part came away, revealing a deep slash. He pinched some powder from one of his pouches and sprinkled it on the wound and the golden blood stopped flowing.

I jogged up to him, grabbed the piece of armor and then looked at Cynthia's legs. "You're gonna have to lose the pants, dear," I told her.

With a defiant face, she shimmied from them and held them up.

"Anything left?" I asked Mihr.

He took a deep breath and shook his head. "Only what you have in your hands."

"Great, see you in a bit. I'll lead them astray. Maybe I can find a cave that still has a few monsters left." When I started walking toward the exit, Mihr snatched my wrist and twirled me around so I landed square against his naked chest. With so much of his gorgeous skin open and close, my breath hitched. "Be safe." He kissed me. "And hurry back." Another kiss.

I nearly melted and was about to pull him closer to deepen the kiss, when a disgusted sound had me jerking back. I glared at the she-Angel, who grimaced.

"Really? Be glad you saved his life, or I would drag you out and leave you somewhere to be found by your oh-so-holy kin." I turned from her and stomped off, a curious mix of anger and elation bouncing through the depths of my being. Time to lead some Angels astray. Huh. That sounded a lot naughtier than it was.

Chapter Twenty-Six
Mihr

Hell, the maze between
the first ring and the Deep

I understood her. But it took a considerable amount of effort to be quiet. And Fane was right, had Cynthia not saved me and flown me to where we were now, I would have dragged her out this cave myself. I clenched my fists and told myself it didn't matter right now, and even so, she had been taught to think a certain way, just like I had. It left me feeling both angry at her and sorry, but right now, I didn't have the energy to talk to her.

Fane had left us in the dark, and when a sudden glow became visible, illuminating Gabe's face, I wondered what it was and loomed over him.

He had piled together a set of small bones and ignited a tiny, purple fire that didn't seem to consume them. We both ignored Cynthia's gasp and the way she scrambled back as far as she was able. She would have to learn to deal.

"A Warlock's Flame, they call it," Gabe explained, then nodded over to the piece of wall Fane had vanished from. "Will it work?"

"It should. The more pressing question is, how will we get out once it did? The whole place is crawling with fighting Angels and Demons." Kasha sniffed at my broken wing, then sat down behind me. Gently, she lay her chin on my shoulder and let me scratch her.

"Which is a good thing for us," the half-Demon mused. "We can slip through the chaos and commotion."

"Have you found Dax?" I asked.

He shook his head. "I'll get to it right away." Sitting down, he did the same weird flourish and sprinkling of sand, he had done to look for Fane. The sand turned dark, resembling runes and symbols as it dropped to the stone-floor, and I left Gabe to ponder his magic. Feeling the wound on my abdomen, I discovered it had spread further. If Kasha hadn't stood behind me, I likely would have swayed with the effort it took to stand.

The problem was, there wasn't much one could do against a Gargoyles wound, and I was certain Gabe would have no idea either, seeing as he hadn't really seen many Demons during his time.

"He is close," Gabe's voice reached me through the fog of my mind. "The boy is… he is close to where Kasha and I found Fane."

"Where was that?"

"No idea, man. There were lots of houses, grand mansions, and it was right behind the desert of black sand."

"The first ring? What was Fane doing in the first ring?"

"Getting her ass almost kicked by a set of Ember-twins," she said as she slid back into the cave and drew the stone closed behind her. "I deposited your bloody bait in a nook. It leads to a cave filled with Hellhounds who can't get out, as I have cornered them in." She smirked. "Your Angel-followers will have a nasty surprise waiting for them."

My Demon narrowed her eyes at me and let her veins glow to light things up a bit. "Now to you. I guess your wing will heal soon, the stab on your back is only a scar by now, but what the heck is that grayish, flaky, weirdness on your abdomen?"

"That's a Gargoyle wound," I said. "Nothing much can be done–"

Fane placed a palm to my wound and shushed me. "I need silence, Greta." Her brows drew together when she felt around, prodding and squeezing my wound softly. Then she clapped her hands together, which started to shimmer and move like clouds. The sand had covered her fingers like a set of gloves. Slowly, Fane pressed both hands to my side and I felt the sand tickle my skin when she did.

I got pulled to her hands, my skin stuck to them, and pain cracked through the wound as the graying area decreased. A grunt left me, courtesy of the pulling and cracking pain, shooting out from the wound. I winced and hissed when it increased.

Fane drew back her hands and my skin felt like it was being ripped off as it still stuck to her. "Dammit," I cursed, making her smile at me.

She kept pulling and I concentrated hard on holding as still as I could. The gray got sucked into her hands as though they were vacuum-cleaners and the moment my skin snapped back, it was its usual color once more. There was a remaining throb of pain, but I felt the lethargy lifting already. Feeling over the space where the wound had been, I came up against a dry cut that would soon heal fully.

"Thank you," I said.

"You ripped a Lilithium collar apart for me, so no biggy. What did it do to your hands?" She took them and held them palms up to scrutinize my flesh. It was blistered a bit, but I hadn't touched the cursed metal for long, so I barely even registered the added ache.

"Gabe has found Dax," I informed her and she glanced from my hands to my face.

Her expression lit up and she sank down to hug the magic man. "You did? Thank you so much!" She hugged him again and kissed the top of his head. "Where?"

"Close to where we found you. In that general area," Gabe said, looking at Fane with a mix of wonder and surprise.

"You are a marvel, Gabe. Once everyone has rested a bit, we will go and find him." Fane pouted her lips, looking at me. "We will have to think of something to hide your obvious holiness, or we'll have to sneak the whole time."

I held my hands up. "Hey, I'm good with sneaking. After all, it is almost as dangerous being a Demon in Hell as it is being Angel. At least at the moment."

****

I leaned my back against the cave wall and sank down next to Cynthia. The she-Angel eyed me for a second, then went ahead to stare at Fane, Gabe, and Kasha, who had taken to resting on the other side of the cave.

"You are a Fallen because of them?" she asked.

"Not really. I was caught by Demons and held in Hell. Fane freed me. We found Kasha in these very tunnels and escaped this realm together. We have been together ever since. They both saved my life and I wouldn't give them up to Michael, who insisted. So, I ended up killing him to save them and myself from certain death."

She nodded, a coppery strand falling from a braid she had twisted her hair into during our time in here. "Michael could be… stern. But Shamal," Cynthia shook her head. "He made us leave her. That's when I knew I couldn't trust him." Her blue eyes found mine. "How could I trust a man who valued the lives of his soldiers so little?"

"Who did you leave?"

"Karina. She's the one who followed you from Heaven. The one who found you and some Demons fighting. An Ifrit sliced her open and I offered to take her up to be healed, but Shamal ordered to search for you and leave her." With a shaking hand, she tucked the loose strand behind one ear. "He said we would take her body up once we left."

I cursed underneath my breath. "You left her?"

"N-no. Not really." Cynthia sniffed and swiped her face with the back of her hand. "I took her to a small village. I hope they were able to help her. I-it was all I had time for, or he would have found out." Her shoulder trembled but she didn't cry. I awkwardly patted her back, not knowing what to say to that.

"You told Shamal he stole us. What does that mean?"

"I don't think now is the time."

"Now might be the only time. We are in Hell and you seem to have a plan. I have no idea whether to trust or follow you, or make my own way. Tell me."

Her expression was hard, it seemed misplaced on her soft features, but I knew what she was capable of and I understood her need to know. She needed something to hold onto, even if it was only the shitty truth about her origins.

"We Angels used to be born. Like all living things. But when Lucifer fell and landed in this very realm, He swore to conquer and annihilate Heaven. Souls from Earth travel to the above, or the below, based on who they were in life. The good ones go to Heaven, the bad ones to Hell. Somehow Lucifer and our Lord discovered a way to give them bodies. I don't know when, or how they found out, and I have no idea how it works. But when the war cost many lives on both sides, we went over to use made Angels and made Demons to bolster our numbers.

"Humans are always asked whether they want to fight and help our cause when their souls enter Heaven. Those that don't are ushered to paradise and spend their time with loved ones, until life calls for them again."

Cynthia's gaze was fascinated and she pulled up her legs to hug her knees, looking way more comfortable in my presence than she had when I sat down.

"When everything happened with me being in Hell and escaping and Michael hunting me, Kasha, and Fane, I found out that he was stealing souls, to build his own army. Shamal was part of it. You... you were never asked whether you wanted to fight. They made you into Angels without teaching you anything about who you are, whom you fight, or why."

"Th-they told us we were important. That we had one job, and that was to make God proud by slaying Demons and protecting Humans." Cynthia threaded her index finger through that same strand of hair, over and over. "I-I used to be a Human? Why can't I remember?"

"Because you entered a new body. When your soul travels into flesh again, it erases memory, sets the mind to zero. Unless you move onto paradise, it is better to not know, to forget. Otherwise, you wouldn't be able to do your job as an Angel. There will be… echoes of your life on Earth, small flashes of who you were or whom you loved, but that's about it."

She was quiet for a whole while, processing the information, while twisting and twirling the strand of hair in her fingers. "Why would they do that to us?" she eventually asked.

"Maybe because they thought we needed more warriors. Demons aren't asked and there are way more of them than us."

"Yeah, that's not it." We looked up and saw Fane strolling over. The shine from her skin flickered across the walls as she moved and I couldn't help but stare at how magnificent she was. "I found out that you guys were made to overtake Hell and end the fight between our realms. Shamal and Michael had a deal with my former Maester, Rhys. They were going to kill Lucifer and rearrange Hell," she shrugged. "Probably planned to do the same up top."

"That can't be," I said. "Michael would never strike a deal with a Demon. No way."

Fane flopped down, cross-legged and I noticed Cynthia not moving away.

"He did. Big time. He was also… involved with my former Maester." She waved a hand. "But that doesn't matter now. Fact is, they planned to end the war together and they were going to use your secret army to do so."

I nearly choked on my own breath. "Michael would never… This can't be true, Fane. I have never met anyone more driven to eradicate Hell – no one who hated Demons more – than Michael."

My Ember gave me an unbelieving look. "My former Maester was an Incubus. An exceptional one. He could have charmed the pants off God himself had he ever set his mind to it. You met Horace and Valo. Rhys was to them what I am to other Embers: transcendent. Also, I have been told your God and all his followers kinda turn their noses up at same-sex inclinations. If Michael loved men, it would have messed with him bigtime, living in Hell."

For a moment, the teachings I had been drilled with my entire life threatened to spill from me. How homosexuality was unpractical, as we needed more Angels and our number were few already. But that was eons ago. Fane was right, it had turned from an impracticality, to being outright banned and abhorred. If what Fane said was true, I hadn't known my friend at all. I swallowed. Would I have accepted him if he had told me? I would like to say I would have, but the fact that I wasn't sure, lay heavy in my gut.

"Did he love him?" I asked.

"Oh, absolutely not. Rhys has never loved anyone but himself, and his own grand ideas. But they did have a plan and I am guessing it went further than invading Hell. Rhys provided Michael and Shamal with Lilithium, which they used to open temporary, hidden portals for the souls to pass through. Lost souls, that no one missed." She glanced at Cynthia. "Sorry about that, Cyn, but you are one of those."

The she-Angel held Fane's gaze for long heartbeats. "What are you planning to do now?"

"Us? We will go and save the soul of our Dax and bring him back to his Human body, then? I'm thinking of stopping Shamal and his soul-stealing business. Kasha already took care of Rhys." Fane shrugged and smiled at me. "If we are alive after that, we will live. Simply, live."

The smile and warmth seeping into me was divine. I held out a palm and she placed her hand into mine. Pulling her to me, she slid over the stone and I turned her so she came to sit between my legs, her back to my chest. I hugged her closely, reveling in the smell of her hair and feel of her warm skin. "We're finally on the same page then?" I asked.

"We are. I have discovered that I do care about those unfortunate shits." She fluttered her lashes at Cynthia. "No offense."

"I will join you," Cynthia said, dropping the strand of hair and straightening her shoulders. "No matter what it takes. I will not let what happened to me, happen to anyone else."

Chapter Twenty-Seven
Ragon's Ploy

Hell, the first ring

"This is a shitshow," Ragon rasped, looking from his balcony at the carnage happening in the streets, in the sky and all around them. An Ifrit rolled past, slicing into an Angel, who hacked at the fire-Demon while yelling at the top of his lungs. Within moments, they were both gone.

He didn't feel compelled to enter the fray in no way, shape, or form. No, this was all Lucifer's business. Ragon sighed and went back inside, shutting the fight outside from his mind. His guards were amongst the strongest of the ring, they would hold out until Hell's forces lay waste to the Angels. There was no way the feathered fiends would win. Not in Hell. Also, he had Jinx. The Succubus was wounded, but she was still able

– and charged with – erecting a protective shield around the mansion.

The doors burst open and Jinx hobbled inside, flanked by what looked like a female Ember he had seen around Rhys' household. That Incubus and his proteges...

"What is this?" Ragon asked, waving at Jinx and her companion.

As the Succubus came closer, using crutches to make up for her lost leg, she wore a grim yet determined expression. "This one has news for you, Maester," she said and nodded at the Ember.

The woman slumped to his feet, sobbing and hiccupping. *Pathetic.*

"And?" Ragon asked, glaring at the woman ruining his carpet. She was bleeding from several wounds, but most of all he detested her tears. They were a sign of weakness.

"My Maester and my brother are dead. W-we were tasked to bring that Ember from the Surface."

This got his attention. "Fane?"

"Y-yes. We waited for the call, and when so many went up, we snuck past and grabbed her. It wasn't hard finding her. She used immense amounts of her powers." The woman sniffled and more tears ran over her face. "We brought her to our Maester's home, collared. A-and we secured her, but sh-she got loose and…"

"And what? Speak up, woman!" Ragon barked.

"We almost had her, almost. But then a Hellcat arrived. I-it killed Aaron with one swipe and then plunged my Maester to his death," her voice broke. "He fell into th-the twisting stone I used to corner her. He g-got crushed in my power. It happened so fast…" She doubled over and whimpered.

"Why did Rhys send you to get Fane, and where is she now?" Ragon thundered. When the Ember only shook with sobs, he snatched her by her hair and pulled her face up so he could look at her. "Focus! Where is she now?"

"She flew off with the Hellcat. We followed, but then the Angels came. I-I don't know where she is."

"Then feel for her. Look for her. Now!"

The Ember nodded and placed both palms on the stone floor. The silence following was tense and only broken up by her pathetic sobs and snivels. "I c-can't–"

"Think hard before you speak another word," Ragon snarled. "Because if you are about to tell me you can't feel her, I will end you."

"Maester…" Jinx began but Ragon held up a hand.

"Shut your yap, you one-legged whore. Thanks to you, Fane and that Angel of hers escaped last time."

The Succubus' lips tightened, but other than that, her expression didn't change. She stepped back and stayed quiet. Good. Ragon wasn't in the mood to argue.

"I-I can…" the Ember stammered and opened her eyes. "I feel her."

In that very moment, the wall leading to the entrance hall exploded. Black dust, rocks, and grains of sand flew at him like missiles and he let his body fall to the floor and covered his head with both hands. When the noise subsided, he glanced at the wall. There was now a hole. A hole in which Fane and her cursed Angel stood, hand in hand. Her other palm was spread out in front of her, no doubt she'd used it to make the hole. On their sides a Hellcat, a she-Angel, and what looked like a Warlock – but not quite – stood, facing the room.

"Hello, Asshole," Fane said, looking at Ragon. "Jinx, Agatha." She nodded at the Succubus and Ember.

"Fane!" Ragon laughed as he scrambled to his feet. "This is a surprise. Have you come because you missed me?"

The Angel at her side snapped open his huge wings and flashed through the room. Faster than anyone could react, he had grabbed Ragon by the throat, picked him up, and slammed his back to the nearest wall, pinning him there. The air left Ragon's lungs on impact and he clawed at the hand surrounding his throat like a vise of iron.

The Angel's gray eyes began to glow, a snarl resting on his face. "No. She came because you have something of ours." The Angel slammed him into the wall once more, making little rocks crumble down. "*I came to kill you.*"

"You!" the female Ember who had been busy soaking Ragon's carpet screamed and sprang up. She pointed at Fane and burst into a sprint. As she went, the stone at her feet ripped open, and she flung the unearthed boulders straight at Fane.

Fane swatted the rocks with her whips and they burst into nothing but dust and sand, hitting the floor with a soft woosh.

The Ember screamed and sank to her knees, plunging both fists into the rock and opening the earth at Fane's feet. "I'll kill you!" she roared.

Fane raised a brow and rose from the earth as if by magic. The Warlock-similar man strutted towards the wailing Ember and blew something into her face. It looked like a load of glitter. The woman slumped down immediately, crumbling into a heap on the floor. The she-Angel bent down and arranged her gently into a sleep-like position.

Ragon hacked and coughed past the grip on his throat. "What. The. Fuuuch?" His antics resulted in him being slammed into the wall again. He was sure his body was molded to the wall by now.

"Careful, Mihr," Fane trilled as she walked closer. "We still need him to speak. Don't break him before he had the chance."

"Kill them!" Ragon managed to rasp.

Jinx hopped on her foot once, glaring at Fane with hate-filled eyes, but she didn't act. Not even as the guards finally stormed the room, brandishing their weapons and roaring before mounting an attack to free their Maester.

"Now you die," Ragon whispered at the Angel holding him in place, his feet dangling. Utter shock and horror struck him when the Angel's lips widened into a radiant smile. It was like nothing he had ever seen and as Ragon was drawn into the presence of the Angel, hating every part of his fascination, the Angel slowly shook his head.

"I don't think so," it said.

Chapter Twenty-Eight

Fane

Hell, Ragon's mansion,

the first ring

With a burst of energy, my veins came to life. I stomped my right foot once, feeling the sand covering it happily amping up my bidding. It almost seemed like the sand enjoyed this as playtime. With one move, the oncoming guards sank into the floor to their hips, stuck for the time being. They grunted and shouted, clawing at the stone, or hacking at it with their blades. It would take them a while to get out of their encasings. Meaning, I had time.

I sauntered past Jinx, who hobbled back, but said nothing as she killed me with her looks. Coming up to Mihr, who held a flailing Ragon to the wall, I placed my palm on his arm until he lowered my former Maester. The fact that he had tackled the Demon Lord across the room had been a major turn-on, and I bit my lip when my Angel glanced at me. I liked this protective side of his. More than I cared to admit.

"You have a core of Lilithium, Ragon," I said, switching my focus to him. "Where is it?"

"Wh-I have a wha-t?" he pressed forth, rubbing over his throat when Mihr let go of him.

"Lilithium. Core." I snapped my fingers in front of his face. "Pay attention."

He frowned, looking thoroughly confused. "I have n-no idea what you are talking about."

I turned to Gabe and opened my hands in a 'what now' kind of gesture. The magic man let a bit of sand from one of his pouches drizzle on the floor and spoke his curious-sounding spell, making the sand darken, draw together and form symbols at his feet.

"I don't know what to tell you," he said. "It is here. *He* is here."

"What do you mean by 'he'?" Jinx suddenly asked.

"The reason we came," I said. "A Human child lost his soul and we think a Lilithium core is involved. We are trying to save him."

Jinx looked taken aback, then her eyes swayed to Ragon, and back to me. She hopped once.

"Do you know something?" I asked.

"Even if you do, I forbid you to say anything," Ragon spat.

The Succubus glared at him, but her mouth stayed shut.

"Ragon, you little bitch, rescind that order," I said.

"Never." He chuckled and I felt the soft zing of metal, scraping against the stone behind his back. He was readying a dagger, or something similar. I punched my fist into the wall by his side and two things happened at once – the metal he had drawn to attack us, fused to the wall and stuck, no matter how hard he yanked. And the impact made a slate tilt from the wall, above one of the cupboards lining the far side of the room, behind his desk. A square, a hollow space opened up above the cupboard.

While Ragon blanched, pulling and wrenching at the weapon behind him, I shook my head and walked over to the little square, leaving Mihr to corner him if he tried something.

"Fane! Don't you dare. That is private," Ragon fumed.

I ignored him, more intrigued by his behavior than anything else. The square seemed to be empty, as I could only sense a hollow space, but nothing more. When I reached inside the hole, my fingers felt something odd. Something I hadn't expected. I grabbed hold and pulled out a wooden box. A box I had once longed to touch, to be able to feel what wood was like. Before I had ever seen the Surface, before I had met Dax and Cam. Before Mihr. It was the music box Lev had bought, alongside me. The one that had gone missing on the day of his murder.

I turned it over in my head, opening it. A languidly sad tune crept from it, washing over the grunts of the guards I had sunken into the ground, blurring out the fighting outside, suffusing my mind.

Very lowly, I turned to face Ragon. The expression on his face was all I needed to confirm what I knew to be true. "You killed him," I whispered. "You killed Lev."

Ragon let go of the weapon he was trying to dislodge behind him. He elbowed Mihr to the side, who let him pass after one look at me.

"Of course, I fucking killed him!" Ragon raged. "He stole you from me. You are mine. You have been since the first time I set eyes on you. And when he took you, I knew what I had to do. I knew I had to…" His mouth opened and closed, but no sound escaped. First, he looked confused, then angry, until panic flashed across his features.

"You killed him?" Jinx snapped. Her fingers danced through the air as if she were holding invisible strings. Her expression was beyond dark, her presence chilling me to the bone. "I have entered your service to find the one responsible, thinking it was Fane." She gestured at me. "I knew the only one who would look for her as fiercely as myself was you. But all the while… it was you. You, who shared my bed, who ordered me to hunt down Embers to look for her. Who made me kill them when they turned out to be inadequate." A shaky breath left her and she crooked her finger. Ragon stumbled over, his eyes fixed on her.

With a shiver, I registered Jinx's strew, thick and heady in the air. My hair stood and goosebumps covered me entirely. I looked at Mihr, dreading him doing the same thing Ragon did, close in on Jinx. My Angel casually strolled past Ragon, to draw an arm around me. I trembled at his touch, almost moaning with pleasure. His muscles clenched in answer and I looked back at Ragon to see what was happening.

Kasha rolled her red eyes and snapped her wings at Gabe and Cynthia, who – wearing looks of complete abandon – tried to make their way to the Succubus, as well. When the snapping sound didn't have effect, Kasha grabbed Gabe with one paw and Cynthia with the other, clutching their struggling bodies to her while sitting on her hunches. She looked like an overgrown meerkat, with pups in her arms.

Meanwhile, Ragon had reached his Succubus, who licked her lips and raised her hands. Placing one clawed palm on his shoulder, she rammed the other hand straight into his chest. His chest-cavity crunched as she broke through it, a small gasp hovering from his lips. With a squelching sound, Jinx pulled out his heart, dripping the black blood over her face, she licked it, then bit down. While Ragon stared, sinking to his knees slowly, she ate his still beating heart, looking every bit like the feral Demon she was.

When my former Maester dropped to the floor, the light in his eyes dimming, the guards stilled, looking around as though they were waking from a dream.

"Let them out, Fane," Jinx said. She breathed out, the black blood shimmering on her lips, chin, and chest. Swiping at it with one bloody hand did nothing but add to the mess.

"Once we are gone, I will," I said. I waved a hand at Ragon. "Well done, Jinxy. I knew you had it in you, but damn, that was cold."

A sigh floated from her and her strew was pulled back. Cynthia and Gabe blinked stupidly and Kasha let them go.

"What in the Hell did you do to me, Demon woman?" Cynthia growled, sliding her blade free.

Gabe patted her arm and pointed at Ragon. "I think we just got caught in the crosshairs," he said when looking from Jinx to Ragon. "Your doing? Good job, that guy was an idiot."

Jinxed mouthed the word back at him, frowned, then shook her head. "Never mind this piece of shit," she prodded his body with one of her crutches, "but we have little time."

She pursed her lips, looking to me and Mihr. "I hate you, Fane. And I hate you, Angel. You took my leg." Jinx fingered the stump of her right leg. "And I couldn't care less whether you got ripped to shreds down here or not, but I know one thing – I am done bowing to whims of Demons thinking to order me around. If you are truly here to free an innocent soul, I will let you, as you have given me the opportunity of satisfaction. That which you seek is beneath Ragon's bedchamber. He had no idea it was there, but Sathanas told me, when I started my servitude to Ragon. Leviathan's father wanted the cores protected, for what purpose I don't know. And I have the ability to send mental messages. He instructed me to let him know if and when someone came looking for it." She turned from me and began hobbling toward the guards at the entrance. "He knows you are here, Fane. If I was you, I'd hurry. And then get out of this shithole." Jinx tapped one of the trapped Demons on the head. "You wanna come with me?"

"Yes, mistress," he answered. The others nodded frantically, straining against the stone.

I stomped my foot once and the space encasing them widened. They clambered from the holes and followed Jinx from the room. We heard her click-clacking down the hall and leaving through the front door.

I shrugged off what had just transpired and pulled Mihr with me, heading for the bedroom of my former Maester. When I reached the arch I had made and decorated into the onyx wall, the day before freeing Mihr, I stopped short. My feet told me there was nothing underneath. Had Jinx lied to us?

While I flexed my toes to feel around, Cynthia went through drawers and cupboards, pulling out clothing. She grimaced as she held up a few pants, but soon settled on a pair and drew them on.

"You heard her, we have to hurry," Mihr said at my side, squeezing my hand reassuringly.

"I don't feel anything," I told him.

He tilted his head to the side. "It won't hurt to look and be sure, right?"

I let go of his hand and stepped into the bedroom, grimacing at the decadent bed and wall carvings, still able to hear his cloying words and feel his leering gaze on me. Thank Jinx he was a goner. And the way she'd done it? Scary. Badass. Mostly scary, though.

Crouching to the floor, I planted my hands and feet to the onyx and drew it apart gently. Like melting butter, it opened between my hands, revealing – I gagged – maybe an elbow deep, a wall of Lilithium spanned the ground. No wonder I hadn't felt a thing. It couldn't be thick though, just enough to shield it from Embers such as myself.

"Will you be so kind as to hit this, Gabby, preferably with a sword?" I asked.

Gabe stuck his head past Mihr. "I have no sword. And Gabby? That is a bit much, don't you think?"

I flew into a giggle fit, the tension from the last hours unloading themselves in laughter and tears. My Angel even chuckled a bit. "She means me, Gabe." He still huffed out small hiccups of laughter when raising his sword. Then he brought it down, smashing the wall – it was thin, as I had thought – into millions of pieces. Mihr happily hacked at it until the hole was big enough for Kasha. He stuck his head inside and whistled. The sound echoed eerily.

"It's pretty big down here," he said, pulling his head free. Nodding at his Hellcat, he jumped inside. Kasha followed within a second.

"It's empty," Mihr shouted from below. "You can come in."

I pushed myself off and launched my body through the hole. My Angel caught me and set me down gently. With little to no effort, I made my veins glow to see better. The… room, for lack of a better word, was black. The deep, light-swallowing kind of black only Lilithium had. Matte. Almost silken. If it wasn't for the havoc it wreaked on my insides, I would have found it pretty.

Behind me, I heard Gabe and Cynthia drop down, while I took a step. "Ugh. Nuts." The ground, the walls, everything was made from the Devil's stone and I couldn't feel a thing. The sensation was similar to what wood had felt like in the beginning. Like losing a sense, like being cut off from it entirely. It took me a few steps to get used to it. After those, walking became easier. The sand traveled up my legs in clouds of distaste and anger.

Finally, settling on the very top of my head like a hat. From way up there, I felt it chide and sulk. I reached up and ran my fingers through it. "It's gonna be fine." The thousands of tiny mouths quieted down somewhat, but there was still the overall feeling of peevishness.

The room was kind of roundish-long, like a pipeline. I glanced back, seeing that it cut off into a solid wall, but the other direction? I couldn't see the end. "Looks like we're going that way," I said.

"Are you sure?" Cynthia asked. "We have no idea where it leads to."

"Yes, we do," Mihr said and passed me, with Kasha by his side. "It leads to Dax."

We saw fine with the light I provided and while we walked on, I took deep breaths to quell the nausea swarming my belly. Not far in, the pipeline widened into a huge, round room. The surfaces looked botchy, like clay having been plastered to natural walls. All of it had to be His work. No one else could work or control Lilithium. Lucifer Himself had made this place. The question was why? He had oodles and mounds of the stuff beneath his castle in the ninth ring. What was so special about this place?

"What the heck is this?" Cynthia asked, standing close to one of the rounded walls. She poked at a lump of black, and it wiggled.

The she-Angel screamed and stumbled back, furiously wiping off the finger she had done the poking with. Mihr unsheathed his sword with a zing, and Kasha growled lowly, her hackles rising.

"That is some sci-fi-type shit," Gabe mumbled, his eyes as round as saucers.

I crept up to the lump and narrowed my eyes.

"Careful, Fay," Mihr said.

Very slowly, I extended a finger and prodded. My nausea reached its boiling point and I doubled over, emptying the contents of my stomach onto the floor. The sand on my head pelted me with pinpricks of panic, and my whips coiled and uncoiled at my sides. When I heard the shuffling of feet behind me, I held up a hand. "Don't come closer. Not nice," I croaked. I dry-heaved, then sucked in air. Mortified, I ripped off one of my sleeves and tried to clean myself up.

"Are you okay?" Mihr asked, right behind me. I jumped when he stroked my back slowly, in soothing circles.

"I told you not to come closer," I said.

"Don't be an idiot." He continued to stroke and I felt better with each circle he drew on my back. "What happened?"

"This lump is what we are looking for," I said. "By my reaction to it, I'd say we have found ourselves a bona fide Lilithium core."

"I hate to be the one telling you this," Gabriel said, "but maybe that isn't the right one." He poked at an identical one next to him and I groaned when I looked around, finding lumps hiding in the blackness of the walls all around us. There had to be at least fifty.

"And we really think Dax is somehow held by one of these?" Mihr asked.

"They look… alive, so it makes sense," I said. "I just don't understand how his magic found them and why. Or how it is possible for one of these things to hold him prisoner and take over his body. It sounds… surreal."

"Gabe? Can you tell which it is?" Mihr asked.

The magic man held out his palms and turned, a low chant growing from him. He took a pinch of powder from his pouches and threw it from him, but the glittering dust just fell to the floor, lying there motionless. Gabe stopped his chanting and blinked at his powder. "That's never happened before."

"Magic doesn't work on Lilithium, maybe that is why. The stone saps all supernatural power."

The half-Demon raised a brow. "Don't you think you could have told me that?"

"How did you find Dax during the whole... floating thing?" Mihr asked. "Maybe that can help?"

"That was the magic itself, shielding him from me," Gabe paced through the room. "I guess it was amplified by this stuff, but if it saps magical energy then it makes no sen – oh sweet ti !khutse!"

"What?" I asked, when Gabe stopped. He opened his mouth, clapped it shut and smiled.

"It is a portal. An exchange of energy. Everything is."

"What are you talking about, man?" Mihr asked, a deep frown gracing his face.

Gabe snapped his fingers and nodded. "Of course! That is why Human souls pass through and we need some way to open them! It is life." He belted out a laugh that had all of us staring at him.

"I think he lost it," Cynthia said drily.

"Yup," Mihr added.

Gabe bent over and slapped his knees, laughing his ass off. "Ahyeh, I should have known. I should have seen before. Lilithium is what shields this realm from the next, just like it would open a passage to Heaven. Meaning the stuff you carry around," he pointed at my head, "can open passages to Hell. The only thing capable of travelling from one to the other without the aid of either Lilithium or heavenly sand, is a Human soul. The sand and the dead stone repel each other, which is why they can rip tears into each other and create passageways. Dax made a spell… Now I get what he was doing. The boy…" Gabriel huffed out an unbelieving laugh. "He wrote a spell to portal all of Heaven's elements back to Heaven and all of Hell's back here. But when he used the demonic and heavenly language, not made for him, the demonic side pulled back. The moment his soul passed into this realm, it was fused to the one thing capable of absorbing and harboring his magic," Gabe waved around wildly, indicating at the lumps around us.

"Nice, very nice, but not entirely right," a cold voice said. We spun to face whoever had spoken and my heart dropped right through my pants. Sathanas, Lev's father, the Lord of the eighth ring and close consort of the Devil Himself, stepped from the pipeline and into the room. His black skin, infused by deep red, glinted in the fire he carried with him in one hand. His six horns curled backwards over his temples, polished to perfection. Yes, there were Demons lining him and behind him, but he could as well have come by himself. His aura filled the room to near bursting and I suddenly felt like I couldn't breathe.

Jinx had said she'd called for him. Should have listened and hurried a bit more.

"It is true, Lilithium has a mind of its own, it is also true that it saps magic and can open passages to Heaven, just like Saliphe can open the doors of Hell. And yes, the boy's soul is tethered to one of these." Sathanas indicated at the lumps. His face hardened. "But it is *my* magic infusing him, *my* mind that will see through his eyes, walk with his feet and live inside his body. We have countless of husks above. Why do you think I keep these here for? Decoration? No. They are our eyes and ears on Earth. Unearthing conspiracies against the Prince of Darkness and his reign. You, Ember, have found the roots of one and were you anyone else, I would be inclined to let you live on behalf of it. But you have been nothing but trouble.

"Freeing an Angel, a born one, one Lucifer could have used to gain dominion over Heaven. Finally. Then you escaped, killed your own kind, lived with Humans and your Angel, only to lead the armies from above through our gates?" He glowered at me and it felt like he was choking me. "You are the reason my son is dead. For that alone, I will kill you."

"Touch her and die," Mihr snarled, twirling his sword and stepping in front of me. Kasha roared and shook out her impressive mane, focusing on the Demon Lord.

"Silly children. You think I won't swipe you away like the gnats you are?" Sathanas smiled evilly. "Come then. Let's see what Mihr the Fallen, and his young kitten can stomach."

Chapter Twenty-Nine
Daxter in Lilithium

Hell, a room filled with Lilithium,
the first ring

The darkness and hopelessness was absolute. He had no idea how much time had passed since he had been pulled from his body and stuck inside this… nothingness. Dax still heard his mother scream, he felt the echoes of her shaking him, begging him to come back.

He had told her he was there. But she hadn't heard him. Then he had sunken deeper, unable to rise back to the surface of his mind. Something had pulled him, steadily, slowly. Until his mother was gone. Fighting it had been exhausting and eventually he had given in, only to wake in total darkness. There was no way of knowing whether he was dead, awake, or asleep.

He had nothing to hold onto for guidance. No light, no sound, no scent. Nothing.

He had panicked. For quite a while, fear had been the only real thing around and inside of him. But eventually, even fear was something one could get used to. Who'd have thought? It had saved him in a way, through his terror he had discovered that he could indeed feel something. And while his panic had gone on forever, he was able to pin his existence to it. *I am*, he had thought. *I might be afraid, but I still am something.* The thought had spun into others and soon he had enough to be sure who he was. His being expanded and hit something. Like lungs being too full of air, there was a certain boundary he could not extend over.

If he could hit something, he could feel it. That was sound logic and he expanded again and again, until he knew exactly how big the boundary around him was. It was dark and cold, giving off a sense of malice and detest. Which led Dax to the conclusion that he was inside something or someone who could feel such things.

He puffed himself out and lined his consciousness against the boundary, listening, feeling.

And all of a sudden, he heard voices. Voices and steps, echoing from blank walls. A deep voice registered within him. It was the same he had encountered during the weaving of his spell. A genius spell, but something had gone wrong. That voice had noticed, then chased him. Looked like it had gotten hold of him. Maybe stuffed him inside this... thing.

The voice and steps drifted past him and vanished, then it was back to silence and pondering.

He didn't know how long he waited and listened, straining to get something. Anything.

After a sheer eternity alone he thought he heard something. *Was it real?* Dax concentrated. *There.* Faint and slow, cautious steps vibrated through him, but this time, the encasing bristled and shivered. Someone was coming his encasing didn't like. Something it was... afraid of. Dax nestled himself against the boundary and felt it tremble, trying to shrink in on itself, but Dax wouldn't let it.

Then he heard a voice. One he knew. And another. Voices he loved. *Fane. Mihr.* The recognition made him hum with joy. They had come for him. He tried shouting their names but he had no lips, no mouth to shout with. He wanted to bang his fists against his encasing, but he had no body. He was helpless as they spoke, so close but unreachable.

Dax concentrated with all his might and sent out a thought, pushing it into the encasing until it was punched back. He tried again. The boundary bristled and fought him, but it was also afraid of what was outside. He only needed a crack, a dent, any kind of weakness. As he searched and prodded, pushed and scraped, a conversation was taking place very close to him. More voices – ones he didn't know – joined Fane and Mihr. Hold on. Dax stilled and listened. That one voice. He knew it. Had he dreamed of it? A man, chanting in Damara, calling for him, beckoning him. Had it happened?

Gabriel. Dax knew his name. This one had tried to free him, but he had been too far away, and the one with the dark voice had fended him off. Right? Gosh, he didn't know. But if he was right, Gabriel was able to do magic. He could help.

Dax pushed at the boundary once more, expanding to his full capacity. One dent, one crack, one weakness. The boundary vibrated with fear when something zinged through it. A touch. Dax swayed from side to side as the encasing moved around him. The boundary scrambled and pulled together just when Dax pushed with all his might. A tiny crack sounded and Dax punched at it.

He had found the weakness and threw a thought outside, not knowing with what or whom it would connect. Someone stiffened when he hit them. *Fane? I'm here!*

"Boy?" a male voice whispered back.

Gabriel?

"You know my name?"

Yes, you tried to bring me back.

"Where are you?"

Stuck, over here.

"I can feel you. But you have to lay low. Some kind of big boss just showed up."

Dax listened and heard the cold, dark voice. *He is the one, the man who caught me and dragged me here.*

"Seems like it."

You have to get us out of here. Or he will kill you all.

"Kid, if I knew how, we wouldn't be standing here."

What did he put me in?

"Excuse me?"

I am stuck. Inside what?

"Lilithium."

The Devil's stone. *That means you can make a portal to Earth.*

"What? How?"

Fane. She brought the sand with her, didn't she? I felt it. The Lilithium is scared of it.

"She did. But how do we…?"

Normally we would need a core of Saliphe – the material the sand is made of – to open a passage, but we have Fane. And you. Dax thought of the correct wording for a few seconds.

"I have propped open numerous portals leading to Earth, way above in the Ascend, if there was a way to connect us to them…"

So we only need a portal from here to another part of Hell? Another part filled with Lilithium?

"Right. Why haven't I thought of that?"

The timing and wording has to be exact. I can act as a conduit, to help you pass. I'll be the key. You have to be ready. What we need now, is –

"–Time we don't have."

In that moment, Kasha roared, signaling she was about to attack. *Let's go!* Dax thought-screamed and felt himself get pulled firmly from the crack in the encasing. He held on to Gabriel as best he could and suddenly, found walls around him he could feel. Walls that did not capture but ground him.

"You hold on now, boy, we have much to discuss when we get out of here," Gabriel whispered down at him.

Chapter Thirty

Mihr

Hell, a room filled with Lilithium,

the first ring

Cynthia appeared at my side, taking a stance and facing off against the legendary Sathanas, without so much as blinking. In each hand, she held daggers, looking like the one she had stabbed me with not long ago.

Her whips coiling at her sides like living snakes, Fane marched up from behind me. She threw back her auburn hair and clicked her tongue at the Demon Lord. "I loved your son, and his death broke me. Regarding the other stuff." She shrugged. "Meh? I just wanted a change of scenery, and not serve a Maester. It's insane the lengths a woman has to go to in order for her needs to be met. Now quit your yapping and come get me, if you dare."

Sathanas stood flabbergasted for a heartbeat, then his evil smile was back. "I see the appeal. But you are right. Enough yapping."

I drew my blade across my arm, making a shallow cut that would bleed adequately. Jophiel and his charge, Abraxas, had escaped the trap Fane had laid for them and had searched for us in the first ring. On our way to this mansion, we had dodged them a few times. They were looking for me, focusing on finding my blood. It was about time they did.

A bit irritated, Sathanas watched my blood drip from my arm, but he shrugged, drew a huge sword from his side and blew into the ball of flames sitting on his left palm. A flame shot at me and I let my sword whistle through the air, deflecting it with ease.

"Nice weapon," Sathanas conceded. "Now let's see how it does in real combat. Charge!"

He and his men lunged at us, but courtesy of the narrow pipeline behind them, not all could exit and surround us.

Cynthia dashed around a Raider, sprang to his back and sank both daggers into his neck. She proceeded to rip them back to her, opening the Raider's throat from ear to ear.

Fane looked like she was dancing, as she twirled and snapped her whips, severing limbs, heads and slicing into oncoming Demons as she went. As though she were a snake charmer, her whips stood and swayed at attention, protecting her from all sides. Even the sand which had taken refuge on her head, sank to her neck where it formed a protective collar.

Kasha bounded into the fight horns first, impaling an Ifrit and nailing him to the ceiling. When she pulled back, he dropped to the stony floor and didn't move anymore.

I found myself up against the Demon Lord himself. Sathanas' sword sang through the air and was blocked by mine. He swung it again, and again. Testing my skill, all the while having the ball of fire in his left hand. He even let it bob up and down as though he was bored.

"Arken," I barked and brought my sword down on him in an arc. It hit his and was swatted to the side.

"A sword with spells? Nice. Mine has them too, meaning none of yours will work on it." Sathanas blew a fiery ball at me and I barely dodged it, too surprised by my sword not working on his.

I focused and started trading blows with him in earnest. He was an exceptional fighter and I got the feeling that he could have obliterated me in moments had he wanted to. But he seemed to enjoy our fight, I even got an indulgent smirk here and there.

As time went on and none of us landed a hit, he sighed, snuffed the flame in his hand and grabbed his blade with both. "Time to end this, Mihr. I truly enjoyed our exchange, but it is time for you to die. You have fought valiantly and I will speak of you with respect from this day onward." He gave me a curt nod, then said something in demonic. His sword glowed red-hot and when I blocked his blow, the power with which it hit me jarred through my arms painfully. I changed my stance immediately. Rather than blocking his heavy hits, I derailed them, changing their course to fly past me and hit the ground, rather than my flesh.

Sathanas grunted in surprise, but soon changed his game, too. Hit hits came faster, building up momentum and strength in a way I barely countered.

Soon, his blade sliced into my upper leg, then my side, then slashed across my left shoulder.

I bit my teeth together and kept my focus, ignoring the steadily growing number of wounds.

The Demon Lord didn't tire, but his face drew together in a scowl the longer I endured. When a commotion behind him distracted him for a split second, I yelled "Seyrich" and swiped my blade up. He blocked it, but not before it had lodged itself into his side.

Sathanas stepped back and dabbed a finger to the cut in his side. He stared at his own blood in wonder. "Huh. Haven't seen this in a long time. Well done, Angel."

The commotion grew into a deafening noise. Weapons clanged against each other and screams sounded from the pipeline. Then Jophiel and Abraxas popped from it, throwing down with the last Demons stuck inside. They obliterated them and went rigid when they saw me and Sathanas fighting.

"Sathanas!" Jophiel cried, swinging his sword, embedding it deeply into a Succubus trying to claw off his face.

"Wait your turn, boy!" the Demon Lord growled.

Fane ran past me, followed closely by Cynthia, as the remaining Demons switched their focus to the two Angels.

I had no idea what they were doing, but it seemed like there was something important happening at my back.

Kasha swiped a paw at a Gargoyle, embedding him head-first into the next wall, then she bounded toward me and Sathanas. She raised a paw and sliced her claws into his right leg as she passed. The Demon Lord yelled and flung his sword at her. It ripped through the skin of her shoulder and I winced, but it left an opening for me. "Arken," I said once more, before pushing my sword – aimed perfectly – under Sathanas arm. It sliced through his skin without effort, piercing his heart on the way. When it exited on his other side, he grunted.

He looked down patting the blade-tip emerging from his flesh and then eyed me.

"It was an honor fighting you," I said. "I too, will speak of you respectfully from this day forward."

I yanked the sword free and Sathanas opened his mouth as he stumbled back, black blood flowing down his lips and glittering on his chest. He gave me a bloody smile and threw his blade as he sank to his knees.

The huge sword went end over pommel, heading straight for Fane. I lunged, but was too late, it would hit her, I was sure of it.

As I landed on the floor and skidded toward my Demon, her whips snapped against the sword mid-air and redirected it into the wall behind Fane. She jerked her face up, looking from me, to Sathanas and then to the wall behind her where the sword stuck.

I almost cried with relief as I scrambled to my feet, gave Kasha's wound a once over then hurried to Fane, Cynthia and Gabe.

"Are you okay?" I asked Fane, turning her from this side to that in order to see if she was wounded.

"I'm good. Almost got impaled just now, did you see?"

"I saw." I pulled her close and kissed her quick but firm and she palmed my face, kissing me back.

"You got him," she said against my lips.

"I did." I glanced back and saw that Sathanas lay on his back, behind him, his guards were still busy losing to Jophiel and Abraxas.

"We're getting out of here," Fane said. "Gabe has a plan."

The magic man had been busy. A huge piece of floor was painted on in the same greenish glow he had used for his other spell back home. But this one looked different.

"Actually, it was the boy's plan."

"What?" Fane asked.

"Dax?" I said at the same time.

"Ijo, he found me. And I managed to free him. Now all we need it to hurry up. What we need is the Saliphe," Gabe said and held a hand out to Fane. "The sand," he added when she didn't react.

Fane blinked at him.

"Quickly. We need a portal."

My Demon held a palm under her neck and the sand dropped into it. "What will happen to it?" she asked.

"No idea, but it will help me use magic so we can get out."

"Mihr, you are dead!" Jophiel cried, stomping our way, fending off a straggler.

Fane placed the sand in Gabe's hand with a worried expression.

The magic man sprinkled it in the middle of his drawing, then he clapped his hands together and spoke words I didn't understand. He plucked one of the necklaces from his neck and placed it on the sand. "Your turn, boy."

Light ignited from the pendant and sand, swirling, green light. Gabe grabbed Cynthia's hand and slipped into the light, vanishing.

"Kasha, go," I said and pointed at the portal. My Hellcat meowed and sprang into it, eyes closed and ears flat. A Demon hit the ground not far away and I reached out for Fane. We glanced back, seeing Jophiel run at us, brandishing his weapon, and jumped.

****

I came to, woken by loud ranting. In a language filed with clicks and ch's. It was Gabe. Surely.

With a splitting headache, I sat up and opened my eyes. It was night. Thousands and thousands of stars spanned the sky, and my hands sank into coarse sand. I turned my head to discover that we were back at Gabe's home. Right in the middle of the circles.

The half-Demon was busy shouting and pacing, throwing his hands up and gesturing wildly.

"He is kinda pissed off that the Angels destroyed his cave," Cynthia said, rubbing her face.

I saw the little slate hill, that had once housed Gabe's home. It was now a pile of rubble and dust.

"He could just ask me and I would make him a new one," Fane rumbled. She was at my side and I drew an arm around her. My Demon nestled into my side and smiled softly. "Home, sweet home," she rasped.

"Where is Kasha?" I asked, looking around. I felt her close by but couldn't see her.

"I think she is off for a drink and a snack, to get her strength up before we fly home," Fane said. "I felt her chasing some unfortunate antelope."

"D-did Dax make it?" I asked. "How did Gabe find him?"

The magic man chose that moment to drop down in our midst. He kept rambling what sounded like curses, before sighing deeply. "I don't know if he made it. That depends on whether he found his way to his body." Gabe continued to explain how he and Dax had connected and how they had come up with a plan during our fight.

"We have to go," Fane said. "We need to know if he made it."

"I'll stay," Gabe said. "Guard the portals for now. I mean I let them close the moment we arrived, countless Angels are now trapped. No idea how that will play out. Please call me with any news of the boy."

I struggled to my feet, my body aching with bruises and cuts. "I think the Angels will be able to leave regardless of the portals. Blessed as they are, all they have to do is fly up the Ascend and it should open for them. I think. Getting in is the hard part for our kind. Regarding Dax, we'll let you know," I said as I plucked up my Demon. "But I bet, him and Cam would love to see you soon."

The half-Demon scratched at the circular scar above his temple. "I'd love to see them too. I have many things to ask the boy and discuss with him. But I have to see how my people are doing first. There is no telling if the battle hit the village. So, I am staying for the time being."

"If you need help, or anything, just call," Fane said.

"Will do."

"I'll be on my way too," Cynthia said. "I need to check on someone. Then I'll come by. We still need to free my kin and put an end to the soul-stealing business."

"If Shamal survived, which I doubt," I said.

She rose as well. "If he survived." The she-Angel drew her copper hair into a bun and fastened it at the nape of her neck.

Fane glanced at her. "You can find us where I drew a heart on the map." She handed over a dirty and worn piece of folded paper she drew from her back pocket. My Demon shrugged when Cynthia took it. "If you need help, or want to talk strategy."

Cynthia nodded once and tugged the map into the pocket of her new pants. "Thank you. For everything." She launched herself into the sky and flew off.

"You know what?" Fane looked after her. "That one is growing on me."

"Yeah, only because she doesn't talk much."

She pressed the pad of her index finger to my nose. "Just like you."

****

We flew as fast as we could, our minds occupied with Dax and whether or not he had made it home. Even so, I found myself marveling at the scenery below us, almost as much as at the feeling of having my Demon snuggled against me. It felt right, flying through the air on Kasha's back, holding Fane to me, while I scratched my Hellcat behind her ears. My two ladies. Hellspawn and loves of my life. Who would have ever thought it? Certainly not me.

Luckily, the fog was thick and low when we arrived, so we could land on my balcony without a problem. Quickly, we filed inside and hurried through my room. When we entered the living room, the TV was on and Cam sat on the couch, facing away from us. We slowly crept closer, afraid of what we might find.

Kasha had no patience for such nonsense and leapt over the couch, eliciting a sharp yell from Cam. A messy head of curls shot up from her lap, a drowsy Dax, who had been sleeping.

That was it. Fane and I vaulted over the couch as well. Hugging, yelling, and – in Fane's case – crying in a heap of bodies.

"You made it!" Fane cried, hugging Dax to her. Then she pulled away to litter his face with kisses. "I was. So. Worried!"

"My turn," I demanded and snatched Dax from her to get some hug-time in myself.

Cam and Fane sat, huddled together, crying, watching us with big, loving eyes. Kasha happily licked Dax' hair until one strand stood up straight. He giggled and wound a free arm around her neck, squeezing us both to him.

Once we had settled somewhat, in a snuggle-pile, Dax told us what had happened.

"I activated the portal and was sucked through instantly. But I couldn't see, or hear, or feel anything. So, I had no idea where I was. I drifted around, searching for something, when I sensed… a voice. Mom called my name, over and over. It was hard at first, to get the direction right, but she never stopped." He smacked a kiss to her cheek and nestled closer to her. "She called until I found her. And my body. It is weird being in one."

He grimaced at his own hands. "But I can finally hug all of you again."

"I would have kept calling you forever," Cam said, beaming at her son. She palmed Fane's cheek. "You guys found him. You said you would, and you did. I can never thank you enough."

"Most of it was Gabe," Fane said. "He led us to him."

"Then I will have to thank him too," Cam said, a small blush creeping up her face. For the longest time, we lounged together, talked, laughed, and simply enjoyed each other's company. We were home. All of us.

****

Fane and I lay in the semi-dark, watching the horizon pale. I felt tired to my bones and reveled in lying there, with her in my arms.

"Are you okay?" I asked.

She propped her chin up on my chest and searched my face with those amber eyes. "No. But I will be. As long as we are okay. Are you?"

"No. But same. As long as I have you, Kash, Cam and Dax, I am fine."

"There is still work to be done," Fane said.

"Yeah, but I have a feeling that Cynthia will want to take point on it, and I am very fine with that."

It was strange. We had allies now, in a way. Angels I could turn to. A half-Warlock who was good company, and others who were… complicated.

"Stop your musing," Fane said and stroked a finger over the crease between my brows. "All will be good. Especially we." She scooted up and kissed me, tasting of sin and secrets. "You know." Fane sucked my lower lip into her mouth and ran her tongue over it. The effect was immediate. "You still owe me an air-boning session."

"A what?" I pulled back to look at her.

"Sex in flight, join the mile high club, only with style." She wiggled her brows. "Up for a morning tour?"

I laughed then pulled her close, kissing her deeply until her breath grew short.

"I told you not to do that," she said, her voice low and raspy. "Those kind of kisses are my undoing."

"Good to know." I continued kissing her.

A snort and mewl from the foot of the bed had us jumping, Kasha got up, stretched and glowered at us, before she flounced from the room.

Fane and I giggled and rolled through the sheets, then I pinned her down, looming over her. I opened my wings and drew them around us, shutting out the world. "I love you, Demon."

She looked at me. Bare, without walls. Glimpsing into my essence. "And I love you, Angel."

The Fairy Circles

Throughout various parts of Namibia and Southern Africa, fairy circles can be found. According to legend, they are the footsteps of God, back when he walked the earth.

They are curious, circular patches of sand where nothing grows. Many theories and stories surround this phenomenon, but as of now no research has irrefutably proven why they exist.

Glossary

Damara

Ijo/Ih – Yes

Dahi – Stop it/Leave it

Axarob – Boy/Son

Etse – Exclamation to utter disbelief

Damara – Indigenous tribe to Namibia

Damaraland – Reservation for the Damara/Nama tribe

Ti !khutse – My God/my father

Axasa – Girl/daughter

Afrikaans

Melkbos – Directly translates to Milkbush. Plant common in the North-West of Namibia. Poisonous to humans and most animals.

Windpomp – Windmill, commonly used to pump fresh water from wells/boreholes

Askies – Excuse me

Groot – Big/large

Gryped – Grabbed/snatched

Mooi – Nice/pretty/beautiful

Aas – Carcass/rotting remains

Tannie – Aunty (commonly used for all women older than oneself)

Skriked - Frightened

Bliksamed – Hit/Punched

Jy weet mos – You already know (figure of speech, similar to "You know…")

Ja, ja, nie die blankes bang maak nie – Yes, yes, don't scare the white people

Afrikaans – Language spoken in Southern Africa (Originating from Dutch)

Hulle weet – They know

Moenie – Don't/Stop it

Nou gaan uit – Go outside now

Blankes – White people

Milliepap – Cornmash/Cornporrige

Biltong – Seasoned, dried meat (Common and beloved snack)

Others

Saliphe – Heavenly, living sand

Aikona – Exclamation, mostly meaning "no"

Ahyeh – Exclamation, can be used in various situations

Sho – Exclamation, can be used in various situations

Oussie – Woman/older woman

Eish – Exclamation, mostly conveying disbelief or surprise

Atatata – Exclamation, mostly conveying disbelief or surprise

Bleddy – Derived from bloody. Exclamation, curse.

Omajova – Large mushroom that grows on, or close to, termite hills

Acknowledgements

There are many people I would like to thank when it comes to writing this book. Angel Falling is special to me, mainly because it takes place in my home country. Meaning it carries pieces of me and what I love most.

Thank you to my mother, who did research, found out certain words and always told me it was going to turn out great. Your faith and pride in me keep me going and baffles me to no end.

Thank you Lizethe, for the right pronunciation and spelling of all the Damara words, and for your love. //am sita geha (I hope I spelled that correctly).

Thank you, special friend, for believing in me and always telling me that I have what it takes. You make my days better and my work more colorful.

To the team at Butterdragons Publishing, thank you for trusting in me and my work. Here's to many more projects together.

To Dazed Designs. Are you kidding me? The covers are gorgeous! You did stellar work, and I am deeply in love with your art.

MJ and Joshua... You rocked my socks off. Thank you for lending Fane and Mihr your voices.

My readers, always, my readers. I hope you enjoy this story, and I was able to bring my true home a bit closer to you.

About Victoria Larque

Victoria Larque writes Paranormal Romance and Urban Fantasy. Her love for the genre is rooted in the fact that she has rules to go by, but they can be bent and even broken if need be. She was born and raised in the wonderful country of Namibia and is now residing and working in Germany where she lives in the woods with her adorable, grumpy husband. She has learned the amazing craft of being a car-mechanic, but her passion is writing, telling stories and dreaming up impossibilities. When she gets home from work, she writes. On the weekends she writes. Her goal is to, one day, be able to do nothing but indulge in her passion.

Other BDP books by Victoria Larque
Terrifying Love A Halloween Anthology
Beautiful Tragedy A Halloween Anthology
Demon Rising (Embers Duology Book One)
Lakeborn

CPSIA information can be obtained
at www.ICGtesting.com
Printed in the USA
BVHW030619071221
623331BV00023B/70